A FANTASY CHRISTMAS

TALES FROM THE HEARTH

A Fantasy Christmas: Tales from the Hearth
First edition.
© A. A. Warne 2019

ISBN-13: 978 0 6485253 6 3 (Paperback)
ISBN-13: 978 0 6485253 5 6 (eBook)

Cover © Pam Hage
Developmental Editor: A. A. Warne
Editor: Adryanna Monteiro
Format by A. A. Warne

This is a work of fiction. Any similarity between the characters and situations within its pages and places or persons, living or dead, is unintentional and co-incidental.

Different roads sometimes lead to the same castle.

~ George R. R. Martin

FOREWORD

Gather around, if reader ye be. I've a tale to tell to thee. Once upon a time—

Just joking. Not *that* type of tale.

What you are about to read is a collection of tales told by a group of people who personally know about hardship, laughter, pain, adventure, broken hearts, and the magic of a moment. And they know how to tell tales of such things.

How do I know?

Each of these stories is penned by an author I know. Someone whose personal journey I have followed and heard about, day after day, as they have created and survived their own life and lived to tell the tale of who they are as they became a published author. In the process we #RogueWriters have supported each other through personal losses, mental health struggles, engagements/weddings, new jobs, learning to write better, book launches, and the business of authorship. And every single one of their tales is powerful.

We are all members of 200 Rogue Fantasy Writers, a tight-knit online writing community. Or, as we say, Castle Rogue —our home base for author questions, thoughts, concerns, and all things writing life support.

Much like the characters we write about, we #200Rogues

banded together for the adventure of publishing the stories that tug at us while the characters wreak havoc in our brains, always telling us what they want to do and demanding their own way. We try to subdue those characters into submission to the plot, but, sometimes, the characters override us and win.

In a world in which people view one another as competition and fight online to prove how they are right or better than others, we devoted ourselves to coexisting for support. We believe that there are enough readers for all of us and understand that, like our readers, we all enjoy something different in a story. We believe that together we are better as a group than we are in isolation. 200 ideas are stronger than 1.

When I was asked to write the foreword for this anthology, faces flashed through my mind. Names. Personal victories they have achieved. Book covers. Character sketches. Writing goals. Questions about how to query agents. Requests to proofread bios. Thoughts on Indie publishing. Resources on writing better. Hours of silliness and online banter. The courage to try something new. Midnight confessions about personal growth.

This is an author community — a little Rogue nation of writers — has remained consistent and connected as a group thanks to the leadership of two fearless administrators. They lead us into battle and refuse to give up on us even when we have considered giving up on ourselves.

What do you say about #Rogues?

Well, read what follows and tell us with your reviews of their fantasy tales.

As for me, I shall say to my friends: thank you for being the brave ones who feel the fear of putting yourself out there and, yet, do it anyway, so these readers get to enjoy what I already know first hand. You, fellow #RogueWriters, are masters honing the age old craft of storytelling.

#GoRogue

M. A. Brave.

A MESSAGE FROM MAMA ROGUE

When the gates to the Castle opened, I don't think I, or anyone, knew how much of a home it would become. What a land of opportunity we had settled. Or even more so, what a supportive family we had just forged. Through everyone's efforts, I am honoured and proud to be Mama Rogue.

A MESSAGE FROM MASTER ROGUE

What started out as a tight knit family has remained a tight knit family. Rogues stick together — and when we do, there's no limit to what's possible.

Stay shady rogues.

~ Master Rogue.

IT'S BEGINNING TO LOOK A LOT LIKE TINKMAS

MICHELLE CROW

Music hummed in the air, lights twinkled about the pub, and all present waited with bated breath for the bubbly shadow rogue to return for the tree lighting. They'd spent a week decorating the pub's interior in preparation for a holiday most present had never even celebrated.

But if the pregnant witchy healer lady wanted a party, they were going to have a party, even if it meant sending Tink shadow surfing to find wiring for their lights.

While the others paced the floors before a roaring fire, shifting impatiently side to side and mingling with drinks in hand, Tink rifled through her belongings in the Shadow Realm—a dimension that connected the fabric of all space and time but only accessed by those imbued with shadow magick. When she enters this realm, she's weightless, like skating across a slick surface, or surfing as she likes to describe it.

As Tink emerged from the shadows, Ann Harming's shoulders sagged and she sighed, dropping her head back so her chocolate curls fell to the middle of her back. "Took you long enough!" she snapped, but stopped, taking in the sight of Tink and cringing into a frown. "Oh my, are you okay? You look like you rolled around in a trashcan!"

Luke, Ann's husband, kept his gaze down on his half-empty stein, a smile forming in the corners of his mouth.

"Yeah, it's kinda messtacular in there," Tink said, pointing to the shadows in the corner. Her tan skin was smudged with dirt and her bubblegum pink hair had fallen from its two top buns. Seeing how filthy she was from the mirror behind the bar, she winced and shrugged.

"Okay, but did you get the wire?" Ann's dark eyes searched the shadow rogue.

Tink pulled a spool of copper wire from a pouch on a utility belt at her waist. "I think so. This was the only brown colored sharp thread I could find," she said, tossing it to the taller woman.

Ann caught it with her left hand, her right one stroking her round belly. It seemed, to Tink, that all Ann ever did anymore was stroke her growing belly. Seeing that Ann would be busy for a while, Tink somersaulted behind the bar and made herself a strawberry shake.

When they first built the pub, Ann had said it looked like an "old western saloon," whatever that meant, but to Tink it looked like any building in all of Alandria: wooden or dirt floors, log and stone, and thatched roofing. She slurped her drink, daydreaming about chocopuffs and swimming in a river of chocolate when Ann called out for her.

"Tink, come here."

Tink jumped into a shadow and reappeared by the witch's side. "Yes?"

Ann held out a shiny bauble and pointed at the last bulb to complete the string of lights. "Would you do the honors of screwing on the last bauble and plugging in the tree?" she asked with a smile.

Amethyst eyes large with excitement, Tink squealed, stamping her feet. "Yes, yes, yes! I do, I do, I do!"

"Okay, okay. Calm down. Here."

With the bauble in hand, Tink sauntered up to the tree and capped the bulb with it, then she squatted down and grabbed the cord with the three prongs on its end, but before she stuck it in the matching outlet she gazed back up at the witchy lady. "Are you sure

I won't get frazzle-dazzled or buzzled when I put this thingie in that thingie?"

"Huh? Are you asking if you will be electrocuted?"

A quick nod of bubblegum strands and Ann chuckled. "No, Tink. You won't be frazzle-dazzled or buzzled. I checked all of the wiring myself. Just plug it in already!"

Tink stared in disbelief at the beautiful, glowing brunette.

With a sigh, Ann heaved forward as if to take over, but Tink growled and batted at her hand. "No, I will do it!" She shoved the prongs into the outlet. Jumping back with a squeal, she pulled her curved daggers from their holsters and shielded herself. After a moment of complete silence, Tink huffed and whimpered, eyes pinched closed. She didn't want to open them and find everyone crispy as bacon.

"You can open your eyes, Tink," Ann whispered softly.

Slowly, Tink peeked around her arms and gasped. The stringed bulbs radiated with light around the freshly cut cedar. They danced by the flickering candles set over the pub's fireplace. It was the second most beautiful thing Tink had ever seen. The first being the tower of donuts she chanced upon after a successful shadow surf a few years back.

"Incredible huh?"

Tink nodded, bubblegum strands falling down around her chin.

"Back in South Carolina, my home state, we took our Christmas tree lighting very serious. My mom and dad made sure we never missed a lighting. We even had competitions and events and everything," Ann said, still staring at the tree, the faraway look she wore from time to time present in her cocoa eyes.

"Neato." Tink circled the tree and re-holstered her daggers, mesmerized by the colors, but gasped when she spotted the very bauble she'd placed only moments before. "Uh, witchy lady, is it normal for one bulb to not light up?"

"Hmm?" Ann moved to stand beside Tink and parted her lips. "Oh, that's okay. It happens sometimes if there's a short or open in the circuit."

Tink had no idea what the witchy woman was talking about, but she knew that most things that didn't work needed a little nudging.

So, she reached out and grabbed the bulb in her hand, ready to shake the life into it when the world around her went darker than the shadows, and she was surrounded by an icy cold chill as if she'd been plunged into a pool of sub-zero water.

Laughter, hearty and full, woke Tink. Her body ached all over. Her head felt like it had been smashed open. Blinking against the light, she peered around her surroundings and quickly scrambled to her feet.

Before her were all kinds of gadgets and gizmos she'd never seen before. A big black box hung on the wall with people inside like a prison, but they were smiling and laughing. On a desk to her left were framed pictures of a man and woman with a baby human in their arms and a human child around the woman's neck. Beside a tall window that stretched from floor to ceiling, stood a giant tree not too different from the one at the pub, though this one also had balls and things hanging from its limbs. Beneath it were sparkling and perfectly wrapped boxes with giant bows and stickers all over them.

"Presents!? Witchy woman didn't say anything about presents!" Tink stomped and circled the tree. Just like the one in the pub, a bulb sat dull and lifeless on the strand. She went to reach for it, hoping to be sent back to where she came from, when a door crashed open and cold spilled into the home. She shuffled back, calling one of her curved blades to her hand, and knelt low, ready to pounce at the sign of a threat.

"Mommy! Mommy, Mommy! Can I pleeeaaase open one present? Just ooone!" a tiny human squealed from the other room. Tink's eyes darted to the picture. Maybe she wouldn't have to shed blood today.

"Felix honey, no! Now take off your coat and go brush your teeth. It's already past your bedtime. If you don't get off to sleep soon Santa won't even stop by tonight."

Slowly, Tink inched along the wall to peek into the hall that led from the living area. The man, woman, and the child was almost as tall as Tink stomped snow from their boots and removed their jackets. Sleeping peacefully in a cushioned seat was the tiny baby human.

4

Tink's eyes bulged at the sight and curiosity almost blew her cover. The man reached down and lifted the snoozing bundle then creaked his way up the stairs. Meanwhile, the woman disappeared into a room that looked and smelled of food. *Felix* groaned, gazing longingly at the living area where the lights twinkled but moved to the stairs behind his father.

With a sigh, Tink slinked toward a shadow. If there was one way to escape this place it would be the shadows. She slipped into their silky cover with a smile, expecting to surf to her little secret dwelling in the Shadow Realm. A moment passed and she was still standing in the shadow of the door of the human's home, not surfing the inky trails that lined the Shadow Realm, and definitely not standing before her collection of yummy snacks and random knick-knacks she kept in heaping piles. It might have been messy, but it was her mess. Panic settled in and she reached out, slamming her hands into the hard wall.

"What the riddle-farts is this?"

Without the shadows as an escape...was she stuck in this strange place? Tink's stomach hit her ankles and her eyes darted around for an escape, any escape. She rushed toward a window, hoping to spot anything familiar, but snow blanketed the surface of everything. Houses sat in a row, all identical to one another, and lights danced across their porches and roofs. Tink's breath fogged up the glass as she stared at the strange world around her. "Where am I?" Footsteps snapped her back to her current predicament and she crept back toward the shadow.

The couple returned downstairs after tucking the children in bed. From the safety of the shadows, Tink observed them whisper in the hall before entering the living room with more boxes and rolls of paper.

"Seriously, Terrance, I can't keep doing all of this by myself," the woman said.

"Not again, Linds. It's Christmas Eve. Can't we just wrap some presents together and enjoy this time?"

The woman huffed and sat on the floor beside the tubing. Lines creased her forehead and a frown set in. Her hands ripped away plastic and tape as she stretched out a long sheet of paper with a pink-cheeked, fat old fart plastered all over it and put a box in the center.

The man groaned, taking a seat across from the woman. Tink watched them, amused by their interactions. He put his hands over the woman's and brushed his thumbs gently over them, which seemed to comfort her as her face softened.

"Can you finish this one? I have to go start the gingerbread cookies and set up Santa's *evidence*." Linds whispered the last part.

At the mention of cookies, Tink perked up. She didn't know what gingerbread cookies were, but she was going to find out.

Terrance sat up straighter. "I can go set that up, babe. You don't need to be out in the cold—plus, it's dark."

Without warning, Linds put down the tape and cupped the man's face in her hands.

"I'm sorry about earlier," she whispered.

"Don't worry about it. Holidays always get us stressed," he said.

Tink silently gagged from the shadows. They were getting all cutesy.

"I know, Ter, I know. I shouldn't have projected on you. I'm just tired."

"I'll set up the evidence of Santa. You just work on your famous gingerbread men, 'kay?"

A gentle sigh escaped the woman's throat before they hugged and kissed. Tink covered her eyes and crossed her fingers that they wouldn't do that gross thing people who like each other do sometimes.

She opened her eyelids to a dark and empty room only after she heard footsteps tapering away. Across the house, the front door creaked shut, the man apparently stepping out to fulfill his promise. Drawers opened and utensils clinked together in the kitchen, and Tink's tummy rumbled. Cookies. The woman would be making cookies!

If Tink didn't get out of here quick, real trouble would come knocking when the cookies exited the oven!

At long last, the woman heaved an exhausted sigh and joined her family upstairs.

For a moment, Tink blinked between the kitchen and the tree.

As the woman had baked, Tink watched sugar and spices mix together, her tummy grumbling the whole time. At one point she had to pretend her boots were glued to the floor for fear of exposing herself to lick a cookie-dough covered spoon!

To her dismay, the cookies weren't done. They sat on the top rack with the oven door ajar, teasing her from across the room.

How long did it take to cool a cookie? She looked again at the dull bauble, the most likely gateway home and figured a few more minutes couldn't hurt.

A crash from above startled her. Knife in hand, she wheeled around and glared at the stairs. She creeped across the black and white checkered tiles and placed one boot on the carpeted stairs, only casting one longing look to the oven. Seriously, just a few minutes wouldn't hurt, right?

Up the stairs she climbed, passing family portraits and random candid shots hanging neatly against the pale-yellow walls. At the top, she had a decision to make: left or right? Her head bobbed side to side before holding left. Something golden danced across the wall from a slightly ajar door. With the quiet skill of an assassin, Tink slipped into the room and took in the sight. Toys were stacked up in one corner of the room and above them, a string of golden lights hung across a curtain rod draped over a small window. A child-sized desk rested against one wall and pushed against the opposite wall was a child's bed, complete with a sleeping child at its helm.

The dancing golden glow came from a nightlight beside the child's bed. A tiny silver figure spun inside its bulb, casting the shadow play. Tink reached out to touch the light show when the small human turned over in his sleep and she forgot about the shiny objects, more interested in the boy.

She'd never seen a human child before. In a few months, Ann would pop one out, but Tink didn't really understand how it would happen. Maybe out of Ann's belly hole?

"Hello?" A tiny voice whispered from the bed.

Tink jumped, scrambling for a shadow.

Felix rubbed his eyes with a yawn.

"Are you one of Santa's elves?" he asked.

Tink had no clue what the kid was talking about. One of whose whats? She held her breath and pressed herself flat in the shadow, but his eyes were locked on to her and it was painfully clear she wasn't able to access the shadow realm here. Nothing in her one-hundred years of existence had prepared her for this sort of social encounter.

"Shh, go back to sleep," she hissed at him, heart thundering in her chest as she glanced to the hallway, half expecting his mother or father to pop in.

"Did Santa get my list?" he said through another yawn.

Tink's mind raced to find a solution. She'd once watched Ann hypnotize a woman before selling the customer medicinal herbs to help with sleep travels. Something about a plane and taking a trip out of body—whatever. Tink couldn't understand the mumbly-jumbly magic mess. Still, Ann had swung a stone on a silver chain while muttering strange words softly to her customer, which must have worked, because the lady fell asleep sitting up and didn't wake up for like an hour.

Without a stone on a chain to swing, Tink started to rock her entire body left then right and in the most monotonous tone she could muster said, "I'm just a fragment of your imitation. Go back to sleep and dream of chocopuffs and plane travels."

Felix squealed with delight and laughed. "You're goofy!"

Heat rose to Tink's cheeks and she stopped swaying.

"Close your eyes!" Tink hissed.

The child sat up, kicked the sheets to the side and climbed out of bed. His feet barely touched the floor as he crossed to Tink's side and made a circle around her. He reached out to touch her blade holster at her hip, making her recoil. Like a cat triggered to action, she smacked at his prying little hand.

"You seem kinda tall for an elf and you look funny. Where are your pointed ears and shoes?"

A cursory glance down to her boots and Tink scoffed. Clearly the child had no sense of fashion. As for his comment about pointed ears, there were only a few creatures Tink knew of with pointed ears and they would have probably already eaten this little bugger. "I'm not an elf, and I don't know any Santana's."

"San-ta," he enunciated with an eye roll. They stood eye to eye,

8

which meant he was taller than her if she removed her boots. "Your hair looks like gum. My favorite is this long roll, kinda like tape, but your eyes are creepy and black. That isn't normal for one of Santa's elves." Once again, his little hands raised as if to touch her. She pulled out her knives, sticking one beside the child's ear.

"My eyes are purple, not black. Thank you about my hair. I have no idea what you are talking about with this Santana character, but you really should have just stayed in bed."

He ducked under her bladed hand and jumped back onto the edge of his bed, crossing his arms as he glared at her. Tink was too baffled to know what to think. His reaction wasn't what she'd expected. Maybe humans were scarier than Ann let on.

"If you aren't an elf, then what are you?" he asked finally.

Tink sheathed her blade and cocked a hip to one side. "I'm a shadow rogue." She waited for his jaw to drop at the mention of her rare nature, but he just sat there unimpressed.

"What's a rogue?"

Tink's jaw was the only one needing scraping from the floor. "A highly trained assassin. A shadow surfer. Me, I'm a rogue. I'm only the most awesome and only one of my kind. Basically, people tell me go stabby and I go stabby." She smiled, putting on a false humble bravado.

The boy's eyes rounded in surprise, but he smiled a second later. "Okay, 'shadow-rogue assassin.' I don't believe you. I think you are working for Santa and he sent you here to scare me back to sleep so he can deliver the last of my presents."

Tink growled and stomped. She turned to face the curtains by the window and stuffed her face into them to pitch as quiet of a fit as possible. Once she'd had it out, she huffed and turned back to the annoying little creature. "No, for the last time, I am not working with Santa-miago! I stab things and I am ready to stab you! Just give me a reason, shorty!"

"Right."

The smell of the cookies from downstairs made its way to her nose again, tickling her senses. Their tantalizing smell drained all her rage and reminded her of the pit growing in her stomach. Food was the one thing that always made her feel better and gave her energy. She needed a cookie, especially after arguing with this kid. Fine, if pretending to be this 'elf' would get her out of this room and to a sugary treat, she'd do it.

With a quick puff, Tink crossed her arms and nodded. "Okay, right, you got me, kid! I am one of Santafrisco's elvises or whatever. Let's work together and get some cookies, hmm? It's what Santan would want."

"My mom says those are for tomorrow. We probably shouldn't eat them."

"Is your mom here right now?" Tink asked.

"Yes. In her bed."

"But she isn't in here, right now, in this very room," Tink pushed.

"No, but she said they are for tomorrow."

"Look, kid, I am going to get a cookie. Now you can come with me, or you can crawl back in bed and go to sleep. Either way, I'm getting a cookie," Tink muttered, pointing at her chest.

He considered it, nodded, and jumped back down from his bed, leading them away from his room and back down the stairs.

"So, uh, what do I call you?" she whispered as they climbed down the stairs.

"Felix. I bet I can guess your name; can I?"

"Yeah, yeah. Go for it," she replied, scanning back and forth to ensure nobody else in the house would catch them on their cookie heist.

"Pinkie. Grumpy. Oh, Bella." With each name Felix stopped on a stair step to look back with a big toothy grin.

Tink stopped, scrunching up her face. "Grumpy?"

"Yeah, 'cause you are really grumpy. Like the old one in the Snow White story," Felix added and laughed.

Not getting the reference, Tink shrugged and thought about the strange human greeting customs Ann went on and on about. Smile, offer a hand to shake, and be friendly. They were at the foot of the stairs, about to go to the kitchen, so she tapped Felix on the shoulder and stuck out her gloved hand. "I'm Tink."

Felix looked at her hand and smacked it sideways then skipped off to the kitchen, leaving a very confused Tink in his wake. She followed, still calculating all the things Ann had taught her that were wrong about her own species. Seriously, shouldn't that woman know her own kind?

"Do you have magical superpowers or something cool like that?" Felix asked as she entered, the sight of the kitchen causing her to hold up short in the doorframe. Like most of the house, it was immaculate and clean. Jars and containers sat in an orderly fashion, labeled and neat on the counters. If Tink could read, she'd be all too happy to dig into what the labels said, maybe even find some extra yummy snacks. An island sat in the center with pots and pans hanging overhead and a deep porcelain sink shone from the side— so clean Tink could make out part of her reflection from across the way.

"Tink?" Felix popped his head into her line of vision. "Do you have superpowers or what?"

Right, tiny annoying human had asked a question. Tink thought on it for a minute. Her shadow surfing was magical, but she didn't know how to explain it. "I don't really have magical powers, but I know a witchy woman who does. Oh, and my friend Vespar, he's a fanger. He has some pretty coolio powers."

"Fanger?" Felix asked, eyebrows raising.

"Oh, uh, I think you call them vampires or something?" Tink touched the counter just to see what the shiny marble felt like. Cold and hard.

"Vampires?"

"Yeah, that's what I said."

"Wait," Felix stopped Tink with his hand on her arm, making her tense up. Every touch and grab brought her right back to the fight stance, but this kid was kinda growing on her so she didn't flip out the blade this time. "Vampires and witches are real?" His eyes, big and blue, seemed to only grow bigger with the question.

"You believe in this Santana-migo-elf guy and elves, but you are having trouble with vampires and witches?" She glanced at his hand still resting on her arm and back at his awe-filled face. His expression relaxed and he let go of her arm, then nodded.

"Well, my mom watches shows with shiny vampires all the time but I just assumed it was all make believe." The awe was quickly replaced with something else as the kid pondered this for a moment. His eyebrows went up again.

Tink realized the kid was scared of this newfound information and felt immediate guilt. He really was growing on her. "Oh, don't worry. Most of them wouldn't be interested in biting you. You know, the fanger. Especially old Vespar. Well, mostly because he is kinda dead, like not dead like a vampire dead, but actually dead dead. Anyways, you are really too annoying to be eaten. I give you a very high surviva-bubble rate." A waft of spice and sugar hit her again and she forgot about being lost in another realm with a very annoying human child.

The deliciously golden-brown cookies, shaped like little bald, fat men, still cooled in the oven where Felix's mom had left them. Tink grinned, clapping her hands together. One, maybe two cookies, and she could get back on her way to the pub and out of here before the parents woke up and freaked out about a strange pink-haired lady talking to their little creature.

"Those are definitely for tomorrow. I don't think we should eat them, Tink."

"I do. I think we should eat them." Tink licked her lips and moved closer to the yummy baked little men.

"But those are for Santa and after we unwrap our presents in the morning."

"Yes, but Santanaman said, 'Tink, go have a cookie for me with Felix.'"

"So, what does he wear?" Felix asked, now sitting on the center island with his feet dangling and his hands cupping the edge.

"What does who wear?"

"Santa."

"Oh, uh, jeans, a black shirt, some strange colorful tie, and he keeps his hair short. Yeah. That good ol' funny elf-dude."

"Wrong."

Tink's eyes darted to her human companion. He was ruining her cookie heist. He hopped down from his perch and stood before the oven, blocking her from the path to deliciousness.

"What are the reindeers' names that drive his sleigh all over the world in a single night?"

Tink growled, annoyed, and shook her head. Counting off with her fingers, she named the few names of people and things she knew. "Uh, Vespar, Ann, Fido, Oreos, and Snickers?"

"Wrong."

Felix cast a smug smile at Tink.

"What's tomorrow?"

Tink glowered at the child and huffed, it was clear that he wasn't going to move aside until she answered him. "I can tell you what it isn't. Today! Ha!"

He didn't laugh—didn't even blink.

"How old are you?" he asked.

"One-hundred and seventy-eight. You?"

His eyes bugged out at that. For a moment, Felix just stared at Tink. She squished up her shoulders, uncomfortable under his blank glare. "Seven, eight next month," Felix whispered.

"Nice. Well if you're done with the questions, maybe move aside so I can get those cookies."

"No, they're for Santa. Not you."

"Oh, come on! Santaman isn't even here! He won't miss one of these fat little lumps of sugar! Look, I will take one cookie and we can leave a note explaining that it was an emergency and you had to give the one cookie to a very needy rogue. But you have to write it, I can't write. Or read. Don't worry kid, your mom won't even know."

He shook his head. "I don't believe you." Felix shut the oven door and placed some strange plastic casing over another piece of plastic with a click.

She studied it from beside him.

"It's a child lock," Felix said, pointing at the strange white contraption. "You can't open it and get any cookies as long as that's there."

She narrowed her eyes and hooked her index between the plastic strap and square then swiped down in one quick motion. It snapped and fell to the floor causing Felix to jump.

"So, you were saying?" She pulled a plate from the cabinet and set it on the counter by the oven to begin her cookie assault, careful not to drop any on the floor.

Jingles sounded overhead and Tink sniffed the air. Something changed from a moment before and it felt familiar, like when Ann was busy weaving her hands over a cauldron and muttering in some foreign gibberish. Magic. Tink stuck her tongue out to taste it, like testing wind direction and speed or the oncoming storm. Magic of any nature had a certain taste, smell, and feel—an unnerving attack on the senses.

"Did you hear that?" she asked a stiff-as-a-statue Felix.

Stamping on the rooftop followed, a clomping as if a herd of cows were somehow running circles above their head. Tink cocked her head up, curiouser and curiouser as the enveloping film of this strange magic encased them further. Goosebumps raced up and down her arms and she narrowed her eyes at her human companion. "Is that..." Tink started.

"Santa," Felix finished in a whisper.

"Oh man, Santa *is* real," he squealed.

"I thought you already said he was real?" Tink asked. This little human was perpuzzlexing.

"I mean, yeah. But, I have never actually seen him. You tricked me!" He placed his hands on his hips. "I actually thought you might *not* be working for Santa." His smile spread wide.

Tink chuckled. "Yeah, that's me. I got the trick bone."

Tink's eyes locked on the cookies. Now that the boy was distracted, maybe she could make a clean getaway with her prize.

"Well, what does he want?" she asked, half interested in the answer, fighting the urge to drool.

"To bring presents to good kids, duh, but you know that! You are so funny!" Felix waved her to follow and ran for the door, calling over his shoulder, "Come on! Let's get him these cookies! I bet you have to go back to the workshop, huh?"

Felix snatched the plate of cookies from the counter and rushed out of the room.

"Wait! Oh, riddle farts!" She huffed and chased after him into the living room where the tree sat. Snow and wind whooshed through from the chimney. "You said he likes to bring presents to *good* kids? Well, how do you know you were good?"

"You just do," he said with a shrug. "Like, when I offer to help Mom with the chores or dinner, or when I listen to Mom all year without talking back or acting wild. You know, doing good stuff, not doing bad things."

Tink scratched her chin. Good stuff. She had helped Witchy Lady with decorations. Maybe that counted.

Felix stared at the chimney, breath held, plate of cookies outstretched before him, reminding Tink of an unmoving tree. When nothing happened, Tink scooted forward and peeked up the brick cave but only saw shadows.

"Uh, kid, there's nobody in here. By the way, why is there a cave in your house and so small too!"

Felix's shoulders sagged, almost sending the cookies to the floor. "It's a fireplace and chimney." Another sigh and the cookies moved to the edge, teetering on the brink of destruction.

"Whoa! Careful with the fragiles!" Tink rushed over and rescued the plate from him. The boy shrugged away from her and plopped down by the tree. Now was her chance! He didn't seem to care about her and the cookies anymore, so she could steal away with the whole lot and get back to her pub! Fighting the urge to scream with excitement, she inhaled and rushed over to the tree about to touch the bulb when a sniffle had her looking back over her shoulder.

Tears streamed down Felix's cheeks. His eyes were sealed tight and his fists were balled up, trembling.

"Riddle-farts," she mumbled under her breath. With a quick sniff of the cookies, Tink pushed herself away from her escape and reluctantly set the plate on a small table by some cushions and chairs. She didn't go empty handed, snatching two cookies she went back and plopped down by the boy.

"Hey." She jabbed him in his squishy side, but he didn't budge. "Hey!" She tried again.

"What? What do you want?" he growled at her, tears still pouring from his bright blue eyes.

"You want a cookie?" she asked, extending a cookie to him while cradling the other closely.

His hand covered it and brought it to his mouth, crunching through the crumbly treat. Tink watched each tiny particle hit the child's shirt and floor. When he didn't speak after he finished it, Tink hugged her knees to her chest and cocked her head to the side, silently nibbling on her own. "So, why did you want to see this Santamaria-elf dude anyway? You don't have enough presents under the tree already?" She pointed at the piles of wrapped gifts.

"I don't care about the presents," he looked down at the floor.

"Then what?"

"I—I wanted to ask Santa if instead of toys he could make my parents happy again."

"Oh." Tink shifted uncomfortably.

"Do your parents fight?" he asked.

Tink couldn't remember her parents. What memories she had from her youth were buried deep.

"Dunno." She figured it was simpler to say that than try to explain her past. Besides he was just a kid.

"Mine fight all the time. They think I don't know about it, but I do."

Tink bit her lip. How could she cheer up this tiny human bugger? She knew just the thing.

"You want to play with my knife?" She pulled her favorite curved dagger out and handed it to the boy. The obsidian blade looked as murky as her purple eyes. He took it with a grin, but as soon as it hit his hand, the weight of it brought both the knife and his hand to the floor.

"Whoa! That's heavy! Hey, you do have super powers! You're super strong, like the Hulk or Thor!"

"Who?"

The boy laughed but didn't try to retrieve the blade. Instead he got up and hustled over to a desk and drawers, rattling around before returning to their spot.

"Okay, Tink. You want to cheer me up?"

"Sure?"

He opened up the little satchel and spread out the contents before them. Tink's eyes grew large and she looked at him with concern. Brushes and squares of color sat in a rainbow palette. A white sponge and a beige one were mixed in with the array as well as tubes of sparkly specks.

"What is it?" Tink asked, smirking.

"It's face paint!"

Tink shook her head. The last time Tink played around with something within a satchel she had coughed out flames for a month. She didn't mess around with things anymore, especially with the things in Ann's lab.

"What do we do with it?" she asked, afraid of the answer.

"We paint each other's faces," Felix added, his face lit up as he arranged the contents of the satchel on the floor at their feet.

He took out a brush, unscrewed a colorful tube, and squeezed out a glob of something bright red onto the brush. "Okay, now hold still."

Tink squinched up her face, the cold, wet brush tickled as the boy swept it across her cheek, but she let him. At first, she held her breath, afraid if she breathed in she would cough up something worse than flames, but then she relaxed the more the child worked on her cheek. When he was done, she got up and looked at her reflection in a window. A blob of brown, green, red, and black sat on her cheek. The kid said it was some kind of reindeer, Rudolfo or something, but she couldn't see it. Still, it was nice of him.

"Okay, my turn!" he interjected.

"You just had a turn."

"No, my turn as in you come paint *my* cheek now."

Tink crossed her hands, waving them back and forth as she shook her head. "No, no. You really don't want me to do that. Trust me."

"Come on! Pleeeaaase!"

His sky-colored eyes softened up at her and she melted. How did the human mother survive this? Would Ann's baby bugger do this?

"Fine," she huffed and sat down. She took out a few brushes, rubbed her thumbs across their soft bristles and chose her colors before deciding to work on the cheek opposite to the one he had done for her. She glanced around the room, trying to find inspiration when her eyes landed on the largest, brightest object in sight. The tree.

First, she drew the lines, then added dots for the lights, and finally, a small golden *x* for the star on top. It looked a bit rough, but she was pretty proud anyway.

"Whoa," Felix whispered as he looked into the glass. "You are bad at face painting. Oh well, I kind of like it. Thanks, Tink."

She grinned in response.

Felix lunged forward and wrapped his arms around her shoulders. Tink stumbled back in surprise, but didn't avoid the embrace. "Thank you so much, Tink," he said, voice soft and breaking.

Afraid he'd cry all over her, she patted him on the back and worked her way out of his hold. "No worries, kiddo. And as for Santanaman, I mean, I don't know where he is or why he isn't down here..." She paused and looked up to the ceiling. The magic still sat on the air, which meant the magical entity still sat on the roof. "But I bet if he knew you wanted your parents to stop fighting more than you wanted presents, he'd think that's pretty cool."

Felix wiped a tear from his eye and went to clean up the face paint when the jingle sounded again. This time, a crash hit the roof and dust fell from the ceiling. Tink looked around, eyes darting all over, waiting for the threat to appear. Felix cowered behind her.

And as they both followed the loud steps across the ceiling to the chimney, they waited patiently, watching as snow glittered down to the chimney floor. The magic grew stronger and more concentrated, making Tink feel light and giddy as it neared.

They held their breath and waited. First, a boot popped into view, shiny and black as night. Then a pair of legs, bulbous belly, chunky arms, and a snowy beard followed. Before them emerged a man with a really red nose, red cheeks, and watery turquoise eyes.

"Ho, ho, ho," he rumbled. "My oh my, Mr. Felix, you should really be in bed." He touched Felix's cheek and then turned to Tink and bent forward with a grin and a glimmer in his eye. "Tink, it's a pleasure to meet you! A bit out of your...realm?" The big man rumbled with laughter at his own joke.

Tink and Felix swallowed hard, looking at each other with their eyebrows raised before turning their attention back to the man before them. Santa moved toward the cookies and stopped, bending down to pick up one, then two, and finally three before stuffing all of them in his mouth in one big bite. When he was done he rubbed the crumbs from his gloved hands and turned back to the two gaping individuals in the living room, smiling at their expressions.

Tink leaned into Felix. "Is he a threat, Felix? I could stabby him if you want." She pointed at the blades sheathed at her hips.

"No need for that, Tink. I would never harm you or anyone. I'm just here to spread some cheer and bring presents. Oh, and enjoy cookies with a glass of cold milk, of course." Santa snapped his fingers and a glass appeared in his hand, full of creamy white liquid.

When he had drained the glass, he smacked his lips together, set it down, and waddled over to the pair still gawking at him.

"You've been busy this year, Felix. Only one fight with your classmate, Arnold, and the rest of the year you did good deeds and acts of kindness. Here, for making the nice list!" Santa turned and snapped his fingers. A giant red sack—bigger than Santa—appeared, and Tink jumped back. How did the man do it? She craned her neck to get a better look at the bag and the magic wielder too. He must be some kind of wizard! He dug around inside and brought out a shiny box, handing it to Felix.

"Thanks, Santa!" Felix tore off the wrapping paper with glee and began unpackaging whatever it was inside.

"And you, Tink! What to do with you? It's been a surprisingly good year for you, my dear shadowy friend, but I must say, your past leaves much to be desired."

Tink shrugged her shoulders to her ears. "I got everything I need, Mr. Santanamiago-elf dude." Although... An everlasting tray of fat, balding cookie-men would be nice. She wouldn't ask this magic man for it though. Wizards were bad news bees where she came from.

As if he'd heard her thoughts, he rumbled into another fit of gut-jiggling, earth-rattling laughter. Seriously, Tink's eyes danced about, knowing the parents would come running down the stairs any second—but they didn't. As his laughter slowed, he continued to gaze at her through his thick glasses, stroking his cotton ball beard. Felix was busy with his gift, the pair forgotten for the time being, so he was no help to her now.

"Tonight, you showed true kindness when dear young Felix needed a strong shoulder. For that, I have something for you as well." His voice rolled with the lilt of someone accustomed to laughing often. It was warm and soothing, much like the magic that permeated the air around him and he couldn't stop chuckling to himself. Honestly, Tink started to think the man was just plain crazy apes. "Just a sec." He touched a finger beside his cherry-red nose and once again rustled his hand through the giant sack before taking out a small silver box and placing it in Tink's palm.

She wanted to jump back and roll away but was drawn to the man, much like she'd been drawn to the cookies. He made her feel...happy, and safe. Even the silver box he placed in her hand felt cozy, and, most importantly, it felt like it belonged to her.

"Th-thank you," she stammered, her mind and body at war with how to manage her nerves. Every instinct told her to attack magic creatures—other than Ann of course—especially after the culling that nearly wiped out her race, but all she wanted to do was be in this wizard's presence.

"Go on, open it."

"Yeah, open it, Tink!" Felix agreed, smiling up at her before resuming with his own gift.

Tink moved the lid to the side. Inside were three perfect balls of chocolate coated in cocoa and sprinkles. At first, she thought the sprinkles were oddly shaped but upon closer inspection she realized they were shaped just like her curved blades. A happy exhale escaped her lips as she let go of her fighter instinct and savored the moment with a smile, closing the box lid to enjoy her treats back home. "Thank you...Santa."

Felix gasped. "You said his name!"

Santa burst into laughter, this time bending forward to brace himself on his thighs as he guffawed a thunderous laugh.

"You two are truly remarkable and entertaining. Thank you for that. I haven't had that kind of humor and wit in at least half a century."

A chiming came from a pocket in Santa's coat. He took out a strange device and made a startled sound. "Oh my, the time! Right, I must be getting on my way. I believe you, too, must be going? Hmm? I'm thinking off to your bed, Mr. Felix," Santa suggested, wiggling his eyebrows at the grinning boy. He turned to Tink and touched his nose again. "As for you, Miss Tink, home is just a light bulb and a jump through the space-time continuum away."

She glanced to Felix, concern present in her eyes. It might have taken stealing cookies, talking about family, and meeting a jolly old fat man named Santa, but she kinda liked the kid.

"Don't worry about him, Tink. He's in good hands," Santa whispered.

With a sigh, she had to assume the old man knew what he was talking about. "And what about—" Tink turned back to find the place where Santa once stood empty. Tink sprinted over to the chimney and glanced up the dark, cave-like tunnel. "Definitely a wizard." The effects of his magic seemingly disappeared with him, leaving her feeling exhausted and ready to climb into bed.

Felix yawned and stretched, and Tink figured she had one last task to perform before she left. First, she collected the cookies and put them back exactly where they were before her heist and run-in with Santa. Felix tagged along but could barely stay on his feet let alone keep his eyelids open. Finally, she felt as if she could leave the kitchen and was almost certain Felix's mom would never know about the events that went down on that Christmas Evening.

With Felix in tow, they climbed the stairs and she tucked him back in his bed, new train set and all from Santa accompanying him.

She rose to leave and he reached out, grabbing her hand.

"Dude, you have to stop doing that!" she scolded him. "I might accidentally cut one of your hands off!"

"Sorry. I just wanted to say thank you," he mumbled, eyes barely open.

"For what?"

"For the best Christmas Eve ever."

"Okay, kid. Goodnight. Be good for your mom."

He snored before she had the last syllable out.

Tink collected her small silver box of delicate chocolates and made her way down the stairs. She peered into the kitchen at the tasty cookies and grinned, then stepped into the living room and over to the tree. In the center of the big tree was a picture of the mom and dad. She wore a beautiful dress and he a lovely suit. Tink tried to remember if the picture had been there before when a jingle overhead brought about a small smile again.

"Well played, wizard!"

Tink found the dull bauble and wrapped her hands around it. The world around her sucked inward with her swirling at the center.

"You have to be joking!" Ann cried out.

Tink's hand cupped the small blown out bulb as she looked around to find the pub just the way she'd left it—as if she'd never left at all. She licked her lips and cleared her throat, about to explain herself when Ann pushed her to the side, still holding one hand on her round tummy.

"I can't believe you'd shadow surf tonight of all nights, Tink! It's Christmas Eve! Where did you go? What is *that* on your face?" Ann grabbed Tink by the chin, jutting it out at an uncomfortable angle and inspected the paint job from Felix. Luke came into her field of vision, shaking his head as if to warn Tink to just ride it out with his wife.

When Ann released her, Tink leaned into to examine the dull bauble one last time.

"Seriously irresponsible and, honestly, just plain rude! We can't just have a normal Christmas without you going off to play in your shadows! Where were you? Hmm?" Ann's questions fell into the background as Tink bent forward to look into the dull light. She caught the faint impression of a chubby man and beard and grinned. "Wizard," she muttered.

"What?" Ann huffed.

"There's a wizard in the light bulb." Tink grinned with a wave and she swore she heard a rumble of laughter in the distance.

"Tink, you're joking, right?" Ann's face grew serious, dark even. Tink should have known dropping the 'W' bomb would set off the witchy lady. Like she'd thought at Felix's, wizards in her world meant bad news bees. At least she'd met one good wizard.

"There is a wizard in the light bulb," Tink said. "But he's a cool dude. He helped my friend Felix. I think he helped Felix's mom and dad too. I don't know about that part." Tink looked down at her hands and the silver box with the delicious looking chocolate balls nestled inside. "He even gave me this silver box of chocolates. His name is Santana." She smirked at her own inside joke. "And he wears this fuzzy red and white suit, and he's really FAT. Like super fat. Like, I think he probably should hold off on some of the chocopuffs, you know?"

Ann shook her head. "Wait, you said he wore red and white? Tink, I have told you the Night Before Christmas story numerous times. There isn't a wizard in the bulb. If there was, my sensors would have detected a dark force present and already eliminated it." Ann cut her eyes around the room as if pointing to all the sensors, like Tink hadn't been the one who physically installed them or anything. Tink did the labor and Ann worked her magic. "We're safe. Don't go around telling anyone there's a wizard in my pub, okay?" Ann sighed and stormed away toward the kitchen. Tink didn't get it. A wizard, Santa—it's all the same thing. Why was Witchy Woman so upset? Plus, Santa was a cool dude.

"But," Tink stammered. "But he's real. He brought toys to the kids."

Luke stood and patted Tink on the back. "Don't worry about it, Tink. She's just kind of moody right now. You know, with the baby and all."

Tink rolled her eyes and then looked to her silver box. She removed the lid, flipping it over. Inside was a small inscription: *For those who still believe.*

"Riddle-farting wizards," she said, then tucked a ball of chocolate into her cheek and laughed.

ABOUT THE AUTHOR

MICHELLE CROW

Michelle Crow grew up on Teenage Mutant Ninja Turtles and Buffy the Vampire Slayer. A lover of anything fantasy or science fiction, she writes her characters like she drinks her coffee: dark but occasionally sweet. This is her third publication, and when she isn't crafting stories, she's helping her college composition students improve their academic writing. She resides in Tennessee with her husband, three little monsters who call her mommy, and one stinky dog named Beezkit.

https://michellecrowscornercafe.wordpress.com

facebook.com/michellecrow.aawarne

twitter.com/BM_Crow

amazon.com/-/B07QF1BHL7

instagram.com/purplecrowcreate

WINTER GARDENS

PAM HAGE

The wheelbarrow crushed the snow as Old Marro rolled it out of the shed and into the garden, and as always, a young silver spruce followed him like a shadow. The tree reached no further than the leather knee pads sewn onto his trousers, but what it lacked in height, it made up in energy. It jumped around as if it hadn't learnt how to dig in its roots and stand still for just a moment. The rest of his garden, displaying a symmetrical, miniature maze of box plants flanked by birch, hazel, and flowerbeds, was far quieter. Winter ruled. It put most plants in a drowsy state and kept them so until spring. Even the evergreens turned less lively—except, of course, for that small spruce. Most gardeners would seek work elsewhere in these dark months, when plants turned uncooperative and people less eager to go outside. Old Marro merely grinned at the cold. He liked a challenge.

He brushed the snow off the young spruce's needles and picked up the plant. It crawled further up his arm until its trunk stood on his shoulder. Roots wrapped around his torso and neck for extra grip. The tree shuddered in brief, intense bursts. It was growing excited.

"What shall we go for today? Another Merannon maze garden, or perhaps a design from the East?" Old Marro thought out loud,

27

fingers scratching his bearded chin. "But Lord Hevris is quite into those natural-looking parks. We should practise them."

Old Marro's usual commissions involved middle-class gardens, but he dreamed of herding the trees of estates. He had plenty of competition, though. Only the best gardeners could do it. Practice was crucial.

He blew the whistle that hung around his neck. No sound came from the device, despite feeling the cool metal tremble between his lips. The garden, however, responded.

The box plants were the first to spring to life, pulling their roots out of the soil and using them as legs as they walked towards their master with a wobbly gait.

He crouched down and scratched their tiny trunks. A warmth spread through his chest; he was glad his plants preferred to listen to him than to slumber. One of his recent compost experiments must have been quite up to their taste.

"Good morning, my lovelies," he told them. "If you would be so kind to stand right over there, next to the overturned flower pot? And shake up those branches a bit, we are going for a wild look today."

They did so without hesitation, all trembling in short bursts of enthusiasm as well. Then the tall firs lined up, curling down towards him as if his words would otherwise be lost. Old Marro placed them in the back of the garden, spacing them in a random pattern as if nature had put them there. Birch came next, still a little sleepy from their winter's rest, followed by hazel, pines, and ivy. He let the flower bulbs be. Some gardeners liked to force those plants to bloom in winter, but Old Marro found that cruel. Such flowers were never as big and bright as those who followed their seasonal rhythm.

His design needed a few tweaks, but after an hour, Old Marro's garden looked like a well-maintained woodland. It appeared larger with the tall plants reaching for the sky in the back and the ground-covering ones in front. The wind whispered through the branches, stirring snow and leaves, and a curious robin navigated the current, eyeing the world below as if wondering how it had changed this time.

Satisfied, Old Marro rolled the wheelbarrow forward and gave each plant a shovel's worth of the compost it carried. He had a unique mix for each species: one was a little richer in chalk, others were more acidic, another was made from pure plant matter, while the next contained manure. The plants showed no difference as they dug into the stuff, wriggling their roots in it like worms in moist soil. The scent of earth flavoured the cold air.

He placed the little silver spruce on the ground next to his shed and gave the plant its share of plant feed when hooves clattered on the cobblestone street. His stomach grew heavy. That sound was never good.

Old Marro walked over to the other side of his house as fast as his ageing knees allowed him. There he saw a column of horses heading away from town. Some carried men with black hunting hats and felt coats with golden tassels. The riderless animals were big beasts of burden, having long stretches of hemp ropes and glass-covered cutwire tied to their harnesses. The length of the cutwires made Old Marro take a step back, shaking. He could wrap one of those around his house with ease, and sever his torso from his legs when getting caught by the wire's coils.

Only one person could lead a hunting party like that. Where Old Marro's stomach had been heavy before, it now seemed to disappear in a hole of dread.

A middle-aged, lean man reined in his silver dapple mare before Old Marro's house, not caring about the people he held up behind him. Or, more likely, he wanted to use them as an audience.

"Good day, old man," Silvester said and lifted his hat, but he carried a mocking grin. "I see you have rearranged your garden. Going for a landscape design? I fear it will never work for trees that small."

A low rustle appeared behind Old Marro. The silver spruce had walked up to its master and was shaking with anger.

"They're big enough," Old Marro said. He wanted to appear as sturdy as the birch he grew, but doubt made his voice waver. When he glanced at the horizon behind Silvester's smirking face, he knew for certain he was wrong. Lord Hevris' trees were so large Old Marro could see them from here.

Silvester followed his gaze and the mocking smile deepened. "I

29

suppose you can care for your herd for a century or two and get a tree of decent height. You would test Lord Hevris' patience greatly, though."

"I'll figure something out. Something more humane than catching wild trees."

"See, that's why you're stuck with your small garden, taking up small jobs; trees aren't human."

And with that, Silvester spurred on his horse, and so did the rest of the party. Old Marro stared after them, hands balled so much that the bone shone through and coloured his knuckles a pale yellow. Even when the hunters disappeared behind a bend in the road, Old Marro stayed tense. Silvester was wrong. So, so wrong.

Old Marro tried to ban the man from his mind as he did his daily duties, but no matter what he did—creating more compost, caring for neighbouring gardens, checking the saplings in his glasshouse—that man's jesting tone never left.

When the sun was about to set, horse hooves clattered again on the road. Their pace was slower this time, and something big and wooden creaked behind them. The hunting party passed by with a redwood tree four times as tall as Old Marro's house. Ropes and cutwire shackled its trunk, lower branches, and biggest roots. The redwood fought its bonds, but the draught horses pulled the wire so tight, the glass sank into the bark like teeth. The majestic plant shivered with pain and smashed its few free branches against the knots that kept it imprisoned. A crack of a whip split the air as Silvester brought the weapon down on the redwood. Its cutwire rope shredded leaf and twig, forcing the tree to stop its struggles.

What Old Marro would give to take that whip and use it on its owner, but he wasn't a brash young man anymore. He watched, again, and saw how the tree ended up in the easternmost corner of the lord's estate, where more giants stood. Men drove anchors into the ground to which the tree got tied. It wasn't pretty. It made a garden static, too. Plants should move, and it was up to the gardener to create something unique and beautiful out of that. But trees like that redwood were so large and impressive on their own, the average spectator wouldn't care about the chains that shackled its trunk.

Old Marro's attention shifted to his own plants: free, happy, but so, so small.

Silvester's ways might be wrong, but his words held a hidden truth.

Old Marro left his home early the next day, carrying a large backpack that had been gathering dust in his attic, and wearing sturdy boots that normally did not travel much further than a few garden paths. The trails of the forest crossed a place so wild, so alive, he almost forgot it was winter. No wind blew, but branches moved and creaked nonetheless. Critters jumped through the snow, or a tree itself roamed about, moving on snakelike roots. The biggest difference was the scale of things. At home, "large" was the greatest descriptor Old Marro ever had to use. Here, "gigantic" wasn't even big enough. The redwoods touched the sky so high up he didn't see their crowns. Other gardeners whispered whole ecosystems lay hidden up there, full of animals that had never set foot on the ground.

Trunks blocked the view on the horizon in all directions. Had the sun already risen? He couldn't tell. Old Marro had to keep walking, though. The biggest trees lived at the heart of the forest, hidden in small valleys that barred the way to harsh winds that might blow them down. Human access wasn't much better; it would take almost a day to get there.

His knees complained after an hour. His ankles followed thirty minutes later. His back gave out next. Hot pain scorched his joints as he sat down against a young redwood tree, puffing like, well, what he was: an old man.

He took off his shoes and massaged his feet. So maybe he couldn't reach the largest trees of the forest without a horse, but the redwood he was using as chair wasn't a small thing either. He looked up. Branches crisscrossed above him, cutting the canopy into countless emerald fragments.

He put on his shoes again, then brushed the bark of the redwood's trunk. "Hello there, I'm a gardener, but I do not use ropes or whips. Tell me, what does it take to lure a fine tree like you out of the woods?"

Roots stirred beneath him, but the giant did not move.

Old Marro's shoulders slumped. "That's a no then. Are you sure? You're missing out on some fine dining."

He took a handful of compost from his backpack and spread it at the tree's base. Small roots poked at the dirt with care, then feasted on it. With a grin, he brushed the last of the dirt off his fingers. At a snail's pace that didn't strain his knees that much, he walked back home and waited by the window for the tree to come.

It never did.

He returned the next day. And the day after that. Still, no redwood wanted to join his garden. Why? Plants cared a lot about the soil they stood in. Considering how much the wild trees feasted on his compost, it must certainly be better than the forest floor. Perhaps his mix lacked the right taste? Old Marro flavoured his compost with various things to make it wilder, ranging from shredded pine cones and needles to flakes of moss. The redwoods seemed to love it, but they didn't leave the forest.

One day, Old Marro left a trail of compost all the way from the woods to his house. One redwood seemed interested, and slowly, it crawled forward on massive roots. Old Marro's heart jumped. This was the best result he had in weeks! He kept up with the giant from a distance. It might not be the biggest the forest had to offer, but it dwarfed the trees Lord Hevris already owned. And unlike those, cutwire and chains hadn't scarred this tree.

The forest thinned when they got near its edge. Old Marro was so close. He saw his garden from here. When he stepped out of the forest, the rustling of leaves behind him stopped. The redwood weaved its roots with those of its smaller neighbours and stood as stone.

"No, no, no! Why do you stop? You have to come with me!" Old Marro hurried to the tree and pushed against the bark. The trunk was so large though that at least four people with outstretched arms were needed to encircle it. Old Marro's pushes did not even make a twig stir.

"What are you doing, old man? You call yourself a gardener?"

Old Marro froze, and his gaze drifted to the source of the voice. Silvester sat on his mare some distance away, his head slightly cocked. More riders travelled up the forest path behind him.

"The tree moved," Old Marro said. "Without using cutwire."

"Sure it did," he said dryly. "Now, perhaps it's better to go back to your own garden and hand this one over to the professionals. You will not move it without brute force."

"But..." Old Marro stared at the tree. By root and twig, it was *his*. It had moved because of him. Silvester couldn't take that away.

The rider rolled his eyes, then flicked a hand at two of his men. They dismounted and with the silent, threatening gait of a mountain lion, they stalked Old Marro. He curved his fingers tightly around rough fissures and crevices on the bark, but the wooden giant didn't protect him when the strong hands of the cronies grabbed him by the arms and dragged him away.

Old Marro kicked at one of his captors, but hardly brushed the man's boot. "You can't do this, Silvester!"

"Actually, I can. It's dangerous to stand near a capture of a tree this size. Safety first, you know."

"I claimed it already!"

"Are you sure? I don't see it moving." Silvester dismounted as well and unrolled his whip of cutwire. His lips showed a skewed smile. "Not yet, that is."

He and his men went to work. Two wrapped a long stretch of wire around the trunk and tied the ends to the draught horses. Others unwrapped whips, too. The horses pulled while the men flailed their weapons at the redwood. The tree shook, pulling its hurt roots close to its trunk like a human protected a broken arm.

Once the whips had freed enough roots from the ground, the horses got the upper hand. The tree moved towards the forest trail, ushered forward with the whips. Bark creaked and got cut and stripped. Branches were torn off. It was a pain to see, but what hurt more was the sound.

Trees were usually so silent that people dismissed stories of talking trees as fairy tales. Old Marro wasn't sure about the talking, but he knew they could certainly cry.

And this one cried his heartwood out.

It was a long wail, a sharp snap, and a deep creak all at once, loud enough to make Old Marro's chest tremble. The redwood reached its branches out to its neighbours but got pulled away before it could touch them. It kept trying, even when the horses had pulled it several strides out of the forest, and suddenly, Old Marro understood. A redwood was never alone. It never left the forest because it never left its kin.

He went back home, tears in his eyes, but a plan rooted in his mind.

The next day, Old Marro didn't leave his shed. The solution was so simple: lure multiple redwoods at once. That required more compost than he had ever seen in his life, though. His stash, which he had almost used up, wouldn't cut it. He had collected all the garden waste he had, then the garden waste of his neighbours, then the garden waste of their neighbours, then the garden waste of the neighbouring village. He chopped leaves and branches into smaller pieces, then let worms feast on it in a special container. It would take at least a month before it was ready.

The little silver spruce jumped behind him as Old Marro worked behind his potting table. Its needles had grown brown tips and looked rather droopy. He hated to admit it, but the other plants in his garden didn't look that great either. Surely, they would understand. Lord Hevris couldn't ignore him once he had caught the largest trees in this land. Other lords would follow. His plants wouldn't have to stand in small gardens but would decorate estates. It was worth it. He just had to bite through this sour apple to get to the sweet core.

Old Marro pushed the spruce away. "Not now, I'm a little busy here. Wait outside, will you?"

The stubborn plant didn't and kept jumping around him. Old Marro sighed, grabbed it by its trunk, and put it in the garden. When he stepped back in the shed, he bolted the door.

The spruce had disappeared the following morning. Old Marro wasn't worried at first—it was normal for young trees to roam—but the plant hadn't returned by the end of the day. That wasn't normal.

He knocked on the door of Mrs Finn, his closest neighbour, with such panic the lucky horseshoe nailed to the doorpost trembled free and fell. When he asked if she had seen the tiny tree in her garden, she shook her head.

"The only silver spruce I've seen is the one you gave me last summer," the elderly lady said as she picked up the horseshoe. "Perhaps it walked the other way, to Bran's fields?"

Old Marro ran in that direction, but the farmer hadn't seen the tree either. "My son might," he said. "Saw one in town when he did some shopping there. He was buying some fabric for the missus, and a tree just walked into the shop! Caused a bit of a mess, too, I believe. No one thought it was yours, though. It's so far away from your home, and your plants are too well-behaved."

Old Marro brought his hands to his mouth. Would that spruce do such a thing? Bran was right, it wasn't the kind of behaviour his plants were known for. Then again, *he* wasn't known for ignoring his garden either. Cold crawled through his veins with each beat of his heart. Moving hurt, as if his limbs were tied to the ground with cutwire. This was his fault. All his fault.

His focus turned to Bran again. "Any idea if it's still there?" His voice creaked.

The man shrugged. "Can't say. It happened this morning."

The old gardener thanked the farmer, then hurried to town. The place wasn't big, having only four decent roads and a handful of alleys meandering between the wood-and-loam houses with their steep, slated roofs. Old Marro looked for tracks left by roots, but so many feet had trampled the snow it had turned to an indecipherable slush. The owners of those footsteps had gone, though. The sun had set. Only moon- and starlight were left, peeking through the clouds, while the lights from candles and oil lamps lit the houses from the inside.

He kicked against the snow, then sank to his knees. Ice water soaked the fabric of his trousers, but he didn't care. He had lost a tree. No gardener with a decent name let that happen. He couldn't look after a large redwood, but a small spruce had been too much as well. He was a failure.

Old Marro didn't know how long he sat there in the snow. Time no longer counted. Nor did the cold. Everything had turned to ice to him.

"Old man! What kind of prank is this supposed to be?" Silvester stopped his mare in the middle of the street. His breathing was faster than usual, his hair was a little dishevelled, and his skin was dotted by drops of sweat. He looked like he had tried to outrun the horse he sat on, but the tone in voice betrayed that anger was a more likely cause.

Old Marro arched an eyebrow at him. "Prank?"

Silvester pointed at Lord Hevris' estate. Despite the distance, the light of candles could be seen shimmering through the windows. Oddly enough, a similar light came from the garden, as if a camp-fire had been lit.

"A stray tree has shown up there. It refuses to go and is destroying my entire garden design. The lord asked me to find its master after I explained to him the thing was far too small to be one of my plants. It has the kind of size you seem to be an expert in."

Old Marro didn't know how he could feel ashamed and relieved at the same time, but at that moment, he did. "Take me there, please."

Gravel lanes, freed of snow, but so white the difference could hardly be seen, brought Old Marro and Silvester to Lord Hevris' home. An easterly landscape design made up the bulk of the estate, but a straight lane of ancient oaks lined the lane towards the round grass lawn before the mansion's entrance. Carriages would follow the road around it to the front door, drop off their passengers, then complete the circle and leave again. It was a dozen strides across, and probably the least interesting part of the garden—usually. Because usually, there wasn't a small tree standing in the middle of it. And usually, small trees weren't covered by ribbons and candles. *Lit* candles.

Old Marro had never seen anything like it. A misbehaving tree was one thing, but a spruce that made a show of it? With fire? In the garden of the man Old Marro wanted to impress? It made him stare at the plant with his mouth gaping wide. He barely saw Silvester glaring at him from his right, and the lord and his daughter standing on his left. His shame wouldn't let him look at them.

"So, can you confirm this is your tree?" Silvester said.

Old Marro couldn't find the words, not even one as short and simple as "yes". He nodded instead.

The lord clapped his hands, making the rings around his thick fingers clatter against each other and the golden velvet of his coat pull tight. "I'm glad that part of the mystery is solved! Now, why did you send it here?"

Old Marro swallowed and forced the air through his voice box. "I... I didn't. It decided on its own."

"The ribbons and candles were also the tree's idea?" Lord Hevris scratched his double chin in thought. "My, I wonder how it got those..."

The old gardener wished he could dig a hole and bury himself in it. He bowed his head. "Please, my lord, accept my apologies. I've been neglecting my garden, and I fear this is the result. Allow me to make up for this mistake."

"Mistake?" the lord laughed. "It's lovely! Especially when little Lara here lit the candles."

The lord's youngest daughter smiled in her mint-green dress like a true miniature lady, and the silver spruce seemed to flaunt its branches towards her. The warm orange light got caught between the branches, flickering between them as if fairies had built their home there. It *was* lovely.

The candlelight reflected in Lord Hevris' eyes when he turned closer to Old Marro. "Do you have more trees available? Or can you train existing ones to hold candles like that? It would be wonderful to have such light and colour in such a dark time of the year. Oh, perhaps we can have a tree indoors! What a delight that would be!"

The daughter's eyes lit up at that idea, but Old Marro wasn't so enthusiastic. "I'm not sure I can, but..." He walked forward and knelt before the tree, and brushed one of its branches. Their colour was far too yellow for his liking. His fault. "I'm so, so sorry. I no longer saw what was truly important. Can you forgive me?"

"It's a *tree*," Silvester snarled. "It can't forgive *anything*."

"And you call yourself a gardener," Old Marro snorted at him without letting go of the branch.

The spruce trembled a little, then pulled its roots out of the ground and took a small step towards its master.

Tears jumped to Old Marro's eyes. "Thank you." He stood up and turned to Lord Hevris again, but not after a long look at his tree. "I think my plants are happy to decorate your estate but only after some well-deserved care. Especially this one."

Silvester laughed in mock again, but the lord nodded. "Understandable. How long do you need? Would a week do?"

Old Marro reckoned that would be enough, and after discussing what trees Old Marro had available, their size, and the costs of candles and ribbons, he and the spruce went home. The tree caused quite a sight. People leaned out of their windows or opened their front door to get a better look and gasped in "oohs" and "aahs". The spruce puffed its branches at them but didn't stray from its gardener.

"I'll light them again tomorrow," Old Marro said as he snuffed out the plant's candles once they reached his garden. "We don't want you to accidentally set fire to yourself, do we?"

The tree didn't seem to mind, but it was stubborn about the ribbons; those had to stay. The spruce seemed to have grown quite fond of its new look. So had Old Marro.

After having watered and fed his plants, he headed inside, smiling. He was a fool. Old Marro had always had the best garden. He just needed a bunch of lights and decorations to see that.

ABOUT THE AUTHOR

PAM HAGE

Pam is an earth scientist from the Netherlands. Dutch might
be her mother tongue, but every
attempt to write a story in that language failed terribly. Only
when she gave English a try, words
started to flow—sort of; she has more hobbies than free time,
so her writing is often interrupted by
drawing, painting, costume crafting, archery and juggling.
www.pamhage.com

twitter.com/queen_of_eagles

instagram.com/queen_of_eagles

pinterest.com/queenofeagles

amazon.com/-/B082497T51

LATE TO THE PARTY

DEANNA YOUNG

T he delivery truck was almost loaded. Chaz took in deep
breaths of cold air and blew them out in stilted puffs, letting a
warm fog coalesce and dissipate around him. There weren't very
many orders for potions, powders, or other magical supplies today,
which was odd for the weekend before Christmas. Maybe he'd get
off early. But then he'd have no excuse not to attend his brother's
Christmas party—the party where everyone would be celebrating
their new internships. The internship Chaz didn't have.

His phone buzzed in his pocket. He opened the text. His phone
buzzed in his pocket. He opened the text, and rolled his eyes. This
was probably the twentieth text his brother had sent him today.

'So, are you coming?' It read.

Chaz blew air through his pursed lips and continued to read.

'...Lila told me she invited Kayla.'

There it was again. The awkward set up. Jeremy and his girl-
friend, Lila, had both been begging him to come to the party for
weeks. He was pretty sure their only motive was to set him up with
Kayla, her cousin. Not that he wouldn't like that; Kayla was totally
the type of girl he'd be interested in. She was practically perfect. But
their pushiness made it weird. Besides, what girl would be interested
in a guy who couldn't secure an internship? A guy who wouldn't

graduate because for some reason no one wanted someone with top marks. It still didn't make sense. He needed to concentrate on sending out more applications before year end, not wooing some girl, practically perfect or not.

Chaz tapped out a quick reply. 'I'm not done with work yet, but I'll try...'

A new text buzzed in his hand before he slipped it into his pocket.

'Just come. It's gonna be fun.' Jeremy followed this text with a GIF of a cat mixing beats on a turntable.

Chaz shook his head and smiled, scrolling through the endless options of GIFs before selecting one that said 'Fine' with a sassy school-girl rolling her eyes and turning away on repeat.

A zip of red streaked past the truck, across the warehouse floor. Right behind it, another streak of blurry color bolted past. Sherlock, one of the warehouse cats, was after something.

Moments later, Sherlock emerged from beneath a shelf with a red fire toad in his mouth.

"Nice work." Chaz hopped out of the back of the truck. "Come on, let's get him back in his cage."

The fluffy orange tabby followed Chaz down the rows of warehouse shelves to an aisle filled with terrariums and cages. Pulling on a pair of leather gloves, Chaz gently removed the indignant fire toad from Sherlock's maw, dropped it back into its enclosure, folded the wire mesh back down, and secured it into place with some metal snaps.

Sherlock mewed, acknowledging his part of the job was done, and padded away. It was almost comical that most of the world didn't believe in magic, yet cats were kept as regular household pets. Their natural magical immunities were what gave them their infamous nine lives.

Clicking chorused down the aisle from around the corner and tiny flashes of light bounced across the floor, then fizzled out. The little Welsh dragon pups had heard someone in the area and wanted a treat.

Chaz grabbed a handful of dried leeches and banana chips and tossed them into the dragon pen. The pups lunged at the scattered treats, climbing over each other and butting heads, each trying to get more than their fair share.

"Hey, I just fed you, I know you're not starving." Chaz said, shaking his head and laughing as he jogged away.

Margo popped her head out of the delivery truck as he approached, "Ah, there you are. I was wondering if you had decided to just head out to the party and leave me here to finish up on my own."

Margo was an elderly woman about a hundred years past normal retirement age. Chaz wasn't sure she'd ever retire. This business was her baby. With her wild, frizzy hair hair, hot pink glasses and brightly colored mumu, she looked like the neighborhood crazy cat lady. Except, she wasn't crazy and cats were just part of the job.

"Yeah, that party is sounding less and less appealing the more my brother texts me. He's trying to set me up with one of Lila's cousins." He shook his head and sighed, taking his hands out of his pocket to grab the last set of orders from the printer tray next to the computer. "Plus, I just don't feel like celebrating with all the other University students. I don't have anything to celebrate right now."

Margo pursed her lips together and put her hands on her hips. "Pish, posh. You're alive and healthy and don't have to walk with a cane. You can dance and eat candy and carbs without worrying about it going to your thighs. That's enough to celebrate right there." She raised her walking stick above her head, then tapped it against her own bulbous bottom to emphasize her point.

He nodded and smiled. "You're right." She couldn't understand the disappointment he was feeling right now. If he didn't get an internship with someone in the next two weeks, he'd have to wait another year to apply, and that was only if his professors allowed him to. Why had he insisted on a magical career rather than a mundane one?

Snatching the final list from the printer tray, he read the list of items he needed to gather. "Wait," he said, snapping his head up, "This invoice is for one of the dragon pups."

"Ah, yes. I'll get a crate," Margo said, moving a tall ladder into place against a warehouse shelf.

"Margo, our truck isn't dragon proof, and we're out of dragon crates. All we have left are flimsy cat carriers. Isn't that against policy?" He knew darn well it was. Bad things happened when dragons were mishandled. Their mischief had been blamed on tornadoes, earthquakes, and even tsunamis before.

"Margo?" When she didn't answer immediately, he waved the list in the air and called her name louder. "Margo!"

"Polo!" she yelled back from the top of the ladder, chuckling to herself.

Chaz crossed his arms across his chest, a furrow in his brow. He wanted to say more, to insist that this was a bad idea, but couldn't. His instincts were at war with each other. He trusted Margo. She owned one of the most well-known magic warehouses in the country. Surely she knew what she was doing, but this seemed careless.

Margo maneuvered down the ladder with a plastic cat carrier tucked under one arm. When she reached the bottom, she waved her free hand in a flippant manner. "It'll be fine. The pup isn't going very far. Just a hop, skip, and a quantum jump, really. We'll make it our first stop. And it's Christmas, for Merlin's sake. You know it's got to be a present for some fairy-eyed kid." She pouted her lip, which was an interesting look on an old woman. "You wouldn't want to disappoint a kid on Christmas, right?"

How many times had he asked his parents for a dragon, only to get shot down? Come to think of it, he'd never gotten a dog either. Not a flying one, or even a mutt from the pound. It would be fun to make another kid's Christmas dream come true.

Chaz took the cage from her, and swung the metal door open. "Right," he said. "It'll be fine." He said more trying to convince himself than to agree with her.

"Besides, Sherlock's coming. He'll keep the Welshie in check." Margo tapped her temple in an I've thought this through kind of way and winked at him.

Hearing his name, Sherlock scampered across the cold metal loading ramp. His toes barely touched down as he made his way into the truck and sprung onto a shelf overlooking the cargo area. Curling into his tail until only his eyes peeked out to keep watch, he became a fluffy orange ball. And that was that. He was loaded.

"Well, get him in the cage." Margo said, startling Chaz as she held out one of the dragons to him. The jet black pup squawked in protest and clicked loud enough to elicit a raised head and perked ears from Sherlock as they stuffed him in the cat carrier.

Chaz carried the creature over the ramp and secured him into place. Hopefully Margo knew what she was doing. "Keep a good eye on him, okay?" He said, looking up at the curry-colored cat on the shelf who looked like he'd been through one too many dryer cycles. Sherlock pointedly looked away from Chaz toward a very uninteresting wall.

"He knows his job," Margo said, seeming to voice the cat's frustration.

Chaz eyed the flimsy plastic carrier one last time and let out a big sigh. Who was he to argue with the boss?

"Okay, let's go," Margo said, climbing into the passenger seat.

The bay doors screeched as Chaz rolled them down and locked them into place. He had just scurried through the side door and finished punching in the security code when Margo rolled down the window and called, "Did you remember the bananas?"

"Margo." Chaz threw as much of an eye-roll into his voice as he could manage, while moving to the driver's side of the truck and climbing in.

Her eyes smiled back at him from under her thick glasses, waiting, as if asking about bananas was the most normal thing in the world.

"We don't sell bananas," he finally said, as if she actually needed an explanation.

"Well, we should," she said. "I like bananas."

Chaz shook his head, pulled his phone out of his pocket, and began typing: Hey, I might be late to the party. We've got more deliveries than expected. He felt a little relieved for a valid excuse to be late as he put the phone on the console and attached it to the charging cord out of habit.

Margo fiddled with some dials on the dash, checking them against the notes on her clipboard.

"Alright, first stop is in Ferris." She punched a few buttons next to the dials and gave him a nod.

The air shimmered and a curtain of colors fell in front of them, transforming the parking lot into a smaller version of the northern lights. They drove through the waving mass of colors, coming out the other side in an identical parking lot hundreds of miles away.

For a brief moment, Chaz's vision swam and his stomach rolled. Traveling by aurora was disorienting. He blinked a few times before his eyes adjusted and he could see the invoice on the dash. Their first stop was only a few blocks away. Thank goodness. The dragon pup wouldn't last long in that flimsy cage.

As if confirming his worries, grating noises sounded from the back of the truck. The tiny dragon was busy chewing on the carrier's gridded metal door.

"Hey, knock it off," he called back, watching the pup in the rearview mirror.

Sherlock jumped off his perch and swatted at the Welshie's snout with a hiss.

The dragon backed away from the front of the cage and clicked in frustration.

"Thanks, Sherlock," Margo said, then patted Chaz's shoulder. "You can relax. He's got things under control."

Chaz fixed his eyes back on the road and merged off the dead side street into traffic.

"Have you had any luck with your internship hunt?" Margo asked.

Chaz blew out a long breath. "No." A heavy weight settled into his gut as he admitted it out loud. "In fact, I haven't even gotten to the testing stage with any of my applications. Well, I did that one time, but you know how that went." He shrugged, "Everyone seems to be afraid to give me a chance because of my age...or something. I'm actually not sure what is going on. I don't want to go to Jeremy's party because I don't even know if I'm going to move on to my fourth year with the rest of them."

Margo gave him an appraising look. "So, what happens if you don't get in? It's not the end of the world. There's always next year."

He grimaced but nodded. "I could technically keep applying for five more years. I just don't know what I want to do. I think that is what is making people not want to pick up my application. They want a commitment from me, and I just can't guarantee that I want to be a mage or a charmer or an anti-architect for the rest of my life." He tapped the steering wheel with his thumbs, shaking his head.

"I can see how that might deter some people. Don't give up, though. You still have a whole week before the new year hits and three before the new school year starts. Anything can happen between now and then."

Chaz didn't think he was going to find an internship between now and the beginning of the next semester, but he nodded, conceding that there could be a chance. "Thanks, Margo. I hope you're right."

The truck hit a bump in the road sending Chaz's phone somersaulting across the dash and onto the floor. It bounced a few times and slipped under the gas pedal. Grunting and biting back a curse, Chaz dug it out with his toe, and tried kicking it back toward the seat with his heel.

The truck lurched as he let off the gas, but the phone was finally free. He hunched over to pick it up, momentarily looking down. A honking horn made him jolt back up and slam on his brakes. A car careened past the nose of the truck, missing them by a hair. It continued to honk as it drove around the corner and out of sight. Their light was green. That car should've stopped, right?

Stiffness gripped Chaz's arms, locking them on the steering wheel. He pushed himself up until his back was rigid and pressing into his seat, trying to steady his breathing.

"Sorry," he said, glancing at Margo.

"For what? Nothing happened." She waved her hand in a 'move along' gesture and turned her focus back on the road. "Close only counts in centaur shoes and crowd charms, right?"

He nodded, puffing out a long breath.

"Now stop breathing so hard. You're fogging up the window," Margo said, turning the heater in the truck to windshield defrost.

Chaz wiped at the window in front of him with his hand, clearing his view, then eased his shaking foot off the brake. Before the truck could start moving again, the air was rent with the sharp sound of screeching tires. Chaz looked into his side-view mirror just before he was hurled forward into the steering wheel, then whipped back against the driver's seat by the belt.

The odor of burnt rubber, hot wires, and other strange smells hung in the air. Light gray wisps of smoke wafted through the cab of the truck. He blinked, clearing the pulsing colors out of his vision. His whole face felt fuzzy and oddly disconnected from the rest of him. What had just happened? Something hit them. Something hit the truck. His ears were ringing and his brain was trying to make sense of the noises around him. He shook his head, trying to dispel the fog.

Freezing air filled the compartment and he shivered.

"...you okay?" Someone shook his left arm. "Hey, seriously, are you alright?" Only then did Chaz notice that his door was open and a large man in coveralls was standing there.

All at once the fog lifted. "Yeah, I think I'm fine." He looked past the man to a group of gawking bystanders. They were talking amongst themselves and pointing to the back of the truck. "What happened?"

"You got rear-ended. That other truck was going pretty fast. Hit 'cha good." The man was looking Chaz over as he spoke. "You've got a cut on your cheek and a bump on your head. Nothing too bad, I think. Should I call you an ambulance? How's your neck?"

Chaz probed his neck and face gently. "It doesn't really hurt. I think I'll be fine." He grabbed a napkin off the dash and pressed it to his cheek, wiping away the blood before it hardened into place.

Remembering where he was and what he was doing, he turned again to see if Margo was alright. "Margo? You oka—" His words cut off. Where was she? The passenger seat was empty.

A lanky teen stepped up next to the coveralled man. He looked back and forth between the two vehicles, never looking directly at Chaz. "I'm real sorry, man. I wasn't paying attention. I mean, I thought you were moving through that green light. I didn't know you'd stopped. It'd been green for a while."

Chaz continued looking around for any sign of Margo as the teen continued to apologize.

Realizing the boy was still talking to him, Chaz turned to him. "Don't worry about it. Accidents happen."

The teen shifted from foot to foot, fidgeting with the keys in his hand, "Um, your cat and dog got out too. I'm so sorry." He held his hands up and added, "But I'll help you find them. They ran off that way right after the accident." He hooked a thumb over his shoulder.

Chaz twisted around in his seat so fast that he almost fell out of the truck. The back door sat wide open and the carrier was upside down with a giant hole ripped out of the side. Two sets of tracks disappeared into the distance against the thin dusting of snow that had begun to fall.

No, no, no, no! A dragon loose in the city? No one would ever hire him as an intern if it got out that he had caused the next 'Hurricane' Katrina.

Chaz unbuckled his seatbelt and hopped out of the truck. Who knows what it could tear up? And Merlin help them all if the dragon found a pineapple. It would start maturing at a ridiculous rate. Thankfully, it wasn't summer; everything was pumpkin spice and peppermint right now.

"Did you happen to see a woman leave my truck?" he asked the people nearby, motioning to the passenger seat. "She was with me in the accident..." Seeing the blank looks on their faces, he added, "Bright orange mumu, crazy hair, kind of plump...really old?"

"No," the teen said. "I didn't see anyone."

The man in the coveralls shrugged and scratched his head. "I don't think I saw anyone either."

Where would she go? It made no sense.

The crowd was starting to disperse and cars slowed as they maneuvered around the accident scene. Chaz's eyes kept darting to the alley where the cat and dog had gone, but he couldn't just leave the truck in the middle of the street. So he waved the men away, and understanding his intention, they stepped off the street. He hopped back into the cab to drive the truck out of traffic. It tilted to the left slightly, and one back tire rubbed against the shifted frame, but it made it the short fifteen feet to the curb.

Snatching his phone, he thumbed through the contacts and placed a call to Margo. The phone rang twice before going to voicemail. Chaz tried again. Nothing. He stuffed the phone in his pocket. There wasn't time for this.

"I have to find my dr..." He paused. "Dog. I have to find my dog. And cat before they get hit or something."

"The city'll probably have 'em picked up soon," the man in the coveralls said, pushing himself into the conversations again. "You should probably stay here and get this all taken care of."

Chaz couldn't breathe; his ribcage squeezed in with each breath but didn't let out. Of course these guys didn't get it. They thought it was just a dog and cat running through the streets. Even if it was, they could still get hurt. Every second he stood around here they'd get farther away. Sherlock could only do so much.

"You alright? You're looking pale. Maybe we should call that ambulance," Coveralls said.

"No." Chaz shrugged away from the man's hand resting on his shoulder. "I have to find them. This is a big city." He tried to put an extra bit of panic in his voice as he spoke the next line. "What if they get hurt. I can't wait and hope that they get picked up."

Coveralls put his hands up in surrender. "Okay, just trying to help."

Trying to be in control was more like it, but Chaz just thanked him and ran around to the back of the truck to close the door. He slammed it a few times before giving up on getting it to shut against the mangled frame leaving it slightly ajar instead.

"I can help..." the teen offered.

Chaz waved him off. "Someone needs to stay at the accident scene. I'm not sure how long this will take. My insurance info is in the glove box. I have to get my dog!" he said and took off down the side alley indicated earlier.

Despite the cold temperatures, the small skiff of snow they'd gotten was already starting to melt. The footprints were gone. The pup was small and couldn't fly yet. That gave him a small chance of catching him before he did any damage or someone figured out he wasn't a dog.

While he was inspecting a set of overturned wooden crates, his phone buzzed. Maybe it was Margo. He pulled it out and stared at the text bubble. No, not Margo. Jeremy. The party is starting bro. I gotta go play host. Kayla should be here soon. This was followed by a GIF of Anna Kendrick waving one arm over her head in a circle, doing the Cowboy dance. Huh. Kayla does look a lot like Anna Kendrick. He'd never realized that before.

Chaz tucked the phone back into his pocket without replying. There wasn't time for this.

Up ahead, a busy street crossed the alley. He looked up and down the road and across the intersection. Which way would the dragon have gone?

Faint music lilted above the sound of city noise. On a hunch, Chaz turned toward the source of the music. He passed a shopkeeper picking up a toppled basket of candy canes, muttering something about wild animals in the city. Chaz smiled. He was on the right track.

The music got louder as he neared a barricaded section of the street. Some sort of Christmas festival was in full swing. A band played lively music music, mixing strangely with the Christmas carols broadcasting over speakers, while people wandered past stalls and carts of handmade goods. Strings of lights hung low, crisscrossing the street. They gave off a welcoming glow in the waning daylight. Within a circle of craft booths, a line of kids at least twenty deep waited to sit on Santa's lap.

A sea of people shifted and shuffled through the festival, and Chaz moved along with them. His eyes were drawn to every yellow or black item he passed. A lot of boots, shoes, and scarves caught his attention but no dragon or cat.

Just as he was about to head back and try somewhere else, a flash of black zipped behind a nearby vendor booth. Chaz skirted around a young family who had stopped to fish something out of a diaper bag and ducked behind the awning.

By the time he got there, the dragon was gone.

The man in the vendor stall selling paintings and hand-crafted frames looked confused. "Um, can I help you?"

Chaz opened his mouth when a yell erupted from behind him. He spun to see a man swatting at a small black animal.

"Shoo. Get out of here!"

The dragon clung to a palm tree sign wrapped in Christmas lights. Sherlock hissed and pawed at the air beneath the pup.

"Good job, Sherlock!" Chaz called out from across the aisle, his breath coming out in visible puffs. "Stay there, keep him treed." Relief radiated from his chest as he shimmied through the crowd.

Moments later Chaz stood below the sign, looking for something to stand on so he could reach the pup. The creature's seamless black scales rippled in agitation, and his extra-large eyes blinked as he stared down at the crowd.

"What is that thing?" the vendor asked.

"Um," Chaz's palms began to sweat and he tried to think fast, "just a porcupine."

The vendor squinted at the creature and looked back at Chaz with a cocked eyebrow.

Before the man could contradict him, Chaz added, "He was burned in a forest fire. Lost all his quills. Very tragic. We call him Quill-less. Quill for short." That was never the pup's name, but Chaz felt like it added to the believability of the crazy story. "He can't grow fur and the reconstructive surgery for his face was just a waste of money. Poor thing."

The vendor continued to stare at Quill, mouth hanging open and his head tilted slightly to the side, obviously trying to digest this information. Finally, he shrugged and handed Chaz a wooden crate to stand on. "I guess I just haven't seen a naked porcupine before."

Chaz laughed, plucking the pup off the sign. "Yeah, it's like giving a cat a bath. You know?"

The dragon didn't struggle, he just clicked his tongue a couple of times, thankfully without the sparks that usually accompanied that action, and settled into Chaz's shoulder.

"I'm glad to see you too, Quill," Chaz said, reinforcing the made-up name.

"Hey, before you leave," the vendor said, "you're gonna have to pay me for the stuff your porcupine ate."

"Oh, yeah." Chaz felt for his wallet in his back pocket, leaning back to accommodate the dragon's weight while only holding him with one arm.

"He ate a whole box of my tropical fruit."

"Fruit! Tropical Fruit?" Chaz said, looking up at the palm tree on the sign.

"Most of my bananas and half a box of pineapple. I'm going to have to buy more."

Chaz's jaw dropped. "Pineapple? Are you sure?" His chest felt like a vice was squeezing it tighter and tighter with each breath.

The vendor crossed his arms. "Yeah. Piña coladas are a favorite here at the festival. And pineapple isn't exactly in season."

The box of overturned pineapple and the shredded remains of banana peels littered the ground behind the booth. Pineapple tops lay everywhere. There were so many. Goosebumps trailed up his arms as horrible scenarios ran through his head.

Chaz looked around, trying to find the quickest way through the crowd while calculating if he'd have enough time to make it back to the truck. Forget not getting an internship, he'd probably be washed and sent out to live in the non-magical world as a consequence for destroying Eastern America.

The crowd parted and Chaz took a step forward to dart through the gap. His ears were ringing from the rush of blood, when a hand clamped onto his shoulder.

"You gonna pay me for that mess?" the vendor's formerly sympathetic face was now an angry glare.

"Oh, yeah. I meant to... I thought I heard my mom," he lied, digging for his wallet in his back pocket and grabbing out all the cash he had. "Keep the change for your trouble. Sorry about the mess! C'mon, Sherlock." He melted away into the crowd, not waiting for a response.

Clutching the squirming dragon tight to his chest, he ran through the crowd, out of the festival. Sherlock dashed ahead, zigzagging around people and clearing a path for Chaz as people paused to watch him or move aside. Once the crowd thinned, Sherlock slowed, keeping pace with them until they reached the side alley once again.

Pulling out his phone, Chaz dialled Margo again. Still no answer. He hung up and went through his phone searching for the magical emergency number. Why couldn't it be an easy number to remember like 9-1-1? He took a deep breath. There was still a chance he could get the dragon back to Margo, and no one would have to know that anything had happened.

The sun had slipped below the buildings, and the cold air blowing through the streets bit at Chaz's fingertips and nose.

Quill smelled pleasant, like grilled pineapple. That couldn't be a good sign.

"How long until you start growing out of control?" Chaz muttered, scratching the pup's bumpy head.

They were almost to the truck. This would all be over soon. Margo would be there waiting for him, right? Because where else could she be?

The dragon squirmed, arching his back and slammed his scaled head into Chaz's jaw.

"Ow!" Chaz blinked, and worked his mouth back and forth, fighting the urge to let go of the wriggling creature.

Quill stopped moving, and Chaz adjusted his grip, lifting the pup higher. With that motion, a burp rumbled out of the dragon, rippling through him in a wave. He expanded like an accordion, his scales shifting and shuffling, until he was the size of a large dog.

It all happened so fast that Chaz staggered back, dropping the pup. He lunged forward and grabbed his tail before he could run away.

The dragon clicked in annoyance and tiny sparks did escape from his mouth this time as he tried to yank his tail free.

Chaz fought to calm himself as he desperately thought back to his potions and anecdotes classes. The pineapple anecdote was something fairly common. But what was it?

Laughter interrupted his thoughts; a group was walking down the sidewalk toward them.

Chaz tried to hide Quill, who was very obviously not a porcupine at this point, while pinning him down.

"Hey, man?" someone asked. "Are you okay?"

The group stopped and stared down at him as he tried to contain the thrashing beast beneath him.

"Yeah, I'm fine," Chaz said with a grunt, moving one hand to clamp the dragon's snout shut so he didn't release any clicks, growls, or sparks.

"My aunt's dog just doesn't want to come back home. He'll calm down in a minute. I've got a leash. It's all good."

"Okay, if you're sure," one of the young men said with uncertainty.

As they moved down the street someone said, "I really don't get the trend with all the hairless pets these days. It's kinda creepy."

Others in the group made comments back, but they'd gotten too far away to hear. Chaz took that as his cue to move. He straddled Quill, and hooked his arms under his front legs, dragging him into the alley, back toward the truck.

Quill hiccupped and burped again, lifting Chaz off the ground with his expanding body. Chaz tried to lock the pup's legs in place and make him hold still, but he was too big. Too strong.

Sherlock strutted up to the pair and sat on his haunches, eyeing them. The tip of his tail flicked back and forth on the ground.

Chaz had been so busy with the dragon he'd forgotten about the cat. "Sherlock, go find Margo! We need her! Go!"

Sherlock looked them both over and sniffed the air, lifting one paw off the ground. He turned and began to bound away.

The dragon burped yet again, spewing a column of fire this time. It singed the tip of the cat's tail from several yards away.

Sherlock jumped and hissed, darting into the alley's shadows, making the dragon scramble backward and bolt in the opposite direction.

Quill was now the size of a horse and Chaz had to wrap his arms around his neck to keep from sliding off. He had wings now, too. When did that happen?

The wings continued to expand and grow as Quill ran, fanning out to scrape against the walls of the buildings, filling the alley with a gritty cloud of dust.

They exploded out of the alley and charged back toward the festival. Quill burped again and Chaz found himself sitting level with the second story windows of the shops along the street. The wings made a thwap, thwap sound as they struck the bare trees along the sidewalk.

Chaz held tight with his legs bucking off the lumbering beast until he regained control. Looking down, he realized with shock that he could see through the dragon. Quill's skin was translucent, as if he had been stretched thin. Chaz's body sunk into him the more they bounced along. It was like sitting on top of stiff black cherry Jell-O. His stomach lurched in time with the enormous footfalls.

The shops along the sidewalk were all closed now and no cars were coming down the street, but the festival was far from empty.

Quill dipped his head and slowed just long enough to eat a barrel of plastic Christmas oranges on display. They appeared to float in the air as the dragon bounded up the street, disintegrating piece by piece until they were gone. The dragon's feet filled in with a solid blackish-red color as the oranges disappeared. The shop windows rattled now with each whomping step.

The scent of roasted almonds blew past them on a breeze. Quill stopped, tilted his head back and sniffed loudly, then leapt forward in a full run. The pound of galloping dragon feet drowned out the music and the chatter of the festival as they drew nearer.

All eyes turned to them. The whole crowd went still. Quill slowed and crept closer to the almond cart. He dug a claw inside and spilled several bags on the ground. The vendor fell down, then screamed when the dragon looked his way, breaking the collective trance. People scattered, running over each other and knocking things down in their haste to get away.

"Great," Chaz said. "Just great." How was he supposed to stop the dragon from eating any more food or trampling people or destroying property? This was going to be a mess.

The authorities would have to get involved now. He needed to call them. Why didn't he ever think to put that number in his phone? and the actual cops -—the non-magical ones—would probably show up soon. Margo was going to lose her license over this for sure. He'd be kicked out of school. No one would hire him once word got out.

His ears were hot with anger and frustration. "Margo, where in the blistering white ash are you!" he shouted. Even if she had run off in the wrong direction to begin with, she should have figured it out what was going on by now and come to help. Where could she be?

He gritted his teeth and forced himself to think. The fact was—

56

she wasn't here. This was up to him. Maybe he could find something the dragon couldn't resist and lure him back to the truck? If only he had actually brought the bananas Margo was teasing him about earlier.

A child's cry broke above the chaos. Quill stopped and looked up.

Chaz held his breath, not daring to make any sudden movements. The dragon sniffed the ground and headed in the direction of the sound.

Chaz's heart dropped into his stomach. *Crap!* What would happen if the dragon found the child? Surely nothing. Quill wasn't trained yet, true, but he also wasn't a wild dragon. He was just a curious and hungry pup. With every step closer Chaz doubted the logic of calling the dragon just a hungry pup.

A careless swipe of the dragon's tail sent several decorated Christmas trees and a hotdog cart crashing to the ground. Quill rounded on the noisy clatter. After pawing at the mess for a moment he realized some of it was food and eagerly gulped up the gravel peppered links.

With the dragon busy eating, Chaz slid down its back. The wing tilted under his weight and lowered him toward the ground. Just before he dropped off, his coat caught on one hard scale hidden among the jell-o-y ones, ripping his jacket zipper apart.

Quill shook Chaz loose as if he were nothing more than an annoying fly and continued lapping up the briny hotdog water.

As soon as Chaz's feet hit the ground, he leapt to a safe distance. A sudden spark of inspiration hit him and he cursed under his breath. Why hadn't he thought of this earlier? Still scanning the low-lit grounds for the child, who had stopped crying, he pulled out his phone and called the Departments of Magic Directory Service.

A musical voice answered after one ring. Thanks for calling the DMDS. We are out of the office for the holiday weekend. Please leave a detailed message, and we'll get back to you. Merry Christmas!

He rolled his eyes, and left a rushed message. Figures.

Straining his ears, he examined the shadows looking for any movement. Nothing. Good, *maybe* the child was gone. He explored the nearby booths, more certain with each second that the child wasn't there. The first booth he came to was lined neatly with paintings and ceramics. The second had cookies, cakes, and sweets displayed on the table. He stuffed a few cookies in his pocket and hurried along. Rugs, shirts, winter hats, garland, and lots of other trinkets filled the stalls, but no child.

A noise drew his attention. Twenty-five yards or so past these booths where a group of people huddled together against a building, looking trapped, including several children. Good they were safe there. He just needed to keep the dragon from heading in that direction and they'd be okay. But how?

Chaz looked back over his shoulder— the dragon was clawing at the cart. With a quick swipe, the door came off its hinge letting buns and condiments spill out. He was still occupied for now, at least.

Jogging past the empty stage, Chaz paused. An industrial fog machine caught his eye. He ran over and flipped it on. It might freak the pup out enough to act as a barrier. Within seconds a sweet smelling cloud rumbled and hissed its way out of the machine.

The noise caught the attention of the dragon. He looked up from where he was eating funnel cake, powdered sugar covering his snout. The color on his body had solidified and darkened halfway to the knees now. He lumbered over to the fog machine, dragging his jiggling belly on the ground. Great. That was the opposite affect he wanted.

More fog rolled out and a fire filled sneeze exploded from the dragon, blowing several instruments off their stands and singeing the garland lining the stage. Quill bit the machine in retaliation but soon lost interest with the non-food item, wandering away snorting and shaking his head.

It worked! At least for now. Next, Chaz needed crumbs for a trail, like in Hansel and Gretel. But what could he use? He turned in a slow circle, taking in the carnage. Destroyed Christmas decorations and pillaged food carts littered the ground. Nothing useful there.

What else? He needed something the dragon couldn't resist. Milk! Milk was like candy to dragon pups.

A food truck along the sidewalk sat with its ordering window wide open. Chaz ran up, and climbed inside. He landed heavily on the floor and immediately yanked open the fridge. They had cream. Even better. He pulled several quarts out, tucking them under his arms as he jumped from the truck. The cream made a hollow half glug sound as he shook the carton that had already been opened.

"Quill! Little Welshie! Over here. Come on. Fresh cream…"

The dragon looked up from where he was biting corn off a rotating spit. His body now had even more solid color. His eyes locked on Chaz and he moved slowly forward, skirting around a new cloud of fog as he passed near the stage.

With the dragon's attention on him, he poured the cream on the ground and ran backwards towards the alley as fast as he could without breaking the line of cream.

Quill's rough tongue flicked out, testing this newly presented treat, he rumbled out a happy purr and licked up the spilled cream with greedy strokes.

Chaz's heart pounded so hard he could hear his heartbeat over the carols still aimlessly spilling from the festival. He fumbled from shaking so hard while opening each new carton of cream.

Police sirens ebbed to life in the distance and his pounding pulse quickened. He had to hurry. Just one more block. He shook the final quart out, sprinkling the last of the cream on the ground.

The dragon's stomach grumbled, coming out like a roar. He stomped toward Chaz, his nostrils flaring in and out.

A trickle of sweat ran down Chaz's face and he stretched out his hand in a calming gesture. "Whoa, boy. Good boy."

Quill slowed, cocked his head and took a tentative step forward. His big eyes were curious and innocent, not menacing. He was just a hungry, oversized pup, not a wild rampaging adult...yet.

Chaz held out one of the empty cartons of cream and walked backwards, going at a steady and careful pace. The dragon licked at the air, following Chaz.

It was working. They just had to get through the alley, then Margo would be able to help. If she was still anywhere in this universe. Either way, getting back to the truck was step one.

Without warning, Quill leapt forward and snatched the cream carton out of Chaz's hand with his teeth. He swallowed it whole, then bent down and licked Chaz's jeans where he'd spilled some cream.

The dragon nibbled the corner of his jacket and Chaz became more forceful. "No!" he yelled in a dog-scolding voice while pushing with all his strength against the beast's face.

The dragon relented and licked Chaz's hair with his hot tongue. Steam from his breath collected in a cloud around them for a moment before Quill spun, knocking Chaz over with his tail and headed back toward the festival.

Chaz threw his arms in the air. "Come on!"

The dragon wasn't moving as quickly as he had before. He seemed tired.

Remembering all at once the cookies in his pocket and something Margo had told him about baby dragons, Chaz started clucking his tongue, mimicking a mother dragon. He held up the cookies and continued making the noises. He was doing a terrible job, but the dragon paused, and turned toward him.

At that same moment, a young woman with dark brown hair in double French braids stepped into view behind Quill. She had a gun out, and it was trained at the dragon's head.

"No! Don't shoot!"

She adjusted her stance and squared her shoulders to take aim. "Move out of the way!"

Chaz dove to the side just as a blue stream of light shot from her gun, freezing the dragon in place. It wasn't a real gun. Chaz collapsed on the ground, relief flooding him, his skin tingling from the spike of unused adrenaline.

He focused on the woman with the gun. "Kayla?" What was she doing here?

"Thanks, Kayla dear," Margo said, appearing out of nowhere with a large silver dragon cage.

"Aunt Margo?" Kayla said, holstering her gun. "I wasn't told it was your dragon on the loose?"

"Apparently so," Margo said, raising the cage into the air and flipping a latch that simultaneously threw the door open and activated some sort of device. It whirred and hummed as she set it on the ground, getting louder and louder, building to a crescendo.

"Aunt Margo?" Chaz said, raising his voice over the noise and looking back and forth between the two women.

Margo nodded. "Great Aunt, technically, but yes." She smiled at Chaz, then put her hand on her chest as if just realizing something. "You two know each other?"

"Yeah. I mean, we've never formally met, but we went to school together last year." Chaz's ears heated, stinging against the cold. Did she know that Jeremy and Lila were trying to set him up with Kayla? Lila and Kayla were cousins, so was Lila related to Margo, too? Was she helping them?

The dragon let out a strange mewling noise, mercifully dragging all their attention away from the awkward conversation. The pup's legs struggled against the magic holding him fast, his eyes twitching with obvious panic.

Chaz stepped closer and Margo put a hand on his shoulder to stop him. "He'll get his mobility back once he's in the cage. You can't touch him or you'll be trapped by the magic too."

"He's terrified though. Poor guy," Chaz said. Holding his hands out, he spoke softly, "It's okay, boy; you're okay." Then with an embarrassed glance at the others he started making a soft clicking noise. Again, the imitation of a mother dragon was terrible, but it worked. Quill stopped struggling, and sat still.

The cage rattled and the hum it had been making built into a whirring buzz. In a flash, the pup was transformed into a whirlwind of glowing dust. He floated as disorganized bits through the air and into the open cage then coalesced again on the other side.

A puddle of shiny, sweet smelling liquid stained the ground where he had been frozen. The pineapple must have drained from the pup somehow. He was a bit bigger than he'd been before the pineapple fiasco, but otherwise seemed to be back to normal.

Fascinating. Without an internship, Chaz would never learn how magic worked so seamlessly alongside technology like this. He'd end up doing some mundane job instead. Which reminded him...

"Kayla, I thought you were a dental hygienist. I didn't know you had taken on a magical career?" Then realizing he probably shouldn't know so much about her, he added, "Your cousin Lila was talking about you last week."

"I am a dental hygienist, but I also do this." She ran her hands over her braids, tucking wisps of hair behind her ears. "We—me and the other staff there—work for the dentist and we also do this kind of stuff. We keep both teeth and society from slipping into decay," she said, then grimaced at her awkward joke.

"Ba-dum-tis!" Margo said from where she was locking the cage and shutting off the still vibrating mechanism.

Kayla smiled appreciatively, made a flourished bow, and stepped over the puddle of pineapple goo to drop a few mints into the cage. "Just in case," she said, looking back at Chaz.

That's right—spearmint was the antidote to pineapple! Duh.

"So, how long have you been doing this job?" Chaz looked down and realized he was a total mess. Dragon slobber soaked one of his legs where the dragon had lapped up the spilled cream. The zipper on his jacket had separated, leaving a gap near the bottom, and his hair... He couldn't see it, but he could feel it wasn't laying right.

Running his fingers through his hair, he attempted to straighten it. "I mean, I don't know anyone who does this kind of stuff."

Kayla kicked at some loose rocks at the base of the cage, "I don't know. I guess I feel a little out of place with the other girls, so I don't mention it when they're around."

"I get that. I don't mention my warehouse job either because it intimidates the other guys. They already can't compete with my style," he said, plucking at his milk stained jeans and slipping his hand casually through the gap in his broken jacket zipper. "It just wouldn't be fair to them."

She laughed. "See, you totally get it."

Smoke wafted out of the cage obscuring Kayla's face for a moment. Quill yawned, dropping with a thump. He looked so sweet and harmless now.

Chaz shook his head. They had come so close to a different ending here. So close. "Margo, where were you? You didn't answer your phone."

"Oh." She waved away his question. "I was keeping watch. I would've stepped in if you needed me to, but you had things under control."

"Under control?" Chaz forced calm into his voice. "Letting the dragon turn into a giant piece of rampaging Jell-O is under control?"

"Oh, it wasn't that bad."

Chaz stared at her, his mouth agape.

"We can talk about this later, Chaz. As for the mess, Kayla's friends are already cleaning that up." She winked. "Plus, I never get to use my dragon insurance. It's nice to see those premiums going toward something for once."

Kayla raised an eyebrow and folded her arms across her chest, but said nothing.

Chaz rocked back as if he'd been shoved. "So you didn't help out just so you could use your insurance?"

Margo pushed her hot pink glasses up the bridge of her nose and managed to somehow look down at Chaz, though he was a foot taller than her. "This was part of your training. A written test is no good. I had to see you in action. You were a bit slow, but you'll do better next time."

"Next time!" Chaz shook his head, "No. No next time. I will not be transporting a dragon without a proper crate ever again."

"See! Learning already."

Kayla laughed and quickly covered her mouth.

Chaz rolled his eyes. "Okay, but he"—Chaz pointed to the dragon—"destroyed that festival, and the city cops are there now."

"Like I said, they'll take care of it. That's what they get paid for. Don't worry about it."

"Are you doubting our skills?" Kayla asked, putting her hands mockingly on her hips.

"No. I just haven't ever...I don't know." He hesitated, running their answers through his mind. "It was more than a little destroyed back there."

"Believe it or not, this'll be an easy cleanup compared to what I'm used to. My very first week on the job we had to go round up a clutch of lost Blue Ridges in California. They started the biggest fire in the state that year."

"Seriously?"

"Yep." She smiled. "This really is an easy cleanup. Just a few charms and a little bit of elbow grease and everything'll be back to new."

The pup snorted in his sleep and shifted to his back, putting his paws in the air. Margo seemed to take that as her sign. She straightened up and clapped her hands. "Well, we better get going. Gotta finish this delivery. Thanks again, dear."

"No problem," Kayla said somewhat distractedly while typing on her phone. She waited, typed again, then turned to Margo. "Do you mind if I come with you?" Her eyes darted toward Chaz for a fraction of a second. "To make sure the pup makes it to his new home safely."

"Great idea! We've got a cozy middle seat in the truck." Margo gave a not-so-subtle nudge to Chaz in the ribs.

Chaz brushed her arm away, hoping Kayla hadn't noticed.

"Are you sure you've got room?" Kayla asked, adjusting her pack's straps on her shoulders.

"Definit—" Chaz started, then froze and slapped a hand to his forehead. "The truck is pretty messed up." He turned to Margo. "After the crash, the back doors wouldn't even close."

"All fixed," Margo said.

"What? How?" Chaz asked, lifting the handle on the dragon cage and unlocking the wheels that allowed it to roll along like a piece of luggage.

"Being a part of the magical world has its perks. I know a guy here. Does emergency repairs on aurora trucks."

"But those were a lot of repairs."

Margo waggled her fingers. "I told you: maaaagic..." She turned and headed to the truck with Sherlock on her heels.

When the other two didn't immediately follow her, Margo looked over her shoulder. "Come on, you two, I have other things I want to do. Like fall asleep watching Netflix. And you've got that party."

He gave a sideways glance to Kayla. "I suppose I should show up to part of my brother's party."

"What party?" Kayla asked, moving closer to Chaz as they walked.

"Um…" Chaz felt like he'd been caught for some reason. "My brother's Christmas party at the University commons."

"Wait, my cousin Lila is throwing a party there tonight."

"Yeah. Same party." He lifted the dragon into the truck and closed the magically fixed door with ease.

"I didn't know Jeremy was your brother." She puckered her lips in thought and scrunched her brows, looking him over before climbing into the cab. "I can see some resemblance now."

"Weird. He's actually my stepbrother."

"Oh." Her eyes widened, and she looked like she was trying to decide whether to apologize or not.

Chaz laughed. "I'm kidding. He's my older brother. We do have different moms though."

She squinted at him, skeptical. "Really?"

"Okay, we have the same mom, but we've never confirmed anything about our dad through DNA testing. So there's a chance we're only half-brothers."

It was Kayla's turn to elbow him in the ribs after she buckled her seatbelt. "How am I supposed to believe anything you say now?"

He laughed and shrugged. "I guess you can't," he said, feeling much better about how the night was going.

A few blocks down the road, the cab of the truck fell silent, and Margo piped up. "So, Chaz, you were wondering what I was doing while you were chasing the dragon?"

"You said you were watching me," Chaz said, confused.

"I was. But why? Did you wonder about that?"

"Part of the training for the warehouse?" Chaz's words slowed as he thought about what he was saying. That didn't make sense. Why give him a high pressure situation to deal with for job training without telling him, or helping him?

"Nope. I've decided that for the first time in over twenty years, I'm going to sponsor an intern. But, I needed to give him a test first —which he passed with flying colors, by the way—so I'd have time to file the proper paperwork before the new semester started."

"Margo?" Chaz said, too stunned to say anything more.

"Polo!" she said, cupping her hands around her mouth, megaphone style.

"Are you serious?" His mind raced and he tried to replay her words in his head. "You were talking about me, right? I'm the intern, right?"

Margo laughed. "Of course you. Geeze, I thought you were smart. I need to pass on my vast mountains of knowledge to a worthy pupil." She let out an exaggerated sigh. "But I guess you'll have to do."

Chaz released a barking laugh. "Thank you, Margo. I just don't know what to say." A weight lifted off his shoulders and his skin tingled, sending goosebumps down his arms.

"I was going to put the letter of internship in an envelope as part of your Christmas bonus tomorrow, but it looked like you needed to hear it tonight."

Chaz reached across Kayla, who was also beaming happily, and patted Margo's knee. "I really did. It's been a rough week. And today…" He shook his head, chuckling. "I wondered what in the world you were thinking when you put that dragon in the cat carrier."

"Yeah. That was totally planned." She said in a monotone voice. "Totally."

The new owners were waiting excitedly for the delivery of their dragon pup. They had a good laugh when they learned what had caused the delay. They even decided that they liked the name Quill, and somehow that made it easier to leave him behind after all they'd been through.

The other deliveries had been sent out with another courier after the accident happened, so now that the dragon pup was with his new owners, the night was coming to an end. Chaz punched in the coordinates to the warehouse and they headed out. Within minutes, they were back in their city.

Kayla sat back against the seat and let out a sigh. "It's been such a long day."

Chaz smiled. "You can say that again." A long, crazy, but eventually good day, he thought. "Do you need a lift back to your vehicle?"

He turned the truck around and craned his neck to watch his mirrors as he backed up to the loading bay.

"Yeah. That'd be great," Kayla said, sounding relieved.

A gurgling growl tore through the cab and Kayla grabbed her stomach, groaning with embarrassment. "Sorry. I kind of skipped lunch today, then had to run off to catch a baby dragon before I could eat dinner."

Chaz grimaced. "Yeah, sorry about that."

The truck's bumper lightly kissed the rubber barrier on the loading dock and Chaz turned the vehicle off. "You should let me take you to dinner before I take you back. I owe you at least that much."

Margo pretended to not be paying attention, but Chaz caught her smile reflected in the window before she turned back to them all wide-eyed and expectant. "Yes! That sounds great."

"You want to come too? What about your Netflix date?" Chaz said, hoping to deter her from tagging along, but not wanting to be rude.

Margo's smile split so big her dentures fell out. "Dang it. Darn teef."

"You might need those for dinner…" Kayla said, giggling as Margo swatted at her arm.

"Watch yourself, or I'll throw these at you. They bite!"

They all laughed.

A series of coughs interrupted Margo's laughing, "Dang. I can't handle this much fun, apparently. I think I better stay in tonight. I'm beat, and I have some paperwork to file. What kind of food were you thinking of getting? Chinese? Italian? Mexican?"

Kayla looked back and forth between Chaz and Margo. "Italian sounds good, I guess. Do you want us to bring you back something?"

"No, no, I'm fine. Got some Cheetos and chamomile tea waiting for me. But why don't you take the aurora and go for some real Italian food? In Italy." She waggled her eyebrows at them.

Chaz's jaw dropped. "Margo, that'd be an expensive jump." He shook his head. "We're fine. There are plenty of places around here."

"Nonsense. You should celebrate getting your internship. It'll be fun." She popped open the door and snapped her fingers, calling Sherlock to hop onto her shoulder. "I insist. Go. Have fun."

Kayla looked at Chaz and smiled, giving him a half shrug.

"Are you up for that then," Chaz asked her, trying to clarify before committing to taking her out to dinner halfway around the world.

"Yeah. Why not? Sounds better than staying home or going to a rowdy college party," she said. "No offense to your brother," she added.

"I'm totally offended," Chaz said, with a gasp and a wide-eyed, serious stare.

She laughed. "Great, let's get going then."

"Have fun, you two," Margo said, swinging the door open and hopping out with more dexterity than someone her age should have. "See you on Wednesday."

"Goodbye, Auntie." Kayla said.

Chaz waved. "Thanks again."

"You're welcome. Now, get outta here." She waved over her shoulder as she walked away.

Kayla leaned across the gap and pulled the door closed.

Noticing they were sitting closer than they needed to be now, Chaz said, "There's an extra seat now if you want it?"

"I'm fine," she said.

He turned away to hide his smile and stole a glance at the in-dash-clock while tuning the aurora dials. Good thing Italy stayed up late for the tourists.

"How about Florence?"

"Sure."

He pulled out his phone to tie up one last loose end: I won't make it to the party. I'm going out. With Kayla. ;) His brother would somehow take all the credit for this, but right now Chaz didn't care.

A curtain of colors fell in front of them. Chaz grinned, enjoying the way his heart raced as Kayla clasped his upper arm and leaned in a little closer.

ABOUT THE AUTHOR

DEANNA YOUNG

Deanna Young was born and raised amongst the sandstone mesas of Aztec, New Mexico. Most of her childhood was spent chasing her siblings through sagebrush, cacti and sprawling pastures. Hunting for lizards, milking goats, exploring ruins, reading Tolkien with her dad and inventing crazy things—like a wheelchair for a chicken with a broken leg—teased a dreamer and doer out of a very shy child. Those adventuresome younger years helped stoke Deanna's imagination and fuel her desire to write as an adult. Now she lives at the other end of the same desert under the shadow of the Oquirrh Mountains in Erda, Utah with her husband and four children. It is here; just south of the Great Salt Lake, that she continues to build worlds with words. Fantasy and sci-fi are her favorite types of stories to write, though she's dabbled in a bit of everything. Deanna has published two flash fiction stories and two short stories in other anthologies, one of which had the honor of being selected for the cover art against other applicants from across the country. Her work can be found on Amazon in both volumes of Once Upon a Future Time (Volume I is the issue containing her featured cover story, and is also available on Audible), and in the kindle only versions of Something Lost, and Something Found by LDS Beta Readers. Follow her on Amazon, and on Facebook by searching for Deanna Young, and Author Deanna Young, respectively.

facebook.com/authordeannayoung

instagram.com/author_deannayoung

amazon.com/author/deanna_young

FRANKENSANTA

A. A. WARNE

Just before lunchtime, three elves left footprints in the snow, crunching the iced surface with their pointy-tip shoes as they hurried towards Santa's shed. Ryo, the shortest of the three, shoved a small box beneath his shirt.

"Why did you do that?" Trislar eyed Ryo's stomach then checked their surroundings, hoping no one else had seen.

Ryo tsked. "We don't want anyone taking it from us, do we?"

Ilrune rolled his eyes. "No one cares what we do, and besides,"—Ilrune leaned in closer— "no one will even know what it is."

Trislar flashed his pearly white teeth and put a little kick in his step. "I can't wait until we show Santa."

Ilrune and Ryo stopped. "Shush!" they demanded.

"What?" Trislar flopped his head to the side under the weight of their judging eyes.

"No one needs to know," Ryo grabbed Trislar by the arm, forcing him forward. "Remember?"

Nodding, Trislar took back his arm. "Yes, yes," he said in a mocking tone. "Don't tell anyone. Keep my mouth shut. And when we do talk about it...whisper!"

Ryo sighed.

"What is it now?" Trislar skipped ahead, not bothering to wait for the answer. He was so excited that a small laugh escaped his lips. Reaching Santa's shed first, he slid open the large wooden door and closed it once they were all inside. He turned and noticed the giant-sized, fully electric red sleigh taking up most of the space.

"Santa?" Ryo called out.

Santa sat up straight and peeked over the door from within the sleigh. "If it isn't the trinity of..." He mumbled something under his breath. He reached for the grease cloth and wiped his hands.

"It's nearly lunchtime." Trislar bounced on his toes. "So we knew you'd be finished working—"

"Finished?" Santa said, cutting him off. Shaking his head, he laughed. He rocked the sleigh slightly as he stood. His red overalls stretched over his bulging stomach and his long-sleeved white shirt showed signs that he'd been fixing the sleigh for some time.

Reaching across to the side cup holder, Santa retrieved a glass of milk.

"Sooo..." Ryo began. "Santa?"

Santa raised an eyebrow, but kept the glass at his lips.

"We made something," Trislar squealed.

"Well I sure hope so," Santa said, as his stomach rumbled. "It's the first of December and all Elves are busy preparing for Christmas."

"Er..." The trinity looked at one another then back to Santa. "We've made something for *you*."

"Ah," he cradled his stomach. "Wouldn't be some cookies now, would it?"

They laughed and Ryo pulled the box from beneath his shirt. "Actually, it's better than any cookie in the entire world," he squeaked.

Santa scoffed. "I highly doubt that." He took the box anyway, lifted the lid, glanced inside and then closed the lid again.

"What are you three up to now?" His voice was low and deep.

"It's not a repeat of 2011," Ryo said, averting his eyes.

"Or 1999!" Trislar added.

An awkwardness settled between them.

"Or," Ilrune broke the silence. "1995. '88. '83. '82. '76—"

"Alright!" Ryo snapped.

Santa laughed. It came at them in a wave, surrounding them like a cuddle. He breathed in deep, filling his lungs, then let out another chuckle until they all joined in.

"You know," Santa said, after catching his breath. "Whatever this is, I don't want it."

The trinity moaned in unison. "But Santa!"

"But nothing." He handed the box back to them. "Twenty-four days left and you three are here annoying me instead of helping the village prepare."

"But this"—Ryo took the box from Santa's hands and held it up higher to his face—"*is* help!"

"Think about it," Ilrune said. "Imagine delivering the entire planet's presents in half of the time it usually takes."

Santa scoffed again.

The elves glared at him. They weren't joking.

"You can't be serious," he said. "We retired the reindeer years ago and this beast"—he gestured to the fully automatic flying sleigh —"is amazing! Why would I let you touch it with that?"

"Because..." Trislar held up one finger in the air to make a point. "It's an enhancer."

Santa's eyes widened in surprise.

Ilrune bounced on his toes. "Just try it once. And if it works, it works." He shrugged his shoulders like it wasn't the biggest deal of their lives.

"And I reckon," Ryo said, "it's the best invention since the automatic sleigh itself."

The Elves nodded.

"An enhancer, you say?" Santa rubbed his thumb along his chin. "It is a good idea," he said slowly. "But—"

The trinity moaned.

"But," Santa held up his own finger this time, quieting them. "We will put it in place next year when we have more time to test it first."

Trislar's eyes instantly filled with water. "But, but..." His bottom lip stuck out. "That's ages away."

"Can't we just test it once?" Ryo added.

"Just this once," Ilrune pleaded. "And if it works, you won't see us until after Christmas. But if it doesn't work, then we can fix it so it's ready for after Christmas."

"Either way," Ryo lowered his voice, "you won't see us until after Christmas."

Santa's nostrils flared. "By the guidance of the Northern star, how did I get you three?"

He leaned out of the sleigh. His bulging stomach scraped the top of the door as he collected the box straight out of Ryo's hands. "Once," he snapped. "And only once!"

The three elves giggled as they bumped fists.

"Okay," Ilrune said, the first to calm down. "This is what you need to do." He quickly fetched a ladder from the back wall and climbed it so he had a better view inside the sleigh. He was careful not to touch Santa's sleigh. There had been too many bad experiences to name, and they were forever on strict conditions never to touch the sleigh again.

Ilrune pointed to the dashboard, explaining exactly what to do and how to do it.

"Now," Ilrune said, "when you're ready, start it up and take it for a run."

"Okay, Elves," Santa said, sitting on the bench seat. "A promise is a promise. None of you are going to break their promise, right?"

"Right!" they sang in unison.

Santa reached for the round green ignition button. His wide, plump finger touched the silky surface, slowly moving inward, and brought the engine to life. But the initial spark jumped over the button, encompassing his finger, burst in his hand, ran up his arm, across his chest and down throughout his body.

Santa jolted back and forth.

Then went limp.

The elves stood there, eyes wide and jaw hanging open, unable to move a muscle. After a long moment of silence, a sound eventually escaped Ilrune's lips. "Um..."

"Oh no. He's dead," Ryo reached for the sleigh door.

"Don't touch that!" Ilrune shouted.

"Shush!" Trislar barked back. "Someone will hear you and find
—" He went silent, his face blank.

"Wait!" Ilrune took a bolt from the shelf behind him and
handed it to Ryo. "Throw this at the sleigh."

Ryo did as he was told. The bolt hit the sleigh door and bounced
onto the ground.

"Did you see a spark?" Ilrune asked.

"Nope."

"Good. Now open the door."

"You open the door!" he snapped back.

"I'll open the door," Trislar said. "Just be quiet, will you!"

"Oh, now you want to be quiet." Ryo rolled his eyes.

Trislar took a step closer, hovered his hand, then grabbed the
handle. In unison, the trinity let out a sigh of relief.

He opened the door and climbed in. Santa was slumped half off
the bench seat, with his head resting against the dashboard.

Trislar turned to the other two, his face pale, eyes bulging.

"What?" Ryo snapped.

"He's..." Trislar whispered. "Dead."

"He can't be!" Ryo yelled. "He's Santa!"

"It's the first day of December!" Trislar said, running his finger-
nails deep into his own scalp. "What are we going to do?"

"The High Elf," Ryo moaned. "We have to tell him."

"No," Trislar cried. "Anything but that!"

"I know." Ryo reached for him, wrapping his arm around Trislar's shoulder for support. "But what choice do we have?"

"There is one thing," Ilrune finally spoke. The other two looked
up, watching him climb down. "Remember the reindeer defibrillator? We could use that and bring him back to life?"

"Er..." Ryo's eyes darted between Trislar and Ilrune. "Are you
serious?"

Ilrune climbed back down the ladder. Trislar jumped out of the
sleigh. The three of them huddled closely together.

"Serious about what exactly?" Ilrune said. "That the reindeer
defibrillator works or that Santa is dead? And if we don't bring him
back to life, he'll remain proper dead!"

"But doesn't it have weird effects?" Trislar's voice went high. He shoved his hands in his pockets as he took one step back.

"Yeah," Ryo added. "That's why they retired the reindeer. Half of them went blind, two had uncontrollable bladders, and one is in a permanent state of comatose."

"Not to mention Rudolf," Trislar added.

"Oh yeah. I can't believe they made a song about it." Ryo shook his head. "That nose was toxic! And to think, that atomic bomb rode around the entire world in one full night."

"Wait." Ryo turned back to Ilrune. "You want to use it on Santa?"

"Think about it!" Ilrune paced the shed. "The reindeer were hundreds of years old, and we used the defibrillator how many times?" He shrugged his shoulders.

"Enough to create zombies." Ryo pointed east where the reindeer were now kept out in a paddock, waiting to die.

Trislar shivered.

"That shouldn't have happened," Ilrune said. "And it won't happen if we do it only once."

Ryo's face fell into his hands. "Fine. But if it doesn't work, you're telling the High Elf."

"Fine," Ilrune said sarcastically as he slipped out of the shed and returned moments later with the defibrillator.

Climbing into the sleigh, Ilrune placed the device onto the bench seat. He unclipped the forks from the side of the machine and held them up.

"Do you remember how to use it?" Ryo said, arching his neck to look inside the sleigh.

"In a sense..." Ilrune drifted off, lost in thought.

"What does that even mean?" Trislar's hands went back to his head, holding it for support.

"It means," Ilrune snapped, "he's no reindeer."

Ryo looked to the door. "Maybe I should've—"

Ilrune cut him off. "Not until we get this over and done with." Ilrune stuck the prongs into Santa's ears, clicked the machine on, and reached for the defibrillator pads. Pressing them together, he felt the charge between his hands. His eyes remained on the machine as he waited for the charge to rise. One little red bar lined up beside the next, until it reached maximum. The lights flickered, and the bulb overhead popped! The dull emergency light above the door came to life, illuminating just enough to see. Ilrune quickly pulled the pads apart and pressed them to Santa's back.

The body jumped. In one swift movement, his back arched, then dropped further down than before, flopping onto the sleigh floor.

"Did it work?" Ryo jumped up, standing on the sleigh's edge.

"The power's out!" Trislar said, rushing to the shed door. "The entire village is in darkness." He closed the door again, latching the lock.

"How much charge did you put in him?" Ryo glared at Ilrune who shrugged. "You're suppose to give him enough to bring him back to life not make him permanently dead!"

Ilrune rolled his eyes.

Moaaarr.

The trinity jumped.

"Did he just...moan?" Ryo whispered.

"Move!" Ilrune pushed Ryo in the back, forcing him out of the sleigh. "Move!" he screamed, jumping down after him.

Huddled up against the door, the trinity stared at the sleigh. First, a hand banged against the dashboard.

Rroooaaa.

"It worked!" Ilrune whispered, squeezing the other two elves' arms with excitement.

His arched back rose first. Slowly lifting his head, he stood tall. His hand came up and ran down his face.

"Um..." Ryo stepped forward. "Are you alright?"

Shoulders forward, Santa's head turned in their direction. His eyes remained closed.

Ilrune leaned close to Trislar and whispered, "I don't think he's breathing."

Santa opened his eyes. Cold, charcoal and black, he glared directly at the trinity.

They stumbled back, grabbing one another for support.

A moan escaped Santa's lips again. He turned back around and sat on the bench seat.

"I told you this was a bad idea," Trislar said. His whole body shook.

"When did you say that?" Ilrune snapped.

"He did," Ryo said. "But never mind that. You said if it didn't work, you'd tell the High Elf."

"Er..." Ilrune shifted his weight from one foot to the other.

"Hurry along then," Ryo added.

"But why me?" Ilrune shook his head. "We're all in this together."

Trislar and Ryo exchanged looks.

"I'm scared of the High Elf." Trislar's arms wrapped around himself like he was trying to keep it together.

"And," Ryo paused, trying to think of an excuse. "I'm staying here so I can keep an eye on Santa."

Just as Ryo finished talking, a vicious, loud sound ripped throughout the shed, as the sleigh smashed through the side wall.

The trinity were blown into the air and crashed into the floor, metres from where they were standing.

Ilrune stumbled to his feet first. "Oh no," he cried. "Now we're in trouble." He watched the sleigh lift high up into the dark night, disappearing out of sight.

"You think!" Ryo screamed. "I'm not going anywhere near the High Elf. He'll kill us."

Trislar brushed off the dust, checking his coat. "No, he won't."

"Then you go," Ryo glared, "and explain all this!"

Trislar rapidly shook his head.

"Exactly. Now we've lost Santa or whatever that thing is, and it's December. December!" Ryo yelled.

"Let's calm down," Ilrune put up his hands, closing the distance between the other two. "I've got a plan."

"Another one?" Ryo sighed. "Because that one"—he pointed to the sky where Santa had disappeared—"worked so well."

Ilrune glared. "Do you want to listen or what?"

"Fine." Crossing his arms. Ryo tapped his foot.

Trislar gulped.

"The High Elf told us not to bother him, right? So, what if we get someone else to help us bring him back, fix him, and then Christmas will be saved!"

"But who?" Trislar asked.

"I don't know about this," Ryo said.

Trislar blurted out. "The Fairies."

Ilrune rolled his eyes. "The Fairies won't ever talk to us again. You know that. I was talking about the Easter Bunny!"

"Him?" Ryo moaned.

"Have you got a better idea?" Ilrune crossed the shed, pulled sheeting from the side, and held it up against the shed door.

"But he's got a bad attitude," Trislar added.

"I know." Ilrune pulled out his handy gift gun from his belt and glued it in place, reaching for another sheet.

"Fine." Ryo started to help, gluing the bottom half. "But, so you know, I don't like this."

They finished fixing the shed, hoping no other elf would notice it once had a hole. Then they ran through the village, careful not to be seen by any other elf. Once they reached the other side, they got into an elf car.

"What are you doing?" Ilrune snapped at Trislar, who was climbing into the car beside him. "The High Elf won't notice one car missing, but he will if there's two gone."

Trislar breathed in, holding his breath. Slamming the door shut, he climbed in between Ilrune and Ryo, to be squashed in the middle. "This is the longest night ever."

Ilrune laughed. "It's just begun," he said as he turned the engine on. He lifted the steering wheel, pressed his foot flat on the pedal, and the car shot up into the sky, disappearing behind the clouds. Careful to remain hidden, the elf car passed over one country after another, and within hours, finally descended somewhere over the tropics.

"This doesn't seem right," Ryo said with his face pressed against the window.

Illrune tapped the dashboard screen. "The location device is telling me this is where he is."

The car hovered above the treetops over a tiny island, the water crystal blue and the sand the brightest of yellows. The sun not only radiated down but also bounced off the water, glaring at them in all directions.

The car lowered between the trees. Illrune held his breath until the tires landed softly on a grassy patch. Ilrune opened the door first. Hot, dry air engulfed the car.

The three of them moaned instantly.

"How does anyone live in these conditions?" Trislar huffed.

They stretched their legs, unclipped their jackets, and stripped each layer as quickly as they could.

"Surely, he can't be here." Ryo shielded his eyes from the sun. "There's no one here."

"No one!" a voice bellowed behind them. "Are you calling me no one!"

"Oh!" Ryo jumped, startled to see the extra tall rabbit, dressed in a Hawaiian shirt, marching towards them.

"You there." The Easter Bunny pointed a finger at them. "Better be thankful that there are no humans on this island—or anywhere remotely close by, for that matter."

The three looked out to the glistening horizon.

"Because," the bunny continued, "hovering above the treetops like some lost tourist is not normal in the human world."

Their faces dropped.

"So that makes me think..." He crossed his arms, leaning all of his weight on his right leg while he tapped his left foot impatiently. "That you three have never been close to the human world in your life, and you're not allowed to be here right now."

The trinity glanced at one another.

"Well..." Ryo began.

"Not technically," Trislar added.

Ilrune stepped forward. "Let us explain—"

The Easter Bunny burst into laughter. He rolled around in the sandy grass, struggling to catch his breath.

"I'm sorry," he said, clutching his stomach as he stood. "But this is way too funny."

"Mr Easter Bunny?" Ryo stepped forward.

"No, I go by Frank now."

"Frank?"

"Yeah, Frank. You got a problem with that?"

"Er..." The trinity glanced at one another then back to Frank. He started laughing again.

"You three are in big trouble."

"Perhaps." Ryo scratched his head. "But—"

"That wasn't a question," Frank said. "And you've turned up to my holiday island thinking I'm going to save you?"

"It would be nice—" Trislar whispered.

"From this!" Frank held out his phone, showing a photograph of Santa's back, racing through the clouds in the sleigh, heading towards a jumbo jet.

Ilrune snatched the phone. "How did you get this?" His hands shook. "How many people already know!" his voice jumped. "Do you know where he was headed?" Looking from the device, he stared at Frank then back to the device. "If you already know, then why are you still here on holiday and not out there saving him!"

"Hold on there!" Holding up his hands to surrender, Frank then snatched the device back. "This is your mess. Your holiday season is in jeopardy. Not mine." He paced along the sandy beach. "And now my peaceful, isolated holiday island is currently being disturbed by you three muck ups."

"So..." Ryo scratched the back of his neck. "You're going to help us?"

Frank's face dropped. "What?"

"We need help," Trislar stepped forward, eyes pleading. "We need to get Santa back to the village so we can fix him, then Christmas will go on like none of this happened."

Frank rolled his eyes.

"He definitely needs fixing," Frank said. "Nearly squashed poor Cupid flat with the sleigh."

"Cupid?"

"Yeah, he's the one who took the photo." Frank wiggled the device in front of them. "You know, he's the last of his kind. Santa might be all about the jolly, but he didn't need to kill love."

"I'll get the car," Ilrune said.

"I'm warning you three. Twenty-four hours and I'm gone. I

81

don't want to be involved. I hate the snow. And none of this is my problem."

"But you'll help?" Ryo said with his hands clasped against his chest, pleading.

Frank lifted a hand and clicked a button. Instantly, a car hovered above the sand beside them.

"Help is a fluid word," he said reaching for the door. "And throw that tiny box that you call a car in my boot."

The trinity managed it themselves, then strapped in, buckling their belts.

"You're like a trinity of nightmares," Frank said, playing with the radio.

Ilrune rolled his eyes.

The bunny threw his foot down on the pedal, and they took off into the sky, shooting much faster than their own car.

Within the hour, they were landing. Unable to reach the windows, the three Elves couldn't determine where they were.

Shutting the engine off, Frank opened the door. The freezing cold hit them first. "Welcome home, boys."

The High Elf's face appeared. His pointy hat was bent, collar scruffed, and his nostrils flared. "You three have a lot to answer for!"

They were too frightened to moan. Climbing out, they saw the entire village had come out to stare. Dropping their chins to their chests, the three elves dragged their feet through the streets and all the way to the High Elf's cabin.

Behind them, Frank and the High Elf whispered all the way to the office. The sound made the trinity shiver. Once inside, they saw no comfort in the High Elf's face when he sat down at his desk. Instead, they sunk lower in their seats, feeling the weight of his glare.

"What did you three idiots do now?"

Ilrune sat in the middle, eyeing Ryo to the left, then Trislar to the right. Did the High Elf not know? How was that even possible? He was supposed to know everything!

"Um..." Trislar began, but Ryo spoke over him. "It wasn't our fault."

"What!" the High Elf screamed. "Everything that goes wrong in

Elf land..." He stood and paced behind his desk. "...is always your fault. What makes you think this time is any different?"

"Because..." Ryo racked his brain for an idea.

"Because is not an answer," the High Elf reminded them.

"If I can step in here..." Frank appeared behind them, arms crossed, leaning against the wall. "They did try and fix their error."

"Right." The High Elf seemed to calm at Frank's words. "Right." But as soon as he linked eyes with the trinity, the red in his face seemed to get even brighter.

"Let's start again, shall we?" He took a big breath in and let it out with a huff. "I believe Santa is currently somewhere in the Eastern district." He paused. The moment of silence did nothing to calm the Elves' nerves. "Why he's there is beyond me. Yet the circumstance of how and, particularly, why he's there will be explained by you three." The High Elf sat down at his desk, laced his hands neatly together, and evened all his facial features before saying, "You may begin."

"He took the sleigh," Trislar whispered.

"Of course he did." The High Elf sounded as though he was holding back a scream. "How else does Santa travel the world?"

Ilrune breathed in and held it.

Ryo shifted in his seat.

"Here's the truth," Ilrune began. "We developed..."

Ryo cut him off. "Santa's dead."

First, there was silence. It felt like it went on for days. Then there was the loudest cackle bursting out of the High Elf's mouth. He slapped the table with a bang, before calming down. "Good one," he said between breaths.

But the three elves weren't laughing.

"Why are you three looking at me like that?" The High Elf eyeballed each of them, his smile still wide.

"That wasn't a joke," Trislar said.

The High Elf's face froze, smile and all. His eyes widened further. A crease indented his forehead, before he lost color.

"Err..." Trislar began, but Ilrune shushed him.

"How is he dead when he's in the sleigh currently zooming all around the world?" As he spoke, his head cocked to the side, left eye twitching.

"It was an accident," Ryo blurted out again. "Honestly,"—he placed both hands up—"a *real* accident."

"Oh no." The High Elf lowered his head down onto the table. "You killed him and then used the defibrillator."

"How'd you guess?" Trislar bounced in his seat.

Even Frank glared at him, but the High Elf kept his head firmly pressed against the wood. "Because you three idiots would be the only ones in the entire world who would do such a thing!"

"But the world needs Santa!" Trislar's bottom lip trembled.

"You really don't seem sad about this," Ryo added quietly.

The High Elf lifted his head. "Sure I'm sad. That Santa was one of the finest that I've ever worked with. But emotions are pointless in a time of urgency."

"Urgency?" Frank spoke up. "Surely Santa can't get into too much trouble?"

"I don't even want to know what *it* is doing out there."

He stood and yelled for his assistant. Two elves came rushing in, each holding pen and paper. "I need you to contact every mythical creature you can. If they've seen Santa in the last twenty-four hours, I want to know every single detail, and don't miss a thing."

"Yes, High Elf."

"And another thing, prepare for arrival."

The two assistants gasped.

"Arrival?" Frank asked.

The three elves still sitting quietly on their chairs looked at one another. They were sure they had heard that term before, but because they often remained well away from their own community, common labels were lost on them.

The High Elf told his assistants to hurry. He then sat, tried to lean back in his chair, then stood and paced the room. "Santa died, did he not?"

"Yes," the three elves whispered in unison.

"At the very moment a Santa dies, his Christmas spirit is transported across the world and into the jolliest man on the planet."

"Like a *new* Santa?" Frank said, now standing tall, waiting for the High Elf to go on.

"Yes. That is exactly what he will be."

"I've always wondered how it worked." Frank ran a finger along his jaw line.

"So..." Trislar smiled. "The world has a Santa then!"

"Don't for a second think this is over!" the High Elf snapped. "We might have an hour, or a week, or even an entire month before the new Santa comes to our very border. But when he does, what do you think will happen?" He looked directly at the elves.

Their bodies went rigid. "Um..." Trislar looked around the room for an answer. "He becomes the new Santa?"

The High Elf sunk his face into his hands, speaking after a long moment of silence. "This is an Elf tradition that all Elves should know as it's just as important as Christmas itself. Anyway, I'll enlighten you all while you think we have the time." He breathed in and out very slowly before continuing. "Once the Christmas spirit is embraced into the heart of the jolliest man on Earth, he will then proceed to make his way from wherever it is that he comes from, all the way to the North Pole. But!" He held up one finger in the air. "At the very moment he reaches our borders, the electric sleigh—and sometimes a half-dead reindeer—will retrieve him and make the last leg, bringing him into the Elf village where he will be named Santa."

"It's so magical!" Trislar clapped his hands.

"When?" Ryo smiled, excited that their troubles were behind them.

Ilrune studied the High Elf's flared nostrils, then side-glanced at Frank. "What are we missing here?"

"How far away," Frank started to say, his words slow and steady, thinking as he spoke aloud, "does the sleigh not work."

"It has world-wide coverage when it comes to magical signal."

"Oh jeez." Frank's shoulders slumped as he leaned back against the wall for support.

"What you're saying," Ilrune said, "is that when the new Santa hits the border, then the sleigh comes to get the new Santa."

"Yes," the High Elf nodded, but it was full of sarcasm. "And who's in that sleigh right now?"

"Oh no!" Trislar jumped to his feet. "The zombie Santa Claus!"

"Oh no indeed." The High Elf lifted his cheeks in a cold smile.

"This is no laughing matter," Ryo added. "We have to fix this."

"But what do we do?" Trislar yelled. "WHAT DO WE DO!"

"We blow up the sleigh," Frank said.

The High Elf scoffed. "Out of the question! I'd approve such a plan if it was January. But *this* close to Christmas? How *dare* you!"

"It was just a suggestion." Frank rolled his eyes.

"We wait at the border," Ilrune said. Everyone in the room went quiet. "Once the sleigh arrives, then we take Zombie Santa before the new Santa gets in."

Pinching his chin with two fingers, the High Elf nodded. "The only issue I have with that is we don't know where the new Santa will be coming from, so we don't know which part of the border he'll hit."

Frank stood tall again. "How big is the border?"

"If we had every mythical creature on the entire planet lined up, it wouldn't wrap around half of it."

"Then do that!" Ryo said. "Get everyone here to help, space them out, and once we know where he hits, all of us go to that spot."

"And do what exactly?"

"Bag him?" Ilrune said.

"Throw him in with the half-dead reindeer," Trislar clapped.

"Let's stop right there," Frank interrupted. "No need to go all morbid. First things first. We have to catch him."

The High Elf called in his assistants again. They rushed in with a stack of papers in their arms. Banging it down onto the desk, they started pointing to one line after another. "Look here and here. This is madness!"

The High Elf's eyes read at super speed, flicking one page to the next, reading through a hundred pages within a minute.

"What's wrong?" Trislar interrupted.

"This is worse than we thought," the High Elf's voice faltered. "Santa has been terrorising families. Stealing from homes. He's been seen in graveyards digging, and then cupid saw him remove his left arm and replace it with a dead one."

Ilrune turned to Frank. "Perhaps we shouldn't wait. We could fly to dead Santa now, catch him before he gets too—"

"No!" High Elf snapped again. He turned to his two assistants. "Get everyone here. I'm calling a world emergency."

The two assistant elves ran straight out of the room.

Ilrune stood. "We should get moving too." The three of them went for the door.

"You three are on border duty."

"Now?" Ryo moaned. "But—"

The High Elf held up his hand to cut him off. "Too bad. Take a radio and report anything you see."

Frank smirked at them as they left.

"We should have gone to the Tooth Fairy," Ryo mumbled.

Trislar hmphed. "Even the Banshee!" A fresh layer of snow crunched beneath his feet.

Illrune shivered. "Why do you say that?"

"Because we would have captured Zombie Santa by now."

"True," Ilrune said as they walked into their cottage to retrieve their thickest jackets, gloves, and snow boots. "What if—"

Ryo cut him off. "This better not be another one of your plans."

Ilrune shrugged. "I'm just trying to come up with a plan to get us out of walking through the dark."

"What I want to know," Trislar said as he fastened the last button on his jacket, "is *how* do we catch him?"

They went silent for a moment, each looking around to find something useful.

"I don't know," Illrune snapped. "Just grab anything that might work, and we'll figure it out when we get there."

"He's very big," Trislar sighed. "So, none of my bags will fit."

"What would we do with a bag? Put it over his head?" Ryo laughed.

"I know!" Ilrune put one finger up. "How about a gun?"

Trislar gasped.

Ryo cocked his head to the side. "To shoot him?"

87

Rolling his eyes, Ilrune said, "Well, I could always jab him in the back of the head with the butt end."

The three of them faced the cold dark night with small flashlights, pockets full of metal tools, and thick clothing.

"If this fails—" Ryo started.

"It won't!" Ilrune snapped.

"But what if it does?" Trislar whispered. "Does that mean we'll have to cancel Christmas?"

There was a silence between them that felt heavy as the chilly wind wrapped around them.

"If we do fail," Ilrune said, "then let's hope the new Santa dies quickly, so the next one has enough time to get here."

"That's dark!" Ryo laughed. "But I like it."

The trinity marched into the thick snow towards the border. "When will we know we've reached it?" Trislar broke the silence. His voice carried far.

"I brought the GPS." Ryo held it up, waving it in the air.

"It should show Zombie Santa's location," Ilrune muttered.

"Yeah, it should have," Ryo retorted. "But the zombie is smart because he disengaged the tracking device."

"Wait, what?" Trislar stopped and glared at him. "But the old Santa didn't even know how to do that!"

Ryo shrugged.

"Let's keep going." Ilrune marched ahead. "I don't want to be out here all night."

And all night they were. Slowly, support started to come in. Elves were the first. Lining up every couple of hundred meters, just far enough to see each other.

Then the fairies arrived in their own small vehicles. They remained inside with the heaters blazing.

Frank called in only some of his troops, because if he had called in all of them, it would have been an environmental nightmare. "Can you imagine," Frank said as he walked up to the trinity, "if I called four billion bunnies to one area?" He laughed. "We'd be all jumping constantly like hopscotch."

"Why's that?" Trislar tilted his head.

"Because of the poo!" Ryo rolled his eyes.

"Oh!" Trislar scratched his head.

A variety of mythical creatures spread out along the border. The trinity didn't know where to stand.

"What's that?" One of the fairies emerged from their vehicles, pointing into the distance.

The trinity and everyone lined up at the border turned to stare. Scanning the darkness, their eyes couldn't focus on anything.

"It's him!" Frank said.

"Who?" Trislar asked.

"Where!" Ryo snapped.

"We can't see that far," Ilrune added.

"The new Santa," Frank whispered.

"Then we have to be ready." Ilrune pulled the metal tools from his pockets and prepared for an attack.

"That's what you brought?" Frank shook his head. "I thought you would be more resourceful than that."

"We're Elves!" Ryo said, glaring out the corner of his eye. "We make things; we don't destroy them."

"Then perhaps you should stand back and let the adults take care of this."

The trinity scowled at Frank.

"What?" Frank shrugged his shoulders. "It's not like all this isn't your fault to begin with."

"How were we supposed—" Trislar started but Ryo nudged him in the arm.

"Save it," Ryo pointed ahead. "It's about to begin."

Just as Ryo said that, the new Santa had reached the border. High overhead, a swishing sound dashed passed.

The trinity ducked down. The noise of its speed popped every now and then.

"That thing is breaking the sound barrier!" Frank whispered.

"Ha!" Ilrune laughed. "I knew it would work."

"What?" Frank glared. "What would work?"

"Our machine!" Ryo smiled.

"It's what killed Santa in the first place!" Trislar added.

"Great," Frank sighed. "Just great."

The sleigh swooped down, brushing against the very top of

Frank's head. Quickly he flattened his ears before dropping his whole body to the ground, then looked up to see the sleigh land. As the sleigh runners pressed to the snow, the zombie Santa stood and looked at the waiting crowd.

His eyes had a brown glow across them. His mouth was black. Any white piece of clothing was white no longer, and now contained blotches of muck.

"He's disgusting," Frank moaned.

The trinity nodded.

"Look at his skin!" a fairy said, hovering behind them at head height.

Santa's limbs were covered in patches, sewed with thick black string, holding it all together.

"He's been replacing himself," the High Elf said as he approached them from behind. "He's no longer the Santa we once knew. He's more death than death itself."

Trislar clutched his stomach. "I think I'm going to be sick."

"Not until we grab him," the High Elf ordered.

"Then let's get this over and done with." Frank stepped forward first, the trinity close behind him.

But Zombie Santa turned his back to them and jumped towards the new Santa. Charging, he raised his hands, smacking down hard as he approached.

The zombie Santa and the new Santa rolled around in the snow. One arm lifted, a fist pumped down. Legs kicked. Knees jolted. A scream here. A dead sound there.

The trinity froze unable to make themselves approach. Instead, they stood back, watching the snow flick in all directions.

"Someone needs to step in and stop this!" the fairy said.

"But how?" Frank yelled.

Cupid flew overhead and readied an arrow.

"What are you going to do?" Frank retorted. "Make him fall in love?"

"Shut up, Bunny!" Cupid squeaked.

The zombie Santa had managed to get on top of the new Santa, throwing one punch after another.

Cupid loosed his arrow, and it went straight through the zombie's neck. He leaned back and let out a deathly roar.

It gave the new Santa just enough time to sit up, reach for the arrow, pull it out, and jam it into the top of the zombie's soft skull.

The zombie's arms fell to his side. Slowly, he rocked back and forth. Dropping to his knees first, he then fell sideways. As he hit the snow, his murky brown eyes rolled into the back of his head, and his tongue flopped out of his mouth.

The new Santa pushed the zombie off him and stood to face the watching crowd.

A celebration erupted and cheers welcomed in the new Santa.

"It's over?" Trislar asked.

"Thank the Christmas spirit for that!" Ilrune said.

Ryo did a little jump as he watched the new Santa hug and greet his new tribe.

The High Elf was the first to shake his hand.

Frank came over and cuffed each of the trinity's heads. "Well, after all of that, I think this is a Christmas that I'll never forget."

"Happy to be of service," Ilrune said sarcastically.

"Thanks for the memories," Frank said as he waved them off to head back to his own vehicle.

The trinity watched him go, then turned back to the Santa who was climbing into the sleigh.

He reached for the on button.

The trinity screamed at once, "Noooo!"

But it was too late! Santa's thin finger pushed the button in. The electricity laced its way around his skin, up the finger, into the arm, and across his chest.

He jolted back and forth, side to side until a strange noise escaped his lips causing the watching crowd to go into shock.

Santa dropped down onto the sleigh floor.

"Oh no," Ilrune whispered. It was the only sound out of the thousands that were watching.

The High Elf glared at them from the other side. "You three!" he screamed.

"What?" Trislar pointed to his own chest. "Us?"

91

"Yes, you!" The High Elf spoke with his jaw locked together. "Sort this mess out now!"

Every single eye was on them. They dropped their heads, avoiding what they could.

"I liked that Santa," Trislar mumbled under his breath. They walked together and stood over the zombie Santa.

"I did too," Ryo added.

"By the Christmas spirit," Ilrune said. "Let's hope the newest Santa gets here soon."

They stood over the body, wondering what to do. The crowd returned to where they had come from, leaving the trinity to their mess. As they stood trying to figure out what to do, a zombie reindeer made its way over.

"Let's be thankful that only the body dies," Ilrune said as he brushed his knuckles over the zombie reindeer's fur. "The magic lives on forever."

ABOUT THE AUTHOR

A. A. WARNE

A. A. Warne writes elaborate, strange, dark, and twisted stories. In other words, speculative fiction.
Located at the bottom of the Blue Mountains in Sydney, Australia, Amanda was born an artist and grew up a painter before deciding to study pottery.
But it wasn't until she found the art of the written word that her universe expanded.
A graduate of Western Sydney University in Arts, Amanda now spends her time wrestling three kids and writing full time.
www.aawarne.com

THE SNOWS AT ASRUM

KIERAN MCKIEL

Alecksi awoke to a soft hum he mistook to be his mother. He could smell porridge, sweetened with honey and juniper berries, and nuts toasting over the fire for Rodestvo dinner. Even his sleep-fogged mind realized it couldn't be real. He laid on frozen wood, stiff and cold despite his thick winter uniform and natural blubber, and heavy boots thumped past his head. Clumps of mud hung on his back where he pressed it into the wall of the fire trench, trying to give his comrades room to navigate the narrow passage. Light snowfall prickled his face.

Mother wouldn't be in such a place.

Officer Vargoski bellowed, "Enemy charge!"

Alecksi jolted fully awake. His fellow soldiers darted past him through the trench. It was not yet dawn, the sky a blank black slate, yet even in the dark he saw how both their white-and-blue uniforms and grey Svar skin stained brown. Their tusks and small eyes seemed too large in their gaunt faces. He knew that after three weeks at the front, he looked the same. That sweet smell he'd taken for his mother's baking had been a translation, his dreaming mind's attempt to rationalize the cloying reek of the latrines and bodies as something tolerable.

We're under attack. Alecksi frantically grabbed around the mud-slicked duckboards lining the floor of the trench for his rifle. Frost coated both his small tusks and the auburn stubble on his chin. The sun had not risen yet, and light snow ghosted down from the black sky. Guns barked throughout the firing trench, each shot like a hammer against his ears. Finally, his hand closed around the stock of his weapon, and he scrambled out onto the fire step. All his fellows already had their rifles steadied on the sandbags along the trench's parapet. Alecksi recognized the humming he'd heard as the machine guns whirring to life in their nests behind his line. *I slept through machine guns.* Should that have seemed as normal to him as it now did?

Alecksi, now part of the firing line, hunkered down as much as he could. With his thumb he flicked down a switch on the back of the weapon. A hum emanated from within the chamber as the weapon formed raw magic into a bullet. That hum lingered several seconds—longer than it should have. Squinting through the barbed wire and foot-long spikes of iron wards along the parapet, he watched shadows dance across no-man's land. Even the snow was stained with mud on that desolate, crater-pocked field. Here and there were ridges and lumps where the snow had covered fallen trees and corpses. A thick, silvery ice fog hung over the ground, obscuring visibility beyond a few hundred yards. In Alecksi's mind, he willed the enemy to reveal themselves. Nothing was so torturous as waiting. *Hurry. Hurry and charge so this can be over.* In his heart, he hoped nothing would come, so that he wouldn't have to pull the trigger.

This was Asrum, the heart of the Ghostlands.

"Hold steady," ordered the Officer as he strode behind the soldiers. White veined his bushy beard and deep bags hung under his small amber eyes. Their squat stature gave the Svar a slight advantage in the trenches. Less care had to be taken to keep one's head down. "And by Belog's bones, don't shoot until you're sure it's a pinkskin."

Muffled gunshots crackled in the fog. A sandbag by Alecksi's head erupted with a puff of snow and sand. Everything in him wanted to lunge back into the trench, to hide there until he gave his superiors no choice but to send him home. Shame would be a small price to pay to escape this. But they wouldn't do that. They'd brand him a traitor and shoot him. The fog hung still, an illusion conjured by enemy mages to hide their infantry's advance. If not for the iron wards negating the magic, it would have flowed into the trench itself and left the Svar blind.

At last, the fog stirred ever so slightly as silhouettes moved through it—too fast to be a fellow Svar, its frame too tall and willowy. Humans. Behind Alecksi the machine guns screamed to life, vomiting a white stream of hard mana bullets at the incomers. Rifles joined next. Gritting his teeth, Alecksi tightened his finger around the trigger until his own weapon cracked, recoil shoving into his shoulder. The hail of bullets stirred the mist and dispelled the shadows, and the Svar found themselves facing a sheer colourless wall again.

The Officer shouted, "What a perfect time for the morning hate." All along the parapets the Svar fired into the mist. Allied artillery joined in, thundering from behind their trenches. A soft whistle followed before a second clap of thunder came as the shells struck the earth in geysers of dirt. They rarely hit anything during the morning hate. Ostensibly the Svar meant to catch the enemy before they returned to the cover of their trenches. He'd once heard the Officer say it was also a way for the men to let off steam. If it helped, Alecksi couldn't tell.

Officer Vargoski ordered, "Cease fire."

Exhaling a long breath, Alecksi slung his rifle behind his shoulder and stepped down from the fire step. As he relaxed, the reality of Asrum crashed down on him: the stench of blood and stormy mana smoke, the throb in his shoulder from his rifle's recoil, the painful ring in his ears, the caw of ravens as they descended on any fresh dead, and the tiredness, sinking deeper into his bones than the early winter cold.

While some soldiers remained on their fire steps to keep watch, Alecksi and a dozen others sat along the fire step to clean their rifles. Mud filled the ammo chamber of Alecksi's again, and he removed the ammo gem to wipe grainy muck off of it. That would explain why it took the bullet so long to form. Sooner or later, mud got into everything. Snow that fell into the trenches immediately melted from the bustle of the soldiers, mixing into the dirt to become cold, thick muck which grabbed like the hands of drowning men at one's boots. Even the duckboards which made the floor of the trench had started sinking into it.

Once the first amber light of dawn appeared above, another officer, Yugorits, came along. With a shrill voice which matched his thin red moustache, Yugorits shouted for the men to stand-to-arms for the daily inspection. Alecksi disliked Officer Yugorits. Vargoski was respectable, as he at least joined his men in the fire trench. But this other fellow reminded Alecksi of the rats which snuffled and clawed through the dirt. He strode in only each morning and each evening, spending the rest of his time in relative of the back rows of trenches. With his beady rat eyes, he checked their rifles, uniforms, and finally their feet for signs of trench foot. Three soldiers showed advanced symptoms and were hurried away into the support trench leading back into friendly territory. Alecksi almost envied them. He still had one more week in the fire trench before he'd be rotated back behind the lines. Job done, Yugorits gave Vargoski a curt nod, then ambled back where he came from as if headed home from the church.

A wooden cart came along next, rattling with cans of food. Breakfast today was the same as the last three weeks: dried-out beef and stale crackers. Alecksi had learned not to taste it. He'd heard from more experienced soldiers, those who'd been in the fire trench several times, that supplies sometimes ran out. They'd then had to hunt down rats for food. This morning, however, he recalled the roasting nuts, baked fruits, and roast elk his mother and sister would be making back home tomorrow, a grand Rodestvo dinner...

"Isn't there any more vodka?" demanded Ertyom, one of said older soldiers. His right tusk was missing after a morning raid a few weeks ago. His thick upper lip was twisted with scars where the tusk once protruded.

Vargoski leaned heavily against a wall of frozen dirt. "We ran out yesterday," he replied through a mouthful of dry meat.

Ertyom threw up his hand. "Not even anymore vodka," he growled under his breath.

The Officer regarded him with eyes colder than the winter air.

"Corporal, have you just volunteered to repair the barbed wire? Good man."

Ertyom ducked his head.

"You two." The Officer pointed to Alecksi and the soldier to his right. "We need a new latrine. You will dig it."

Alecksi and the other man, Grigorye, made no haste to each collect a shovel and pickaxe from a supply shed in the support trench, then find a relatively unspoiled area at one end of the fire trench. When Alecksi had first arrived, he'd resented being assigned these menial tasks. He'd come to take the Ghostlands for his people —drive out the pinkskins with a glorious charge. He didn't see real combat until nearly a week into his deployment. It turned out that there was nothing glorious about combat. Real fighting was chaos, screams, and blood.

Some of the other recruits who arrived with Alecksi, three weeks ago as of today, struggled with that knowledge. All Svar were raised on stories of valor and tenacity, of the wars their people had fought first to unify their feuding clans, then to maintain that peace against foreign invaders. None of those wars had involved weeks spent huddled in mud and offal, or guns that could cut down rows of men like grass. But Alecksi endeavoured to be adaptable. His life depended on it. Ever since his father had been crippled in one of those short, glorious wars of yesteryear, he'd had to become the breadwinner for his family. He loathed digging latrines or setting up barbed wire or any such tasks. But he had learned to begrudgingly appreciate that they weren't combat, nor were they boredom.

In the trenches, however, boredom was as inescapable as the sour-sweet stink of rot. After several hours of hacking up the frozen dirt, once his hands were raw and reddened and his arms ached, the latrine was finished. Sagging over his pickaxe, Alecksi invited Grigorye to a game of cards. The winner would get a cigarette. Said cards were by now smudged and warped by wet filth. Between them, they had a vague idea of how to play, acquired recently out of a need to stave off monotony. It mostly came down to bluffing and dumb luck. Grigorye won and held out his grey bear paw of a hand. Alecksi grimaced as he dug a crooked cigarette out from one of his belt pouches.

"I got a letter from my wife yesterday," Grigorye said, the cigarette bobbing between his teeth as he spoke. His tusks protruded further, curling outwards from his upper jaws, showing him to be older than Alecksi. The dirt and heavy fatigue on his face made it difficult to tell how much older. "She isn't making a Rodestvo dinner this year."

Alecksi furrowed his brow. "No Rodestvo dinner?"

"What's the point if only one of us is there?" Grigorye dug out a pack of matches from his pocket. "She already gave me my gift, anyway."

Alecksi thought of his own family—his mother, his sister, his crippled father—who would at least be happy in his stead. "What I mean is, why are we here if not for our families?"

The red eye of the cigarette glowed as Grigorye pondered that. "Why are we here?"

Alecksi blinked. "I assume for—"

"No, really." Grigorye plucked the cigarette from his lips, waving it around at the trench. "What started this? There's no enemy at home. This, the Ghostlands, is a few rocks in the ocean." He leaned closer to Alecksi, breath foul with neglect. "Why are we here?"

Alecksi scoured his memories. He was sure he'd heard some reasoning, something which had sounded so just and rational at the time. "One of our chancellors was shot," he finally recalled, "by a pinkskin in a town here."

Svar and pinkskins had shared the Ghostlands for a time, allegedly an attempt to foster peace between them. Svar schools had even taught the Human language for a few years. Still, it had gone as dealings with pinkskins usually did. They agreed to a truce to end those old short wars, and then with a single gunshot started a new one unlike any before.

Grigorye took a long drag. Smoke flooded out as he asked, "Why, though?"

"Because..." Alecksi swallowed. He didn't want to sound foolish, but nor did he have any other answer. "That's what pinkskins do, Grigorye."

"But why?" Grigorye rubbed his brow. "Surely they have homes and families as well?" He took another drag and exhaled. Smoke curled up toward the blank white sky, only to be snatched away by the wind as soon as it left the trench. "Surely they are filthy, bored, and hungry in their trenches, just as we are."

Alecksi leaned back against the fire step. Snow had been swept from the step and duckboards into the drainage ditch below, but no matter how the soldiers worked to remove it, more always fell. Heavy boots thumped on wood as Officer Vargoski strode towards them. Surely he would know more about their objective. "Officer," he asked, "what are we doing here?"

"Defending the Asrum front." The Officer kept walking.

"Why, though?"

Vargoski paused to stare down at him with tired, annoyed eyes. "Because we are ordered to." Then he walked on.

Alecksi watched the Officer go, uneasy with that reply. Out of anyone here, shouldn't Vargoski have been able to give him a straight answer? Unless Vargoski didn't know either. The younger soldier sank back against his seat, feeling colder than ever. If he didn't know what he was fighting for, then what were his fellows dying for? His enemies, even? Only one answer occurred to him. He clenched his fists, gripped by sudden anger. They were dying for a few rocks in the ocean. They were dying for the trenches, for snow and mud.

That afternoon, enemy artillery rained on the Svar fire trench once again. Mages wove their mercurial barriers overhead from the support trench, rippling like the Scarred Sea as shells burst against them. Even so, Alecksi and the other infantrymen hunkered down with their backs against the walls. It wasn't uncommon for a barrage to break through the mage-shields. After perhaps an hour, the percussion of shells died away to echoes and the intact mage-shields became still. A shrill ring filled his ears as he got back on the fire step. Artillery strikes were often cover for infantry raids. They stared into the stark white fog until their eyes stung, only for no enemy to come.

Two fake-outs in one day. Ruminating over a dinner of dry pork and old bread, Alecksi thought it obvious that the pinkskins meant to wear them down. Get the Svar to waste their mana and bullets, chip away at their resolve. But Grigorye had planted a seed in his mind, and all Alecksi could think of now was how exhausted the Humans themselves must be. Their forces had been here since the late summer as well, digging their own trenches, staving off their own boredom, stewing in their own anxiety at the constant threat of shell or charge. As dusk darkened the sky and the Svar endured the evening stand-to-arms, he wondered how much longer this war could go on. How long, he questioned as he steadied his rifle on a snow-dusted sandbag, could a war last if no man on either side wanted to fight?

Night fell, bringing deathly cold with it. Alecksi waited out his patrol shift, then tried to get his two hours of sleep, huddled in a dirty and worn bearskin blanket. But rest never came easily at Asrum. He tried to imagine the warmth and smell of his home's hearth. The comforting drone of the clergy in the church at the heart of his town, singing their evening hymns to Belog and Cherog to guard the souls of the townsfolk as they slept. Alecksi had heard there'd once been a clergy here at Asrum, singing the same hymns for the soldiers. Their voices echoed from the camps behind the trenches, safely within friendly territory, extending that same safety to the men at the front. Eventually the clergy were removed for their safety. Now the soldiers had to recall the words for themselves.

The ice fog dissipated the next morning. The Svar were called to stand at arms. The morning hate followed. Inspection, breakfast, chores. Alecksi and Ertyom were assigned to excavate a sunken section of duckboard. Ertyom grumbled to himself all the while, with no words for Alecksi. After that Alecksi tried his hand at cards with Grigorye again. If the older Svar won, he'd get another cigarette. If the younger one did, he'd receive a match with which to light a cigarette. Alecksi had used all of his own. Grigorye won. As he accepted his prize, he handed Alecksi a match anyway. "Happy Rodestvo."

Alecksi regarded the match a moment. "Today is Rodestvo."

Grigorye raised his brow. "You'd forgotten?"

"No." Alecksi shrugged. "It only doesn't feel like it."

"Then I hope this helps." Grigorye extended the match closer. "Please, take it."

Accepting the match, Alecksi examined it. Its head was perfectly red, as was its brittle wooden shaft. Somehow the mud had not reached them. Grigorye's matches must have been the only things at Asrum untouched by mud. But sooner or later, the filth would reach them. They had only just arrived from the Motherland. To be covered with mud there was unusual. Perhaps if one fell off their horse into a puddle. An accident, something to laugh over. Mud did not cover everything with its freezing, groping embrace back home. Guns did not bellow all day and night. Rot and smoke did not fill one's nostrils. One could walk in the open without fear of a sniper's sights selecting him, or a shell falling onto him. At home, his family was exchanging small gifts beneath wreaths of pine and holly, baking porridge, and toasting nuts for Rodestvo.

Looking at the match, Alecksi narrowed his eyes, trying to dull the hot sting in them. He asked, "Do you think they have something like Rodestvo? The Humans?"

Ertyom dawdled past them. He hissed, "Of course they don't have Rodestvo."

"He didn't ask if they had Rodestvo," Grigorye said. "Just something like it." The older Svar seemed to consider the question. "I suppose they might. I don't know——"

Ertyom stopped and whirled on the other Svar. "All we need to know about them is that they are across no-man's land from us."

Grigorye heaved a sigh and began to shuffle the cards for a new game. Once again, however, the notion had seized Alecksi. He tried to imagine the pinkskins in the hot southern plains and forests they had come from, hanging wreaths of their own, giving one another their own small tokens, baking feasts in honor of their own saints, singing hymns to whatever gods they worshipped. However, their faces were a blur in his mind, their voices garbled mumbles, their homes a vague jumble of stone and wood. No matter how much he tried, he could not imagine them as men like himself. Men far away from home, trapped in the icy bowels of these trenches, whose families wrote letters to them and received the same from them, who hoped each night only to survive.

Alecksi could only imagine them as pinkskins.

That was what Asrum had taught him.

But Alecksi did not want to fight today.

He did not want to have enemies.

Not on Rodestvo.

Alecksi lifted his head to the grey sky and shouted, "Hey."

Grigorye stared. "Who are you talking to?"

Alecksi shouted again, "Hey, Human."

Silence from no-man's land. Ertyom cackled. "Will you invite them for dinner?"

Alecksi ignored him. "Hey, Human. Hey."

A distant shout replied, "What, tusk?"

All the Svar went quiet. Alecksi had not expected a response. Getting one, however, gave him a rush of something that was neither quite relief nor fear. "Today is Rodestvo."

A moment passed before the Human replied, "What in rust is Rodestvo?"

Alecksi floundered, unsure how to describe it in the other man's language. None of his fellows offered any help. Some continued to go about their business, Ertyom included. But a handful, including Grigorye, had gathered around to listen. "A holy day," he decided. "Give gifts and feast for Saint Rodest."

The Human didn't answer for a while. "We don't know any Saint Rodest."

"He gave food and wood for fire," Alecksi explained, "to the poor, in winter."

"Do not waste his name." Ertyom stormed back over, looming over Alecksi with eyes in a hateful squint. "Do not waste his name on them."

"Shut up," Grigorye growled at him. He turned back to Alecksi and gave an encouraging nod.

"Sounds like a good bloke," the Human shouted back. "You sure he was a tusk?"

A few of the Svar grumbled and bristled, but Alecksi ignored the jibe. His throat was becoming hoarse from shouting across the expanse. He called out, "Come here."

"Piss off." Even at this distance, Alecksi could hear the Human's voice tremble.

Alecksi chided himself. Of course no one would agree to stroll up to the enemy trench alone. "I want to talk," he replied. "I will meet you at the middle."

Grigorye's eyes widened. "Alecksi, don't."

Ertyom gave a bitter chuckle. "Let him."

Meanwhile, more Svar had gathered to listen. The duckboards groaned under heavy boots as Officer Vargoski approached. "What's happening here?"

From across no-man's land the Human said, "If I leave the trench, you'll shoot me."

The Officer lifted his head to the lip of the trench. "Who's that?" he demanded, suddenly stern. "Private, who are you talking to?"

"No guns," Alecksi promised. "I leave mine here, you leave yours there."

A pause. Then, "Alright. You come up first."

"Alecksi." Grigorye grabbed his shoulder. "Don't. You've spoken to them, they don't have Rodestvo. Isn't that enough?"

Alecksi brushed him off. He did not want to hide in a trench on a holy day when he should have been home, feasting with his family. He stood, unslung his rifle from his shoulder and took his pistol from its holster, and set them on the fire step. "I'm coming up now."

Vargoski lumbered over, his broad shadow falling onto Alecksi. The Officer snarled, "Private, if you leave this trench, understand this. If the pinkskins don't shoot you, I will."

Alecksi ignored the Officer. He likely was going to be shot by someone eventually, whether he did this or not. Perhaps during the next enemy charge, or when the Svar next charged the enemy. At least this way it would be by his own will, before the war stripped that from him as well. He slipped the pristine matchstick into his breast pocket as he stood and moved along the trench.

Behind him, Vargoski chuckled bitterly and muttered, "Let him go, then. He is mad. Let Belog judge his foolish soul."

Every eye followed Alecksi, disbelieving stares on him like so many flies, but no one moved. He mounted one of the ladders up out of the trench, swallowed what he could of his apprehension, and climbed. A sniper could have been waiting for him, or artillery, or a machine gun, or a single man with his rifle. Rung by rung he ascended. He paused near the top to peer into no-man's land.

Asrum, Alecksi had heard, had once been a rolling field of short grass and stone blanketed with lichen. Here and there had stood clusters of cranberry bushes or short pine trees. By the time he'd arrived, artillery had been pummeling it for half a year. A thin blanket of grey snow covered the place. Ridges and craters broke up the field, and many more small bulges laid in the snow—the half-frozen bodies of men who had fallen in dozens of fruitless raids and charges. Much of the exposed rock now littered the place as fist-sized rubble. What few trees still stood did so as skewed grey skeletons, thin and brittle as Grigorye's matchsticks. The bushes were long obliterated. A hundred meters away stood another line of barbed wire and sandbags—the parapet of the enemy trench. Only the ravens spoke, cawing back and forth across the dead field.

Alecksi, jaw chattering, waited a moment for the gunshots. Any moment now. Had this been a mistake? Perhaps he would have survived the war if he'd only stayed in the trench. Or perhaps the next round of enemy artillery would have broken through the mage-shields and collapsed the trench on him. Any moment now.

But no shots came. Stepping up onto the frozen ground, he raised his hands. "No guns," he called out.

"No guns," the unseen Human replied from across the field.

Curling his hands into fists to stop their shaking, Alecksi began his lonely march. His boots crunched through the snow to squelch into the mud beneath. It seemed to take hours, making his way around the bodies and shell holes. Even with the cold slowing decay, the clammy stench of death hung thick here. At any moment, bullets might have come ripping at him. Eventually, Alecksi reached what he judged to be the halfway point. The jagged patterns of the Human trenches marked the earth for what looked to be another mile ahead before dipping down a steep hill, behind which their artillery surely hid.

Alecksi called out, "I'm here."

Voices whispered in the trench ahead. Then a shift in the grey earth caught his eye—a helmet emerged from an obscured sap. The newcomer climbed until his shoulders were visible. He paused, still too far away for Alecksi to see any more than a red face in the grey. The Svar raised his hands a little higher, emphasizing that they were empty. Seeing this, the other man climbed the rest of the way, raising his own empty hands as he approached. He stopped a few yards away. The Human's thick winter uniform must have once been white with subtle accents of black and yellow, but was now dulled by mud and wear. He had no rifle or pistol, as promised. His narrow face was more red than pink in the cold where it wasn't stained with dirt. It almost looked child-like with his large blue eyes and lack of tusks. His gauntness quickly dispelled that, shadows pooling in his exhausted features. Those blue eyes blazed like the windows of a burning house in the grime around them.

"Okay," the Human said, his breath hanging like a muzzle around his mouth. His words came almost painfully precise through lips unstretched by tusks. "What now?"

Alecksi wasn't sure. He hadn't expected to make it this far, a surprise he suspected the Human shared. Then he remembered the day. He reached for his breast pocket. The Human flinched as if struck with a physical blow. Alecksi, realizing himself, held up his empty hands again. "Rodestvo gift," he assured him. "It's just a gift."

The Human demanded, "What is it?"

"A matchstick."

The other man licked his parched lips. "A matchstick?"

Alecksi nodded. "Do you have matchsticks?"

A pause. Then, "No. Mud knackered all ours."

Alecksi, very slowly, reached again for his pocket. The Human watched. After a moment of feeling around the small pouch, Alecksi dug out the match. By Belog's mercy, it was still pristine. He held it out towards the other man.

"Come closer," the Human said, still wary.

The Svar took a few careful steps forward. The Human did the same and plucked the matchstick from Alecksi's fingers. He examined it, then slipped it into his pocket. "Thanks."

Alecksi nodded. "You are welcome."

Their eyes met in that moment. Up until then they had watched each other's hands. Each man stole glances at the trenches behind the other, half-expecting some trap to spring. None had. The Human asked, "You want anything?"

"We have no vodka," shouted Ertyom from the Svar lines. Alecksi looked back to see several of his fellows peering up from over the parapet.

"Vodka." The Human blinked, then caught on. "We have some rum left."

Alecksi turned back to his trench. "Rum?"

Grey helmets nodded along the Svar lines. Alecksi nodded in turn at the Human.

The Human returned into his sap, and several minutes later returned. In his hand was a mud-caked glass bottle, mostly full of dark liquid. He extended it towards Alecksi. "Here."

"Thank you." Alecksi accepted it, took a small swig. Though cold, the alcohol still smouldered on his tongue. He savored it a moment before he swallowed. Then he handed it back towards the Human. "Now you."

The other man stared.

"We both drink," Alecksi explained. "For..." He was about to say Friendship, but that word could not possibly apply here. Whatever happened today, tomorrow they would return to huddling in the trenches in dread of each other, hurling shells and bullets across Asrum, each throwing themselves fatally and pointlessly against the other's lines. Alecksi had thought he'd surrendered to that now, had accepted that reality. But now that he was looking the other man in the eye, had given to him and accepted from him, Alecksi remembered the world before three weeks ago. One without overflowing latrines or barbed wire or machine guns. It was a world he wanted desperately to go back to. He recognized in this other man's eyes that same desire there. "For friendship," he said.

The man stared a moment longer. Then he accepted the bottle and took a small sip before handing it back. "For friendship."

The Svar extended his free hand. "Alecksi."

The Human hesitated a moment before accepting. "Daven."

From one of the Human saps, a second man cautiously ascended into view. Once he emerged onto the field and approached Alecksi and Daven, another climbed up behind him.

Alecksi heard boots squelching through the mud behind him, and looked back to see Grigorye approaching. He, like the Human newcomers, did not have his weapons. More Svar were climbing up to follow him. While the sky remained blank and grey as the world below, the morning snow had stopped. No guns cracked nor artillery thundered that Rodestvo day at Asrum.

ABOUT THE AUTHOR

KIERAN MCKIEL

Kieran McKiel is a poet and a writer of fiction. Currently located in Yellowknife in the Northern Territories, Canada, where the sun scarcely sets in the summer and scarcely rises in the winter. A graduate of University of Victoria in British Columbia, he received a BFA in Creative Writing in 2017.

His work has been published by Metamorphose Lit, Empyreome Magazine, Nudity House, Saltern, and Silver Birch Press. When he's not writing, he's studying for his second degree in Communications. In the meantime, he awaits the discovery of fossils which prove Godzilla was a real dinosaur."

facebook.com/KieranMcKielAuthor

twitter.com/KieranMcKiel

instagram.com/kieran.mckiel.author

amazon.com/-/B0824L8R8D

SUGARED DATES

HASKELL CROW

S tanding on the roof of the museum, she could see the whole city sparkle with lamplight. An earthy smell touched her nose. The evening drizzle had wet the clay bricks that were favored in Sol, but even a little wet clay couldn't dampen spirits tonight. It was the festival of lights. Rolling her shoulders, Aelynn checked to see that all of her knives were there and ready. After two weeks of careful planning, she didn't expect any trouble on tonight's heist, but that never stopped trouble before. As if on cue, she heard muffled whispers and the sound of shuffling feet behind her. There were two guards crossing the roof to the railing at the outer wall.

That's odd, the roof isn't part of their rotation, she thought. Guess now is as good a time as any.

Casually throwing a half-eaten apple over her shoulder, she leapt from the building, the sound of raised voices following closely behind. Aelynn had been a Finder for years, and no matter how careful she was, how hard she planned, there was always something.

Hurtling through the air, she aimed for the balcony just over the museum's garden wall.

This part of the city was the oldest, so it was all crammed together, making getting into homes that much easier—if you weren't afraid of heights. Now, to be crystal clear, she was no thief.

She was a Finder, which meant she found things for a fee. It wasn't her fault if the things she found didn't always belong to the person who hired her. She didn't ask those types of questions.

Aelynn landed with the soft whisper of her feet touching the balcony, turning her momentum into a forward roll...right into a table that wasn't there when she picked this route yesterday.

The clatter was awful. A bronze pitcher of water had fallen to the ground, along with some empty plates and silverware. Scooping a couple of spoons into her waistband, she stilled the spinning pitcher. With any luck, the loud sounds of music and merry from the festival would cover her tracks. Just then, an oil lamp lit inside the home.

Great, just great.

Moving along the balcony, she climbed onto the rail and hoisted herself up onto the roof just before a lantern illuminated the platform below her.

Wiping the sweat from her brow, she got a running start so she could clear the alley between her and the next rooftop. Landing in a roll again, she sent up a prayer for no more surprise tables. She kept her momentum going this time and sprinted across the roof for her next jump. Soaring through the air, she wondered idly why people couldn't do this on their own. It wasn't that hard.

Coming just short of the next roof, she grabbed the edge of the building and planted her feet on the wall with a quiet thud, if just a little louder than she intended. Dropping down to the window below, she pulled herself through. Everything was smooth sailing from here on out.

She picked this window because there was never lamplight after dark. It proved to be an unused guest room as she moved through. Listening for footsteps, she slipped out of the bedroom door into the night air. The clay staircase traveled down the outside of the building to the room she was after. She pressed her ear against the door. Nothing. Pushing, she found it locked. No matter. Aelynn might not be a thief, but she would likely be a good one. Slipping a knife from her sleeve, she stared, puzzled, at the keyhole locks used in Sol. Giggling quietly, she started to chip away the clay door frame near the lock until she could see through to the bolt. Using her knife in a prying fashion, the bolt gave a satisfying click, followed by the angry howl of a wolfhound on the floor below.

Stupid, stupid, stupid. Of course they have a wolfhound.

Opening the door, she practically fell into the room and threw the bolt closed behind her. Turning, she was surprised to find three scared children staring at her.

Kids. A wolfhound OR kids.

Before the oldest screamed, Aelynn put a finger to her lips. Reaching into her waist pouch with her other hand, she discretely slipped the knife back up her sleeve. Her hand came out with a bag of sugared dates she was saving for later. The kids smiled and took the dates, rushing off to their bed to watch the intruder. Even sitting on the bed, the tallest of the three was almost as tall as Aelynn.

"I'm here for a horsey." Aelynn found herself smiling through her face scarf.

The eldest of the girls pointed to the east. "Our farm is a mile that way."

"Not that kind."

Finally understanding, she pointed to a cupboard behind Aelynn. With a wry smile, Aelynn opened the cupboard.

It was filled with many horses, wooden toys, dolls, and even trophies. The one she was after was there, too. It was black with a golden mane. The body was made of some sort of leather, and the hair felt like true horse hair. It was one of the most beautiful toys she had ever seen.

Tucking it away, she noted the children's sad eyes watching her like she was taking their most favored toy. Her heart dropped. She reached back into her pouch to get a very foreign snack—cocoa bars. Handing one to each child hurt a little, but her spirit lifted when she saw the joy on their faces after taking their first bite.

"What is this?" The youngest spoke out of turn.

"Cocoa," Aelynn whispered whimsically. "From the far reaches of Los Nacht."

This brought gasps from all three of them, as they coveted their treats.

"Where is this...Los KNOCKS?" the youngest asked, stumbling over the foreign words.

"Over the hills, south, and deep in the darklands," Aelynn said, moving her hand as if in line with the distant horizon.

"I judge this a fair trade," the eldest said with absolutely no sarcasm, as if her opinion was super important. The other two seemed to agree, so Aelynn said nothing.

Outside the room she could hear raised voices and the low rumble of a wolfhound coming up the stairs. They would soon be at the door, so she motioned the children away from the window.

The window was high on the wall opposite from the door and barely large enough for a child to squeeze through. Luckily for Aelynn, she was much smaller than the average citizens of Sol, being from a place that rarely saw the sun.

She hopped up and planted two knives in the wall above the window then swung her feet through the small hole and twisted as her momentum carried her through as easily as a pole vaulter might twist over their hurdle. Once everything was through but her hands, she planted her feet on the outside walls and worked her knives free, while still holding the inside of the window.

Looking down, the fall was about thirty feet. After all, she had never planned to leave this way. Just then she heard a beating on the door to the children's room, followed by a latch slamming open. Bending at the waist and knee she vaulted away from the building, aiming at an open window in the building across the alleyway. She was about halfway across when she realized... It was definitely too far.

In a last-ditch effort to recover, she threw a knife into the building's wall, halfway between the window and the ground, to use as a foothold. Crashing hard against the wall with a thud, she clambered for the knife to slow her fall but her impact had knocked the wind from her lungs. Falling in a flail of loose-fitting clothes, she screamed very loudly in her head so no one would hear.

She came crashing down in a stack of wooden crates. Wood, dust, and curses flew everywhere. Lucky for her, her bones had broken her fall. Grabbing at her ribs, she hobbled into an adjacent alleyway. Stripping down some of her clothes to reveal a colorful outfit underneath, she left the alleyway and hobbled into throng of partiers celebrating the festival.

That went surprisingly well.

FWEEEEEEEEET!

An ear-piercing whistle rang out over the crowd. "Stop! Clear the street. There is a thief about!"

Surprisingly well... She chided herself mentally as she tried to move with the crowd out of the street. A throng of guards pushed by, and she let out a sigh of relief. Too soon it seemed, as the guards all stopped in place, and she saw why. A wolfhound stood at the front of the pack, testing the air with its nose. Not waiting to see what happened next, she pushed her way through the crowd to the edge of the street. She felt the collective eyes of everyone around focus on her as they all backed away. She turned to see a wolfhound a dozen steps behind her, focused and growling dangerously. Then, just over the hound's shoulder, she saw the leash hitting the ground. The wolfhound crouched to leap.

Turning, she jumped on top of a stack of crates and tossed a knife past the wolfhound. He hardly noticed. That is, until his leash jerked him to a halt mid-leap, the knife pinning it to the ground. Without another wasted moment, she was climbing the building using exposed beams and other footholds. The yelping sounds the hound made when he hit the ground reminded her just how much her own ribs hurt.

THUNK! Her own knife sunk into the wall next to her, and she could see that the guard had thrown it after freeing the wolfhound, who was nowhere to be seen.

"Great night," she cursed to the sky.

That gave her all the motivation she needed to crest the building. Running in a hobble, she leaped from roof to roof. FWEEEET! She heard a whistle go up from the roof she first crested. FWEEEEEEET! Another whistle responded—this time from the end of the row of buildings.

They must have run ahead while I was climbing, she thought wryly.

Running toward the second group, she suddenly made a hard right. There was a rope with lanterns hung from it that connected her building to the one across the street. She made it halfway before she lost her footing. As she fell, she noticed a tear in her pants that was wet with blood. Great, she was bleeding while being chased by an animal.

Straight below her was a man on stilts, dressed as a giant for the festivities. She grabbed him around the waist and the abrupt weight sent them both falling to the street below.

"AAAAAAH!" he belted out as they fell. Aelynn rode him down like he was a Los Nacht desert board skimming down the southern dunes. They crashed through the awning of a street side food stall with the loud thwack of what she hoped was his stilts breaking. Giving him a kiss on the cheek, she got up in a full sprint. She felt a pair of bewildered eyes on her back as she ran.

After a few blocks, she was sure she had lost them, and the crowd had thickened again. Resuming her lazy limp northward, she felt a drop of blood running down her leg.

"Unlucky star!" she spat, tearing a strip of cloth from her shawl to tie around her leg. Behind her, the crowd was parting before something unseen. She shuddered involuntarily.

"Wolfhound." See, trouble.

Up ahead the street abruptly ended. "The canal," she whispered to herself. The small river that cut the city in half is what made it possible for this many people to live in one place. Feeling the jaws of pursuit run up her spine, she ran, half stumbling, for the end of the street. She heard the large strides of the animal closing in, so she reached for a knife in her waistband and flung it while turning as she cleared the railing. Plunging into the cool waters of the Eris, she heard the regretful howl of an angry beast and realized that she had smacked it hard in the jaw with a silver spoon. She couldn't help but smile as the current carried her away.

Finding the herb gatherer's home on the north side of the city was quite the task during all the partying. She had to drink her fair share of cocktails to...uh...fit in. Giving the healer the toy, she asked, "Was it worth all this trouble?"

The stout woman smiled and said, "It always is."

Aelynn watched the older woman cross the room and hand the horse to a teenage boy. She raised her eyebrow in confusion.

Looking at the bedridden boy, she asked, "Why would you want a toy horse?"

The boy looked up. "It was the last toy my father made before passing away."

Swallowing, Aelynn slunk away to retrieve her reward.

"He might make it another day or two," the healer whispered. "But that's it."

Aelynn looked back at the boy and walked out the door without her wad of cash.

Well...without half of it, anyway.

ABOUT THE AUTHOR

HASKELL CROW

Haskell Crow is a firefighter by day, and fantasy junkie by night. When he isn't wrestling his three children, putting out fires, or playing video games, he's reading a good book (usually The Wheel of Time series for the umpteenth time). While this may be his first published work, this rogue has a world of stories to share.

ⓐ amazon.com/-/B0824DMH9L

A HEIST, A PROPHECY, AND A UNICORN

SERENA DAWSON

Taramon ran through the canopy, each step certain, leaping between branches with ease. The Termerdal trees grew tall here. He sped from tree to tree tirelessly. Each breath came easy, his pack was no burden, and the forest stretched out before him. He could run forever.

The forest city of Amarnal spread before him, the living tree-homes filling the valley. The walls were grown of entwined aerial roots, merged with the trunks to form one natural, living whole. Today, the treehomes were hung with bright banners and wreaths, decorated for the Winter Celebration. He dropped to the ground and joined the flow of people.

The Winter Celebration had brought the city alive and roused the Aldan from their treehomes. Taramon wove between Aldan going in every direction, their clothing bright with harvest colours, tassels, and embroidery. Taramon flipped his dark hair out of his eyes and gave his hunting leathers a glance. He'd have to find a robe or something by tomorrow night.

He went first to Marabor's house—Taramon had been away too long, and his adoptive brother would give him grief if he didn't stop in—but the house was cold and empty.

On the way home, he saw Elrazon hurrying towards him, his

normally immaculate braid swinging wildly as he dodged Aldan and hurried up to Taramon. Taramon spread his hands wide in greeting, taking in his friends bedraggled look with deepening concern. "Peace to you."

Elrazon returned the gesture then dropped his hands at his sides. "Taramon." He opened his mouth again, but no sound came out.

"What's wrong?" Taramon asked, his stomach clenched with foreboding. "Where's Marabor?"

"Taramon," Elrazon's voice cracked, and his face contorted briefly.

Taramon wanted to shake him, but the sorrow in Elrazon's eyes stopped him. "Please, whatever it is, just tell me."

Elrazon's eyes closed briefly, as if in pain. "Marabor has been charged with consorting with a human—"

Taramon cursed savagely.

"Taramon, he ran, but the Keepers have caught him. Keeper Daiarkan—"

Startled cries behind them made them turn. Keeper Daiarkan led a bound and blindfolded Marabor through the crowd. The watching Aldan stepped back, falling silent as the pair went past.

Marabor's long brown hair fell over his face, hiding his expression from Taramon, but pain defined every line of his body, and Taramon's gut clenched when he realised the stain on the blindfold was blood.

Daiarkan saw Taramon and shoved Marabor to his knees. Unable to brace himself with his hands bound behind him, Marabor fell face first into the dirt. One side of the blindfold slipped, and Taramon's whole body went cold as he realised what the bloodied eyes meant. Daiarkan met Taramon's gaze, his black eyes shining with triumph.

Taramon lunged forward, but a hand clamped down on his shoulder, holding him in place. Taramon turned to see Elrazon's grim face. His eyes were full of sorrow, but his hand on Taramon's shoulder was like iron.

A memory of Daiarkan standing over another bound figure hit Taramon like a kick to the gut. Daiarkan had loomed taller then, eyes and hair the colour of shadow. A figure of dread. But now,

Daiarkan's hair was as grey as a corpse, his narrow face like some fallen ruin, all abrupt angles and strange shadows.

Taramon fought the urge to drop his eyes. His pulse was loud in his ears as he held his enemy's gaze. Fear and fury—always his twin responses to being in Daiarkan's presence.

Daiarkan dragged Marabor to his feet and sneered at Taramon.

Taramon twisted free from Elrazon's hold, but a second pair of arms stopped him, and Rayloran said into his ear, "You can't, Taramon! That's what Daiarkan wants. You attack him and you'll be executed along with Marabor."

Taramon held Daiarkan's gaze for three more beats of his heart, imagining sinking his blade into Daiarkan's withered heart. But Daiarkan was a Keeper of the Law.

Untouchable.

Taramon glanced down at his fisted hands. When he looked up, Daiarkan had turned away, dragging Marabor with him. Taramon realised he was shaking. He was glad for the steadying hands. He didn't meet his friends' eyes, though he could feel their concerned gazes.

"He's gone, Taramon," Elrazon said quietly.

Taramon nodded, his eyes for a moment seeing nothing. His blood buzzed in his ears. His fingertips tingled.

"Taramon, I'm sorry." He looked up to see Rayloran's eyes were scrunched almost closed in her effort to keep the tears back. Weeping was not something an Aldan could do in public; it was seen as a weakness, and therefore, shameful. Any show of emotion was. Taramon looked away, more uncomfortable with her emotions than his own.

Rayloran squeezed Taramon's hand. "Come to my treehome, both of you. I'll make us tea."

Taramon forced himself to follow Rayloran and Elrazon, though he was hardly aware of where he walked.

Oh, Marabor. Why did you do it? Taramon swallowed the bile that pushed up his throat. Marabor was bound for execution, and there was nothing he could do about it.

* * *

Rayloran led them to her treehome without speaking. Taramon looked at the house with surprise. He had walked the length of Amarnal without noticing a thing.

The house was grown from the traditional four trunks, its branches and abundant aerial roots trained to encompass five comfortably sized floors. Taramon went in and stood in the sitting room, waiting for Rayloran to brew the tea.

He stared at Rayloran's collection. The alcoves, formed of living boughs whose bark was polished from use, were filled with books. She read in many languages and was one of the smartest Aldan Taramon knew. His eyes landed on a book Marabor had given her.

Taramon's breath left him in a rush. Blind. Marabor was blind and bound for death. He'd never read another word. Never again see the sunlight falling through the trees. Never walk free through the forest he loved. Even when led to his execution, he wouldn't see his family and friends.

Grief rushed though Taramon and he gasped at the savage strength of it. The pain made him stagger. He leaned his hand against the living wall, the rough bark under his hand grounding him for a moment.

"Taramon." Elrazon was beside him, a steadying hand on his shoulder.

"I'm alright," he said, pushing himself from the wall. But even as he said it, fury rose up again—the overpowering urge to return Daiarkan's brutality. Taramon realised that his hand was clenching the handle of his dagger. He forced himself to let go. He paced the room, his hands fisted, Elrazon and Rayloran watching him silently.

"He blinded him!" Taramon raged.

"To make it harder for him to run," Elrazon said. Taramon spun towards him. Elrazon shrugged. "It's the only reason to do such a thing."

"Or because he's a sadistic monster?" Rayloran added as she brought the tea tray to the table, her movements lacking her usual grace. She looked like she was carrying a mountain. He would take her grief if he could, but he already carried enough of his own.

Taramon looked at his shaking hands. "I badly want to break something."

Rayloran handed Taramon a teacup with a smile devoid of humour. "I never liked this one."

Taramon threw it against the doorpost, shattering it. Little shards hit the three of them.

Elrazon brushed off the fragments as Rayloran asked, "Did it help?"

"Not really." Taramon closed his eyes, trying to master his fury one slow breath at a time. Finally, the fury at Daiarkan burned out, leaving an aching hollow behind.

How could Marabor have been so stupid as to let his head be turned by some human? Taramon should have been there to stop him. To protect him. He'd been away too long, and now Marabor would die.

Taramon sunk into a chair. "I failed him," he muttered, staring at his hands lying limp in his lap. He'd always known what action to take, but now he was as useless as a broken blade.

"You couldn't have stopped him," Rayloran said. "He was as stubborn as you are. Thern-headed, the both of you." Rayloran began sweeping up the teacup.

Elrazon took a seat next to Taramon. "I have an idea." He paused to make sure he had their attention.

"Spit it out, Elrazon!" Taramon snapped. Elrazon raised an eyebrow at him. "Sorry," he muttered.

Elrazon folded his hands. "I have information that Daiarkan is in possession of a part of the prophecy," Elrazon began.

"A fragment of the forbidden prophecy?" Rayloran looked at him speculatively.

He nodded. "I heard it had been taken from the fortress of Orm. How Daiarkan got his hands on it, I have no idea, but it should have been handed over to the Elders. I've heard from Watcher Zek that Daiarkan has been collecting things he has no right to."

Taramon snarled, "So he's a thief as well as a butcher."

Elrazon leaned back and smiled at them both. "I think we should steal it."

"You're starting to sound like Taramon." Rayloran laughed.

Taramon snorted. "Just because Daiarkan has it? Why should we care?"

"The prophecy could concern us all. The empire forbade anyone from having a copy. They were responsible for it being divided into pieces and hidden. All the surrounding realms are watching for the appearance of this prophesied One."

Taramon shook his head. "I fail to see what a prophecy has to do with helping Marabor."

"It has to do with helping the Aldan as a whole. The parts of the prophecy we have speak about cultural revolution for the Aldan and the downfall of the Empire. What could be more pertinent?"

"More pertinent!" Taramon growled. "How about the law that will see my brother dead within days!"

Elrazon threw his hands up. "That law is exactly what I'm trying to change!"

Rayloran leaned between them and asked Elrazon, "What if the prophecy doesn't say what you think it does?"

Elrazon leaned back. "Then I'll figure that out when I get to it."

Taramon stared at the table as he sipped his tea, turning the problem over in his head while Elrazon and Rayloran talked about the prophecy. He needed a plan. He wasn't going to allow an execution this time.

He looked at them both. "I have a plan but I need your help."

Elrazon and Rayloran exchanged a glance before she said, "you know you will always have it, but what are you thinking?"

"Not just to steal the prophecy."

She put down her cup and Elrazon raised his eyebrows expectantly.

Taramon put his cup down with a clatter that made Rayloran frown. "I will not allow Marabor to die. We steal the prophecy and break him out."

"It's impossible," she said immediately. Elrazon said nothing, but watched Taramon intently.

Taramon looked at them both before dropping his eyes. "It's not impossible, just...really difficult."

"Bold." Elrazon rubbed his chin. "We'd need a team. There's no way you can pull this off alone."

"It will be a small team. Watcher Zek, Saven, the three of us…" He wiped at the tea he'd spilt, his mind turning the problem over and over.

"Consider carefully what you're risking." Rayloran's voice dropped, her tone grim. "What Daiarkan did to Marabor... He doesn't even pretend to wait for the judgement of the Circle, anymore. Judge and executioner in one and completely certain of himself. The council, the Circle—none of them will limit him."

Taramon met her eyes. "I'm not afraid of Daiarkan."

Rayloran frowned. "You should be. He's relentless, sadistic, and has the law behind him."

Taramon folded his arms. "But I have my friends behind me. Don't I?" He gave them both a challenging look.

"Taramon," Rayloran sighed. "You know I'd love to see Daiarkan lose, just once. But I can't see how it's possible, even for you."

"I will find a way." He looked up and their eyes locked. "And I want you to help me."

She leaned in, forcing him to note the fear in her eyes. "I will help you, but you must promise me something. If anything goes wrong, you run. Run far, far away and don't ever return. Daiarkan's been waiting for an excuse to hunt you down."

"I don't fancy being an exile."

Elrazon gave Taramon a sharp look for his flippant tone.

Rayloran sighed, stirring the tea leaves in the bottom of her cup. "This really scares me, Taramon. If you were caught, you'd be headed for execution, the same as Marabor." She glanced up at him. "Unlike you, I don't have the skill to break people out of prison."

Taramon held her gaze, filling his voice with as much confidence and sincerity as he could. "I won't let Daiarkan catch me. I know how he thinks. I'll have contingencies."

She leaned back, her voice resigned as she said, "Okay, let's hear this plan of yours then."

"Well,"—Taramon rubbed his chin—"you and Saven will act as go-betweens. Watcher Zek will help us, I believe, and—" he broke off, embarrassed. "It involves Zannar."

"You're trusting Marabor's freedom and your life...to a thern?" The tone Elrazon said this in suggested Taramon had taken leave of his wits.

"Therns are very smart!" Taramon said. "You know they understand every word we say."

"So do cats," Rayloran said. "And just like cats, therns do whatever they please."

"I'll train her," Taramon said.

"I hope you have more to this plan than trusting a thern to do as she's told, Taramon."

"Have a little faith." Taramon gave Rayloran a roguish smile. "Have I ever made stupid plans before?"

Taramon was heading home when Watcher Zek called out to him from the smithy.

"Getting another dagger?" Taramon asked slyly when Zek limped out to see him. Zek was one of the oldest Watchers on duty but still an Aldan to take seriously, despite his past injuries.

"I know why you're here," Zek said, turning down Ember road as if sure Taramon would follow.

"You do?" Taramon said, trotting to keep up.

Zek stopped and nodded. "What Daiarkan has done is shameful." They stood close, and Zek's voice was quiet enough not to carry as he said, "Never thought I'd see a day I was ashamed to be a Watcher."

"Zek…" Taramon paused, measuring the risk. "I plan to take something from Daiarkan's hometree tomorrow, before the Celebration."

Zek's eyebrows rose, and he said carefully, "Tomorrow night it is my duty to guard Daiarkan's hometree."

Taramon stiffened. "And what about the cell within?"

Zek looked at him. "Eh. And that too."

After a loaded pause, Taramon said, "They won't execute him until after the celebration—"

Zek cut in. "Time gives us nothing, Taramon. Unless you can provide me with some miracle, there is nothing I can do about it. I still have to do my duty." Zek glared at Taramon, as if daring him to disagree.

Taramon glanced around, then leaned forward to say, "I've heard there is only one way to open the cell door, and that is with the key Daiarkan keeps on his person at all times."

Zek glanced in the direction of the smithy, then said grudgingly, "I've heard the same."

"Well," Taramon lowered his voice, "what if I came to have that key?"

Zek stared at him hard. Finally, he asked, "Would you even recognise it?"

Taramon shook his head. "He's got so many keys on his robe he's like a walking windchime."

For a moment, Zek's face creased up as he smiled, but then his eyes turned serious. "If you're caught, it will be the same fate as Marabor: death."

Taramon dismissed that with a wave of his hand. "Can you describe the key to me?"

"Better than that; I'll draw it for you."

Taramon left with the sketch of the key in his pocket.

Taramon walked into the forest towards his treehome and called, "Zhil zhil, zhil." The trilling call could be heard for miles.

Some minutes later, a rustle came from the bushes beside the path. The birds still sang, so he kept walking. Another rustle. The corner of his mouth twitched. If there was a creature alive who could cheer him up at such a time, it was Zannar.

The rustling followed him, sometimes on one side of the path, sometimes on the other, but he pretended he hadn't noticed and kept his eyes straight ahead. When she was being noisy on purpose, she meant to scare him.

A small green form rushed from the bushes, ramming Taramon in the back of the thigh. He let himself be pushed to the ground, rolling onto his back as he was climbed on and licked mercilessly by his sharp-hoofed thern.

"Oh no! The deadly and mythical unicorn!" Taramon said in mock fear as Zannar covered him in saliva. "How will I survive?"

Therns were nothing like the large unicorns of myth as they were closer to the size of a goat, but they were extremely smart and loyal.

"Ow!" Taramon lifted one of her small hooves off his leg. "Zannar, enough!" He tried to rise but she put a hoof on his shoulder and proceeded to lick his hair until it stuck wetly to his forehead.

He started to laugh. "Seriously, Zannar. Enough!" This time she allowed him to push her off and sit up. Wrapping his arms around her deer-like neck, he hugged her and said, "I missed you too." He ran his hands through her green-banded fur and rubbed the base of her horn. She closed her eyes in pleasure.

Taramon spent the next two hours teaching Zannar her part in his plan, using the sketch of the key. He rewarded her with her favourite leaves, in case she needed some extra motivation. She quickly learned what he wanted her to do, but he repeated the lesson several times to make sure.

He couldn't help a little anxiety about how she would perform on the day. I'll figure it out as it happens, if anything goes wrong. He'd done all he could. Zannar's part in the plan just couldn't be played by anyone else.

When they were finished, Taramon took out his fire pouch, and kindling a small fire, he burnt the sketch of the key to ashes.

* * *

"I think the plan for getting the prophecy out of Daiarkan's is as solid as it can be," Taramon said.

"Considering he's going to be in the tree when you take it…" Rayloran arched an eyebrow at him.

Taramon sipped from his cup. "As long as I can make the jump and get into his tree without being spotted, the rest should play out the way we've planned."

"What about the escape plan for Marabor?" Rayloran asked. "You can't expect the Weldren to hide him forever?"

"He will have to go to the Downlands."

"The haunt of exiles and criminals," Rayloran muttered.

"And isn't he both? There is a load of goods going by boat tomorrow night. If we can slip him in, then he will sail right past the border."

Rayloran cradled her mug. "Who's taking the boat?"

"Amarzan."

Rayloran raised her eyebrows. "You sure have a lot of Aldan who owe you favours."

"One of those upsides to a long life." He winked.

Rayloran huffed. "What do you plan to do with the prophecy?"

"The prophecy? I hand it in to the Circle, like the good Aldan I am."

"After making a copy, one presumes?"

He allowed one corner of his mouth to lift. "Naturally."

Taramon ran along the branch, leaping to another tree with the ease of long practice. Trees and treehomes passed under him as Taramon sped through the forest canopy. Somewhere below, Zannar would be running silently, following his course.

Taramon was as sure-footed up here as he was on the ground. He was approaching the most difficult part: getting into Daiarkan's hometree, which grew in the centre of a small clearing, apart from the trees around it. The closest branch to Daiarkan's tree was a near-impossible leap across and upwards. He had to make the jump. There were no smaller branches to break his fall to the ground five stories below. The only other option was to go knock at Daiarkan's front door.

Taramon rubbed his sweaty hands down his pants. Backing up along his branch, he judged the distance, ran, and leapt. The rush of throwing his body through the air was one he'd always enjoyed, but this time he was stretching his faith.

Ashes.

His feet landed but his weight was too far behind. He could feel the crucial shift as he started to tip backwards. He threw himself forward, grabbing a handful of leaves as he scrambled for hand-holds. He managed to not pitch face first off the branch by twisting to wrap his arms and legs around as much of the branch as he could. After a moment of indignity, he righted himself.

His eyes scanned the ground below, panicked he may have been heard or spotted. All was still and silent. Taramon put his head down on the branch and waited for his heart to slow.

Now he just had to climb unseen into the fifth-floor room. Zek had said that when Daiarkan was home he disliked Watchers hanging around. The Keeper probably wouldn't call for Zek until he was ready to go to the feast. The window was a tight fit, forcing Taramon to wriggle through. Landing softly, his quick scan of the room confirmed what Zek had told him—this was Daiarkan's trophy room.

The room was full of items seized from those Daiarkan captured. Taramon's stomach roiled. Daiarkan probably justified it to himself somehow—the just wages of a Keeper, criminals had no rights to their property, or something like that. There was everything from fine clothing, to jewellery, to weapons. Next to the window there was an entire dresser covered in bowls of precious metal and finely carved wood filled with smaller treasures.

He quickly searched through the small containers and there was the brass globe, between a jewelled dagger and an ornate silver jug, just as Zek had said. It was small enough to fit in his palm, the outside carved with abstract shapes, with a silk ribbon attached to its top. Gently, he untwisted the halves. The prophecy fragment was a scrap of parchment written over with tiny runes.

No time to read it now. Tucking the globe in his pocket, Taramon began to climb back through the window. As he wriggled out, his foot collided with a copper bowl. It fell with a clatter.

A shout from below made Taramon shinny down the trunk with all the speed he could. As he reached the ground, he looked up and saw Daiarkan's furious face in the window. Taramon sprinted towards his chosen tree, breath burning in his throat. Stopping at the base, he spun towards the forest and called for Zannar. "Zhil, zhil, zhil."

Zannar appeared from the forest and ran straight to him. He gave her a handful of leaves from his pocket, tying the globe onto her neck as she ate.

"Now run! Run and hide!" He pulled what remained of the leaves away, shooing her towards the forest. She reluctantly trotted into the trees.

Time to go. Dropping the leaves, he started climbing. He was part way up and climbing fast when Daiarkan emerged, panting, from the door below. Daiarkan glared up at Taramon, well out of reach, and then towards the forest where Zannar had disappeared. Instead of running to climb after Taramon, he walked towards the base of Taramon's tree, his eyes on the ground.

Oh, scorch him. The leaves!

Daiarkan looked towards the forest edge where Zannar had disappeared, then picked up the discarded leaves. Daiarkan lifted his head and trilled her call, mimicking Taramon so well that he paused in his climb to watch the forest's edge. A small green nose pushed out. Nostrils twitched.

Don't do it. He tried to project his thoughts to her, but she just did a little prance of excitement at the smell of asana leaves. She paused for only a moment when she saw Daiarkan, but continued walking towards him with cautious excitement.

Soot and ashes.

The little traitor was trotting out of the forest and straight to Daiarkan. He untied the globe from Zannar's neck while she nibbled at his robe. He shoved her away, his eyes on the prize in his hand. Daiarkan arched his neck, looking up at Taramon triumphantly.

Taramon muted his expression, and turned to run across the branches. It was impossible not to feel hurt at Zannar's easy trust of Daiarkan but there were bigger plans in play.

Taramon fidgeted with his robe. Rayloran slapped his hand. Taramon glared at her but dropped his hands by his sides. Daiarkan stood oblivious, only a span in front of Taramon, speaking to a companion. They stood in line with the other royals on the Great Path, Aldan lined up behind them as far as Taramon could see in the waning light. Lanterns lined the path, their soft light glinting off everyone's finery.

Taramon pulled at his robe again. It felt wrong, like wearing someone else's skin. Free of tassels and embroidery, it dangled to his feet, sweeping the ground. While not his hunting leathers, it was a comforting forest-green. Rayloran tugged at his sleeve and he looked up to see that Daiarkan had spotted them.

Daiarkan stalked towards him, eyes burning with anger. Taramon spread his hands open in mock greeting.

Daiarkan said nothing, but his face flushed red and a vein bulged at his temple. The music started up and Daiarkan was forced to go back to his position as the procession started forward.

Taramon smiled at Rayloran. As long as Daiarkan was thinking about what happened that afternoon, he wouldn't suspect they were up to anything else.

Daiarkan strode in front of the other Aldan, his posture proud. The keys of his office hung from the tassels of his robe, tinkling with each step he took.

Zannar better have taken the right one.

The Grove was filled with light, its latticed ceiling hung with rings of lanterns, as if measuring the vast living hall. As they entered, Taramon noted the Watchers guarding the entrance. Rayloran went to join the other dancers, so Taramon scanned the tables. He'd hoped to see his favourite pastries, but food would have to wait. He could see Elrazon walking up to give him the wreath.

"You found a presentable robe!" Elrazon looked up and frowned. "But you forgot your hair."

"I didn't forget." Taramon gave his head a shake, making his hair fall all over his face, then flicked it back. "It's right here."

Elrazon sighed. "Well, one out of two isn't bad. I hope you had a good Harvest Day?"

"Excellent, thank you."

Elrazon gave him a knowing look.

More Aldan entered the Grove. Taramon grew more impatient by the minute while Elrazon admired the costumes of each Aldan who went past. Finally, in walked the Pathmaker, the last of the Aldan to enter. Another tradition Taramon didn't understand. Thank the Creator he didn't have to pace slowly behind the whole population of Amarnal.

The Pathmaker was clothed in the finest of robes, so long it dragged behind him as he walked, a cunning blend of subtle autumn colours edged with silver like the first frost of winter. His hair shone as white as the moon, flowing down his back like a waterfall. His face serene, the Pathmaker paced slowly toward the dais, the Aldan around falling silent. Taramon stepped forward when Elrazon gave him a nudge with his elbow.

Taramon knelt, holding the wreath before him and said, "I present this Wreath of Gathering to you, our Pathmaker, as thanks for leading the Aldan people with wisdom. May our people be blessed."

As one, all the Aldan repeated, "May our people be blessed."

The Pathmaker took the wreath, and Taramon rose and stepped back. The Pathmaker ascended the dais and said a blessing over the people, the celebration, and the food.

Taramon walked towards the tables laden with the feast, where he heard Daiarkan boasting.

Daiarkan intoned grandly, "I am, like the trunks which surround this Grove, a pillar of strength upon which the Aldan depend. Without me—"

His control snapped like a worn bow string. "The Aldan need fewer butchers and fewer laws. What we need are more healers and more artists."

The Aldan nearby fell silent, shifting uncomfortably as they watched Taramon and Daiarkan glare at each other. Aldan did not raise their voices needlessly. The belief that their long lives would grow intolerable if the rules of civility were not maintained influenced their every action. Taramon knew many agreed with him but doubted any would speak their minds. It was not the Aldan way.

Daiarkan sneered at him. "My job is one few are willing to do. I uphold the law, while you take pleasure in breaking it like a spoilt child. You have no respect and deserve none. Your friend reaped what he sowed."

Taramon ground his teeth.

"Come, Daiarkan." Elrazon walked between them. "Can you not leave work for another day? Look at Taramon. Even he left his blade off for tonight."

Taramon stiffened as Daiarkan gave him a sharp look, his eyes going to where Taramon usually wore his dagger. Taramon could see his mind turning. Daiarkan reached to check for his key, but there was only a ragged string where the tassel had hung.

Daiarkan's voice rose. "The key to the cell is missing!" He made a grab for Taramon's robe, his expression furious, but Taramon stepped out of his reach.

"Perhaps," Taramon drawled, looking him up and down, "it got caught on a branch. With all those tassels I wouldn't be surprised. It's probably lying on the path somewhere."

Two Watchers came to see what the disturbance was. Daiarkan pointed at Taramon, his finger shaking with anger, and demanded, "Search him!"

But, of course, Taramon didn't have the key. After a thorough search, they apologised. Daiarkan stalked away, furiously demanding the Watchers check on the prisoner.

Taramon exchanged worried glances with Rayloran, who passed at the edge of the gathered crowd. She would soon have to leave the Grove to change into her costume with the other dancers. Taramon sent up a silent prayer. They were running out of time.

The dancers squatted on the branches above Taramon and the rest of the Aldan. Each dancer held a silken rope, which was more of a ribbon-like cloth, as they waited for the music to begin. As one, they rose with the music and threw themselves from the branches in a glorious freefall. Wrapping the rope about a leg, they slowed their fall, gliding like birds over the heads of the Aldan below. Swooping, twisting, diving, rising as if by magic, falling and rolling until the ribbon seemed tied in a hopeless knot, then untied in a moment. Their dance was mesmerising, but Taramon had eyes only for the one whose rope he held.

Defying gravity with a handful of silk, the skydancers flew. Hidden in the shadows, as all the other dancer's assistants were, Taramon kept tension on the rope, pulling his dancer higher at the appropriate times.

With aching muscles, Taramon worked, his eyes always on Rayloran, for it was her who dove over the Aldan. With her arms outstretched, elegance in every line, she trusted her life to his hands. As he trusted his to hers.

Now came the finale. The dancers had climbed to the highest

part of their dance, and with a crescendo, the music made all eyes turn their way as they fell. Taramon braced his weight with a stuttering heart. Before they dove headfirst into the forest floor in front of the startled audience, they slowed just enough to pivot and land lightly on their feet and were met with great applause.

Rayloran bowed along with the rest of the dancers. She gave one swift look to Taramon and walked through the crowd to change. Taramon gathered the silken rope until he felt a bump in the fibres. Taking the small dagger from his boot, he cut the stitches to reveal the key.

What to do now? If the key wasn't found, Zek would be blamed.

His plan had been to tie it back onto Daiarkan's robe without anyone seeing so no one could be implicated. Now he had to return it somehow without being seen. Taramon suppressed a shiver.

He walked towards Daiarkan where he stood speaking to Elrazon. Taramon approached the table and looked over the food. Daiarkan glanced his way and kept an eye on Taramon as he continued his conversation. Taramon walked past him to grab a slice of crisp, roasted sweet potato from the table and stood not far from the two Aldan as he ate it, apparently surveying the room.

How in the forest do I get rid of the key without being seen? He needed a distraction.

Daiarkan turned as two Watchers led Zek towards their table. Taramon leaned across to grab another crispy vegetable and dropped the key into Daiarkan's bowl of soup. The soft plop as it landed in the almost-empty bowl wasn't heard over the approaching Watchers. Taramon straightened and stepped away from the table. As good a place as any.

"The prisoner has escaped, sir," one of the Watchers said to Daiarkan. "We brought Watcher Zek for questioning."

Daiarkan grabbed Zek by the collar of his uniform. "You will pay for your treachery!"

"I was not aware the prisoner had escaped, sir, until your men here alerted me," Zek said calmly.

"Liar!" Daiarkan gave him a shake. "Are you not the one tasked with guarding my hometree and the prisoner therein?"

"Indeed, I was guarding your treehome, sir," Zek said. "But I could hardly have helped the prisoner escape, since only your key will unlock the door."

"The key has been stolen!" Daiarkan bellowed.

"Is that not your missing key?" Elrazon leaned over, pointing into Daiarkan's bowl with an air so innocent Taramon had to look away before he cracked up laughing.

The Watchers, Zek, and Daiarkan looked into the bowl. Without a word, Daiarkan grabbed the key, soup dripping off his hand, squeezing it until his knuckles turned white.

"You," Daiarkan ground out, looking at him with such fury that Taramon almost took a step back.

Elrazon stepped between them. "Now, Daiarkan. Taramon has already been searched once this evening, and he did not have the key. We'll have no more of these unfounded accusations. Taramon has been here all night, as have you. There must be some other explanation for all this than our good Taramon, who has not left this celebration since it began."

Daiarkan leaned right into Taramon's personal space.

Taramon froze. Surely Daiarkan wouldn't attack him in front of so many witnesses?

"I know how you did it," Daiarkan hissed. "That cursed thern took it from my robe. If you tell me where the prisoner is, your thern will not be harmed."

Taramon swallowed, his hand reaching automatically for his dagger, but he grasped only air. Ashes.

"Think it over. You know what I'm capable of," Daiarkan said before stalking away from a shaken Taramon.

Taramon, Zek, Elrazon, and Daiarkan stood in a ring of Watchers as the Pathmaker questioned them in turn. Finally, the Pathmaker released them, saying, "I consider this event concluded. Since the key appeared in Daiarkan's bowl with as much mystery as it disappeared from his robe, I can make no judgement. In the morning, you may track the prisoner. For now, I want you all to go enjoy what is left of the evening."

"But—" Daiarkan said.

The Pathmaker cut him off, raising an eyebrow. "You hold the only key to the cell in your hand, correct?"

Daiarkan nodded, his face set like stone.

"Then kindly explain to me," the Pathmaker said, "how Taramon could have taken the key and released the prisoner, all while never leaving the Winter Celebration."

"He had help, obviously. We must launch an investigation—"

"Enough, Daiarkan!" The Pathmaker's face turned red, whether from anger or shame at having raised his voice, Taramon couldn't tell.

Daiarkan glared at Taramon with pure hatred and walked away.

Taramon found a patch of shadow to stand in. Some minutes later, Zek left the Watchers to wander over. He stood near Taramon, tipping his head up. "The stars are out tonight."

Taramon didn't look at Zek, his heart racing. "A good night for wandering the paths and seeing where we find ourselves."

Zek said with a smile, "All our rivers run to the sea, Taramon," before walking away.

Taramon almost sagged, his relief was so profound. Marabor was safely gone, and Zannar with him. It had been a hard call, asking them to take her, but he'd feared she would be in danger if Daiarkan suspected her.

Tonight, I've saved and yet lost two of my family.

All through the evening, Taramon talked, ate, and danced as the occasion required, but his spirit was with Marabor on the path he must follow. All the way to the Downlands, into the maze of land and water where even Daiarkan could not track them.

Taramon wished he'd been able to give him more than a blade, but if anyone could survive in that land of outcasts, it was Marabor.

Rayloran found him leaning against a tree, gazing at the cele-bration. "It's been a good night, hasn't it?" she said.

"Yes, it's been a very good night, I think."

"Do you think Daiarkan has discovered that you took the prophecy from inside the globe before he retrieved it?"

Taramon laughed. "No, but when he does, He'll have to decide if reporting me is worth his facing the same punishment. I've already made a copy for you to decipher later."

She laughed. "Rogue," she said fondly before gliding away into the crowd, leaving his heart a little lighter.

Saven came past and handed Taramon a weren lattice with a wink, then walked away. The honey pastry was the perfect counterpoint to the tart weren jam. Feasts aren't all bad.

Across the gathering, Daiarkan stood as still as a predator, his eyes on Taramon, his face twisted with hate.

Taramon held his gaze until Daiarkan looked away, then bit into his pastry and smiled.

ABOUT THE AUTHOR

SERENA DAWSON

Serena Dawson is an artist and writer who wanders the paths of Middle Earth, (New Zealand), in her housetruck. She and her husband built their tiny home on wheels and share it with three kids, a dog and lots of bonsai. When not busy doing "all the things," Serena loves to explore forests, preferably barefoot, and let her imagination run free.

facebook.com/Serena.Dawson.art

instagram.com/serenadawsonart

amazon.com/-/B08249D487

FOR ALL THE CLAINSMYTH

JOSHUA A. BROWN

The land was rugged. A chain of stony, snow-covered mountains ran from the southwest corner of Mourdal to the northeast, essentially dividing the kingdom, with a few passes allowing for travel between the sections. These mountains, known as The Mourdallan Mountains, were unforgiving to any who dared to travel into their upper reaches. Most were wise enough not to, but it was said that there were settlements up there, as well as nests and lairs of things best not spoken of, lest the children find it more difficult to sleep.

The winter solstice was approaching, and the snow and cold weather reigned throughout Mourdal. It was not a season the population of farmers and tradesmen held dearly because of the bitter cold and relentless snow. The winter solstice holiday, though, was held very dearly by them, and though it had not yet come for the year, Rendan smiled when he thought back to past years. The warm, spicy punch and the meager feast with his kin was always a joy.

The holiday itself, called Clainsmyth, was a celebration of the winter spirits, as well as a time for the people of many kingdoms to enjoy peace and tranquility in the cold periods of the year. The spirits were plentiful, but were not to be confused with the gods, who bestowed blessings during Clainsmyth, but did not influence the spirits of the solstice. The spirits were a diverse bunch, but the main three were beloved and storied.

There was Theraylyxus, the Sprite of Frost and Snow, who made sure the winter solstice was beautiful with her creations woven upon every surface. Maratouken, a jolly and rotund spirit adorned in festive robes of gold and crimson, who brought the feelings of joy and mirth to people across the lands. And then there was Gyth, a shadowy figure meant to remind people that should they harbor ill will or bad intentions during Clainsmyth, there *would* be a grim future.

Rendan was seated on the back of a wagon, having quietly caught a ride through the town of Harakol. He was on his way to see about work in the smithy. If there was none, then he'd need to arrange for travel to the castle in the city of Galtros. There was always work within the castle, and he was skilled with various kinds of labor. At twenty, he found Harakol had everything he needed to live a happy life. For a while in his youth, his father had tried to nudge him toward being a page for a knight, but he was not disciplined enough to follow that path.

As the sound of hammers clanging off anvils filled his ears, he hopped off the cart. The driver felt the shift and looked back. He spied Rendan, but merely smiled as he continued on. Rendan looked around at the log and stone buildings surrounding him, regarding the one he was bound for. He checked to make sure the road was clear, and with quick steps, made his way into the heat of the smithy, and was glad for it in the waning hours of the day. Once inside, he looked around before his gaze finally settled upon a burly, bearded man pounding away, fashioning some sort of farming implement.

"Ho there, Tyrus!" Rendan said as he headed toward the blacksmith, who looked up.

"Rendan!" Tyrus boomed in surprise. "I've not seen you in some time, lad. Here looking for work, are yeh? That's about the only time I see you, eh boy?"

"I am, indeed, Tyrus," Rendan said. "Have you any?"

"I did, but the last six lads who showed up here are now doing it," Tyrus uttered with a grin through his graying beard. "Still, there's always something to do for my young friend, eh?"

"I was hoping so." Rendan hooked his thumbs in his belt. "I could use a little coin these days."

"Winter is always tough, my friend," Tyrus said, setting aside his hammer. "The holiday seems to make money disappear for some and appear in piles for others."

"I don't need a pile of it, but I'll take any work you can give me," Rendan said.

"About the only thing to do at the moment would be to deliver these trowels to Kandrek's farm, a few hours ride to the south, along the main road," Tyrus said. Rendan gave a nod.

"I remember Kandrek," Rendan recalled. "Trowels already? He sure is getting a jump on the spring!"

"He hopes for a fairly bountiful year in his fields, so he is taking no chances," Tyrus said, running a gloved hand along the piece he'd just finished. "In having me make them now, he's not in line with the others in the spring. You can ride old Hawlice to get there. I'll help you get him saddled up."

They left the smithy to head for the stable where Tyrus kept his pair of horses. Hawlice was familiar to Rendan, a dark gray gelding who was large and solid. A bit older but still a reliable mount for short journeys. As the pair got him saddled and Tyrus made sure the trowels were loaded into a bag, Rendan rubbed the horse's nose.

"All right now," Tyrus said. "You ride down the road tonight to get those to Kandrek, then come back here and I'll pay you four silver Shrochs."

"That's a deal!" Rendan said, climbing atop the horse and putting his feet in the stirrups. Hawlice fussed at the feel of the rider on his back.

"Still two days to Clainsmyth, as of tomorrow morning," Tyrus said, beaming. "So won't you be the hero to your clan with four Shrochs for the feast?"

"Without doubt, it will make things more festive," Rendan agreed. "I guess I'd best be on my way."

"Now, boy, on occasion, even during Clainsmyth, there's robbers and bandits along that road," Tyrus said, lifting a hand with the palm toward Rendan. "Do you have a dagger?"

"No, I prefer not to carry weapons," Rendan answered.

"No weapon?" Tyrus blurted. "You *are* brave!"

"I've never had need of any in my errands for you," Rendan offered with a shrug. "So I prefer not to carry them."

"A shame, considering how good you are with all of them," Tyrus teased. He tossed a dagger in a sheath to Rendan, who caught it, before looking at it with a wrinkled face.

"I shan't need it, but I do thank you," Rendan said, securing the sheath on the saddle. He brought the horse about and started away from the stable under the gaze of Tyrus, who then headed back into the smithy.

Elsewhere, looming above the kingdom in the mountains there stood a domed structure that had survived the harshest conditions the peaks could dish out. Within this structure there was no regard for the joy or goodwill of Clainsmyth. Within its walls dwelled a coven of witches who had been forced to exile in the mountain by the Order of Divine Flame—the kingdom's holy paladins—forty years before.

From within tattered robes of gray, a gnarled, bony hand extended toward a cauldron where bubbling and glowing liquid seemed almost to whisper. The hand stirred the air for a moment, and a violet flame shot upward and was gone, leaving only a plume of black smoke. Hissing, labored breath came from under the cowl of the robes, and across the cauldron from her waited a figure.

This figure was barely three feet tall, with hard, scaly skin, warts and twisted, spiny ridges along the center of its twisted face. Its long, pointed nose was somewhat crooked from past incidents. Thin lips like small, black worms were parted just enough to show the pointed and jagged teeth. The goblin's chin came to a warty point. Hard yellow eyes, streaked with red veins glared across at the witch. It wore dark, battled-dented armor and waited with its arms folded across its chest. This was Worlyx.

"It is done," a raspy voice came from under the cowl. "She is born."

"You tell me where," Worlyx growled. "I do the deed."

"Buffoon..." the voice of the witch chastised him. "You will not destroy *this* girl."

"Oh?"

"You will bring her here..." the witch uttered, glaring out from under the cowl. "And *we* will destroy her."

"As you command."

* * *

Rendan rode in silence. It had been hours since he passed anyone going in either direction. This would have been a concern in better weather, but the temperature had dropped, and the wind told Rendan that snow was coming. Getting the trowels dropped off and heading home for some pieces of silver was now something he wanted to do quickly. He knew Tyrus, and the big old oaf would be good for a little extra coin if Rendan had to travel in the snow.

Presently, there came a sound like a voice in the very air, and Rendan slowed the horse at its echo in his ears. He briefly eyed the dagger strapped to the saddle but then searched the trees on either side of the road for any sign of bandits lying in wait. Seeing none, he decided the strange noise was either travelers in the woods, or just his imagination. The sound did not come again.

The bitterness in the air stung as the sun dipped behind the horizon, but the snow had not yet begun to fall. He was certain it was not far off, but rode for another hour before the first flakes began to gently descend from above. It was possible he would have to ask old Kandrek to stay in his barn if the snow became too thick to return home in the night. Kandrek was a reasonable fellow, Rendan remembered, and so he pressed on toward the farm.

Some hundred yards down the road, the wind had strengthened steadily, and in it Rendan once again heard what he thought was a voice. Amidst the swirls of faint sound, he made out his own name with a bit more clarity than the last time he'd heard the whispers. He brought the horse to a halt, then turned it in a circle to look around. The trees were sparse, but still there was no visible person from whom the voice could have come. He nudged the horse with his heels, eager to get started again and reach Kandrek's.

He rode up over a tall hill, finding the sting of the elements to be disagreeable. He pulled the hood of his cloak more snugly about his head, and was glad to look down and see the distant farm in the valley. The house had some faint light coming from behind shuttered windows, but otherwise looked dark and quiet. Rendan urged the horse faster and made his way down the hill.

The horse swiftly made its way down the hill to the farm, its hooves stirring up the fresh blanket of white on the ground. Rendan brought the animal to a halt and swung down from its back. Just as his feet hit the snow, the door to the farmhouse opened, revealing the lanky form of Kandrek in silhouette. Rendan lifted a hand as the farmer emerged.

"Who's there?" Kandrek called from the step of his house. He eyed the rider with scrutiny.

"It's me. Rendan," he called back. "Tyrus has sent me to deliver your trowels."

"Very good," Kandrek uttered flatly. "Let's take them to the barn, boy."

Rendan led the horse, with Kandrek trudging ahead of them to the big old barn behind the house. The walk was getting harder as they went, and the snow was piling up as the wind grew stronger. Soon enough, they reached the barn and Kandrek dragged open the big, wooden door. He motioned for Rendan to lead the horse inside, where there was a single lantern lighting the place. Everything in the barn seemed old and covered with ages of dust. Ropes, tools, and buckets were stacked along the sides of the aisle.

"I'll take those trowels," Kandrek said, examining Tyrus' work. "Put Hawlice down in that end stall. I'd be a damned menace if I let you head home in this. Turnin' out to be a right storm, ain't it?"

"It certainly is," Rendan uttered before yawning and rubbing his tired eyes. Kandrek headed off with the trowels while Rendan removed the saddle from Hawlice, who immediately seemed glad to be rid of it. Hawlice shook vigorously for a moment. Rendan then walked the horse to the end stall and led him inside. Kandrek had returned and brought hay into the stall before he and Rendan left, headed back to the house.

"You can bed down out here by the fire," Kandrek said. "I'll make sure you have some blankets. If the snow's died off, you can start back in the morning."

"I hope it does," Rendan said, holding his palms toward the crackling fire. "It's only two days to Clainsmyth, and I'm sure my family will be wanting me home."

"Well, you get some rest, and we'll hope this storm ends soon," Kandrek said with a smile. After he'd provided Rendan with some blankets, Kandrek headed off for his own room, leaving Rendan to settle in by the fire. After the long ride, it took little time for his mind to grow foggy. As he drifted off to sleep, he thought for a moment he'd seen the image of a face in the flames, but disregarded it and closed his eyes.

* * *

Rendan awoke on the floor of the farmhouse and immediately the hairs on his flesh rose. The first sensation was merely cold, but as his senses came to him, it was not just cold, it was *bitterly* cold. The fire was gone, the door was open, and the entire place was laced with ice crystals and snow. Shivering and shaking, Rendan realized that his blankets afforded little protection from the frigid air, and he sat up with a gasp. No sooner was he sitting up that he spied a face to his right. It was lean, feminine, and leering. The hair surrounding the face was short, spikey, and silver mixed with blue. Rendan's eyes went wide and his mouth fell open.

"Hello, Rendan!" the face said in a biting, squeaky voice.

He cried out, scooting back away from the face, which was attached to a thin body with long arms and legs. With folded legs, she was sitting very near to where he'd been sleeping. As he moved, she seemed to extend herself in a rubbery way, and launched across the room after him. He backed into someone else, and turned, expecting to find Kandrek equally horrified. Instead, he was face to face with something in a long, gray set of tattered robes that seemed to have no face under its hood. Again, he yelped and moved away, watching as the now-giggling girl landed next to the robed figure.

"Kandrek!" Rendan called out.

"Don't be as stupid as you look!" the girl said with a dismissive wave of her right hand. "He'll sleep until we tell him not to."

"What?" Rendan stammered.

"Some hero..." the robed thing issued forth in a garbled, unsettling voice.

Now, Rendan held still for a moment, and watched as the pair studied him. There came the crunching of footsteps from outside in the snow, and a shadow fell over the doorway. Rendan had heard of things like ogres, but now as a huge figure stepped inside, draped in some sort of coat or robes, he was sure that the tales of ogres were true. Rendan's eyes darted to the right as he regarded the doorway behind the one who had just entered. Could he make it? His thought was cut off by the voice of the gigantic figure.

"Good," its deep voice rumbled thickly. "He's awake!"

"Yeah, but... Are yeh sure this guy is the other one?" the girl asked and scratched her head, resulting in a sparkle of blue, icy crystals from her scalp.

"I'm very certain," the enormous man said before he turned to Rendan. "We need your help."

"My help?" Rendan blurted so suddenly the other three exchanged a glance.

"That's right, boy," the man said, and took two gigantic steps to cross the room.

"Help with what?" Rendan asked.

"We don't often directly speak to mortals, but something has happened, and if we don't get your help, terrible things could come of it," the man said.

"Then you're..."

"Maratouken!" the figure said proudly, kneeling so that his face was on level with Rendan's. He gestured toward the other two. "And my associates, Theraylyxus and Gyth. You know us as the spirits of Clainsmyth, my boy."

Maratouken's face was flush with warmth, and he wore a set of crimson and gold robes, lined with fur. His hat matched the robes,

152

and Rendan couldn't help but be calmed by the fatherly expression of joy on the spirit's face. As he glanced at the others, he could see that Theraylyxus was grinning from ear to ear, but there was still no sign of the face of Gyth, who moved very little.

"By the gods..." Rendan uttered. "You're real."

"Well, of course we're real," Maratouken said in good humor, but quickly changed to a sober expression. "And why we've come to interact with mortals is also very real. Time is of the essence, Rendan."

"What's happened?" Rendan asked, looking over each of them. "And how can I help?"

"Far away, in a very small place called Elaenyral, a girl has been born to this world," Maratouken said. "A very special girl, indeed."

"That's not right!" Theraylyxus snapped from across the room, and within an instant, had blown over to the other two with a gust of wind. "She was not *born*, Maratouken."

"Oh, all right then," Maratouken grumbled with a roll of his eyes. "Perhaps *born* is the wrong way to put it. But she was created."

"Created?" Rendan asked. "Created how?"

"By the magic of the gods and goddesses," Maratouken answered.

"Why?" Rendan asked.

"As a gift to your kind, and a beacon for ours," Maratouken replied. "In times of darkness, it is the spirit of Clainsmyth which unifies the mortal men. She was created by the gods to inspire the mortals to keep that spirit all the year."

"This is indeed a very blessed event," Rendan acknowledged under the stares of the three mysterious figures. "But, what have I to do with it?"

"The gods and goddesses created her, and it is true their intent will help strengthen the bonds of all mortal men, women, and children," Maratouken said. "She is to be a light which shows us love and hope. Her magic will strengthen all of Clainsmyth, including we three. That is why it is important that you and others gather this girl and bring her to us at our cathedral."

"But if the gods created her, could *they* not have delivered her to you?" Rendan asked and again looked around at the spirits.

Now, the spirits looked to one another, and Maratouken wore a particularly grim expression.

"This child was created by great magic," Maratouken uttered. "The purity of her essence was told to us to be so powerful that her magic would have almost no limits. The gods delivered her to the mortal world to be delivered to us because they wanted to test you mortals, and...their presence here would alert others to the girl's existence."

"Others," Rendan said, and noted a glance between Maratouken and Theraylyxus. "Something tells me that these 'others' found out about her anyway."

"The last we heard from the gods, they urged us to hurry," Maratouken said.

"After they had delivered her safely, the gods learned they had been betrayed, and that those in the hells had learned of the girl," Theraylyxus added, her eyes welling with tears.

"The hells?" Rendan blurted and then laughed. "And you think I can save this girl from the hells?"

"We believe you can save her from the hells' mortal minions," Theraylyxus countered. "So, we cannot wait. You must meet the others. The gods showed us four of you—four mortal souls—who were worthy of protecting the girl and safely delivering her to our cathedral. Now... we must go."

There was a rush of cold air and a swirl of sparkling snow around Rendan. An instant later, he found himself in a quiet valley lined with towering pine trees and lightly blanketed with snow. Rendan turned a full circle in amazement, his gaze coming to rest upon three others, looking stunned at the arrival of the spirits and himself. The waiting trio quickly approached.

"Very good," one of them said. "Is he the last?"

She was tall, and dressed in a well-made set of chainmail. She wore a red tunic over it, with a single white rose in the center, and on her hip was a sword belt with the weapon still in its scabbard. Her lean face was rather stern in its expression, and her icy blue eyes were hard as she studied Rendan.

The second was a man dressed in warm clothes with a dark cloak over the top. He was a little older than Rendan, and unlike the woman, he looked unsure, perhaps nervous. He looked around the clearing, and then set his eyes on the spirits.

Nervousness was not something that seemed to be on the mind of the last of them. It was a stout, burly dwarf covered in a leather coat and hat and carrying what looked to be a very sturdy club. His eyes were dark, and the lower half of his face was covered in a bushy white beard which had grown down nearly to his waist. He scrutinized the newest arrival and presently gave a huff of disapproval.

"Who's dis?" he asked. "Look like a boy."

"Take ease, my dwarven friend," Maratouken said pleasantly. "I assure you, he is strong of mind and of sword hand."

"But he hasn't a sword," the woman said.

Theraylyxus rolled her eyes, and in a flash, Rendan found that his right hand had filled with the handle of a sword. It felt light, but in his mind, he could tell the blade was something more than those which Tyrus could forge. He examined the blade, which had runes etched into it, and looked at the spirits.

"By my lady..." The woman gasped as light reflected from the sword, onto her face. "Surely a blade of such perfection is from the heavens."

"It is," Maratouken affirmed.

"Made for dealing with the minions of hell," Rendan uttered and swished the sword back and forth.

"It is time for the four of you to journey the short distance to Elaenyral, and retrieve the girl," Maratouken said, pointing off to his right. "We cannot interfere directly in the mortal world. Once you have her, meet us at the cathedral where we may bless her. She will then become the light of Clainsmyth."

The woman turned to Rendan, giving an approving nod as she looked into his eyes.

"I am Tanaska of Thaurous," the woman said. "The Order of the Holy Thorn."

"Rendan." He introduced himself.

"Onrozul," the man in the robes said. "I'm still not certain why I'm even here."

"Don't let him sell himself short," Maratouken said. "He is a wizard, and a gifted one at that. Should you run into trouble, his skills will come in handy."

"Fazok Togmok," the dwarf grunted, introducing himself by thumping his own chest. "Call me Tog."

"All right," Theraylyxus said, her tone now a bit more urgent. "You'd better go. The girl is currently being cared for by the town's innkeeper, but I can feel another presence. A dark presence. Others are coming. Go!"

With no more hesitation, the four of them set out through the pine trees in haste, breathing in the crisp, cold air as they went. There was no time for conversation, but the group was swiftly to the edge of the trees. A dark little town was only a few hundred yards away. The snow was light enough they could hurry, and their boots stirred a haze of it as they went.

Though Theraylyxus had said there were others, nothing seemed to move in their line of sight. In a short time they were making their way along the main road through the town. Rendan scanned the small spread of buildings for the inn. He looked around at the many structures, but his mind was still reeling from the swift developments that had led him here. A moment later, Tanaska's voice focused him.

"There," Tanaska said quietly, gesturing toward a two-story building further down the road. A wooden sign hung on the front of the building, swaying in the wind announcing that it was HOLOTH'S HAVEN. Rendan thought about how nice it would be to have a room with a comfortable bed there, but he came back to the moment as they drew close, and Tog thumped a fist against the front doors.

"This doesn't seem so difficult," Onrozul said.

The sound of two bolts sliding open on the inside drew their attention, and then the door opened to reveal a short, portly old man who looked cautiously out at them. His stubbled, wrinkled face studied them a moment.

"Are you them?" he asked. "The ones to deliver the child?"

"We have been sent by the spirits of Clainsmyth," Tanaska informed him. "And come to safeguard the infant girl's passage to be with them."

"Then come," he said, and backed away to open the door further.

Tog was the last one to pass through the doorway. Inside the tavern, Tanaska had stopped, and she looked around the place. Rendan watched her, noting that she seemed suddenly different, like she was more aware. She scrutinized Holoth a moment before swiftly pulling her sword from the scabbard. Immediately, Rendan knew something was wrong, and gripped his own sword a bit tighter.

The sound of a wolf's howl rolled down from the mountains just as Holoth was preparing to close the door. The howl was joined by a second, and then another, and then the song of some dozen wolves filled the air around them.

"What is it?" Rendan asked. "Wolves? Why would they care about her?"

"It's not the wolves," Tanaska said. "I can sense them. Evil. Close that door."

The sound of the wolves came again, much closer. Holoth slammed the door shut and slid both bolts across.

"Quickly, to the girl," Onrozul said. "I'd like to be back in my bed as soon as I can. I'm no adventurer."

"In a moment, this will be no adventure," Tanaska warned Onrozul. There was a fire in her eyes that Rendan had not yet seen. Sounds could be heard on the other side of the door as someone was approaching. Muffled growls from the wolves could be heard.

"Then what will it be?" Rendan asked.

"A fight..." Tanaska growled in response.

There was a loud bang as the doors were struck from the outside, causing the group inside to jump back. Rendan exchanged a worried glance with Tanaska as another blow shook the doors. Holoth hurried away just before Rendan set his eyes on the doors and readied his sword. The doors burst open, and through them rippled a wave of energy that took Rendan off his feet before he fell to the floor. The others had been knocked down, but were quick to recover as the sound of rattling armor drew their attention. Goblins flooded in.

Worlyx strode in behind them. A sinister grin spread across his face just as Holoth returned with the girl in his arms and wrapped in a blanket.

"Easy as festering fly pie," the goblin sneered. "Take her."

The goblins closed quickly on Holoth, who turned to flee, but found that he was faced with a hooded, robed figure that had appeared behind him. He froze, and the robed figure snatched the swaddled infant, staring at him from behind the hood. The goblins were waiting as Holoth backed away from the hooded figure, but before he could react, he felt the hot pain of spears thrust into his back. Holoth crumbled to the floor.

Worlyx caught only the flash of movement before Rendan appeared, launching himself at the goblins. He downed one of the creatures immediately with a single flash of his blade. Worlyx drew his own blade, but was only then aware that two of his others had been cut down by someone in white armor. He scowled and backed toward the doorway while the robed figure receded into the gloom. In a moment, the goblins fled through the front doors again.

"After them!" Tanaska said. "They have the girl!"

The four of them hurried to the front door and rushed out into the winter night. They pulled up short, however, when they realized that waiting in the snow were dozens more of the horrid, scaly things in armor.

Rendan was quick to block the spear of one before Tog swung his club to knock the beast away. Worlyx returned to the saddle on his mount—a large, gray wolf—and he nodded toward the quartet.

"Arrows!" he shrieked at goblins nearby on their wolf mounts. They lifted their bows and drew back the strings.

"Look out!" Onrozul called.

But just as the arrows raced from the bows, the wizard lifted his hands, calling out a word which echoed through the town. The arrows seemed to bounce off nothing and sail uselessly into the snow. Worlyx grunted in disgust at the sight, then turned to the witch climbing atop her horse with the infant.

"Do something! Or they'll follow us all the way to your mistress!" Worlyx snarled.

The witch looked around from the horse, and the air filled with twisted red ropes of electricity. Rendan and the others dove for cover as her magic snapped and slithered through the air. She then swept a hand from right to left in front of her and gazed at Worlyx.

"Ride! Our mounts will use my magic to travel with all haste!"

Worlyx signaled his goblins, and with two sharp whistling sounds, the group headed for the mountains while the electricity raged.

Curious townspeople who had begun to peek from windows dove for cover as the witch's magic continued to crackle and burn. In another moment it was dark and quiet again, and Rendan stood staring after where they had gone. He turned to Tanaska, who looked livid at the development, while Onrozul checked himself over. Tog extinguished a small fire on his beard with his fingertips.

"We must go after them," Rendan called out with ferocity. "If she is the hope for Clainsmyth and her spirit will keep away the likes of *them*, then we have to save her!"

"I agree, but we do not know where they've gone," Tanaska said. "If only the spirits could help."

"We need horses," Rendan said. "We can follow the tracks they have left in the snow if we leave swiftly."

"Who knows how long it could take to find them?" Onrozul groaned. "We do not have much time before Clainsmyth, and the girl is to be blessed before that, or it won't matter."

"We cannot interfere," Maratouken said, appearing with the other two. "Meaning, we cannot take her, cannot cross blades with these vile creatures... But we can discover where they have gone. We can deliver you there."

"But it must be quickly," Rendan said, his eyes fiery. "As you've said, time is of the essence."

"Theraylyxus, give chase," Maratouken said, which sent the sprite away with a flash of ice crystals. "You four, make sure you have all that you need. This could be quick. Gyth? To the Cathedral."

Gyth vanished into the air, while Maratouken looked into the forested hills surrounding the town. He drew in a long breath through his nose, and closed his eyes before beginning to mutter quietly. The other four exchanged glances, but then moved closer to one another and eyed Maratouken.

"Are you in need of anything else?" Tanaska quietly asked Rendan.

He shrugged. "I'm not sure."

"Got a sword, got what ya need," Tog growled.

"I cannot argue that logic," Rendan said.

"High in the mountains," Maratouken said, his voice sounding as though he was speaking in a large, cavernous room. "They follow a track which will take them to a tall peak. The rider holding the girl bears a symbol burned onto her left hand; a serpent on a thorny branch."

"The Drach," Tanaska gasped. "They were thought to have been vanquished ages ago."

Maratouken continued to mutter as his eyes remained closed. Rendan shared a glance with Onrozul before shrugging.

"*Who*, or *what*, are the Drach?" Rendan asked.

"Witches," Tanaska answered. "Thought destroyed by the king's paladins a long time ago."

"Witches?" Onrozul blurted in horror. "My magic is no match for that!"

"You don't know that," Rendan said. "Clearly, you were able to protect us from their goblins. We cannot let these witches have the girl."

"We won't!" Tanaska blurted.

There was a pause as each of them seemed to be searching their mind for an answer.

"But we cannot even follow them," Onrozul said.

Maratouken opened his eyes, and smiled.

"You can," he said. "Here they come."

The four of them looked where Maratouken now stared, unsure of what he meant, but in another moment, four of the largest deer any of them had ever seen walked from the trees, directly toward them. The deer all had towering antlers and seemed powerful as their steps brought them to the outstretched hands of Maratouken. He greeted them by softly touching their noses, and he smiled at them as they nuzzled him.

"What are these?" Rendan asked.

"These, my friends, are longtime allies of the spirits of Clainsmyth. They are here to help you," Maratouken replied. "They will carry you to the temple of the Drachs."

"A coven of witches seems like much to overcome. Especially since they are protected by an army of goblins!" Onrozul complained.

"It does not matter," Tanaska interjected. "We must ride, and follow them to where this coven is hiding."

"Yes," Maratouken agreed. "Ride swiftly, but hold on tight, and trust these deer to see you safely through."

Theraylyxus appeared, looking worried as she settled in next to Maratouken.

"It will take a day, even upon these," she said. "I fear we're cutting it very close."

Rendan hurried to one of the deer and was helped up by Tog before Tanaska helped Onrozul up. Tog was nimbler than Rendan had thought, and the stout dwarf was easily able to seat himself on the back of one of the deer. Tanaska was the last up, and she glanced around as the others were steadying themselves on the mounts. She had put her sword away, and she looked down at Maratouken.

"They know the way?" she asked.

"They know the way," Maratouken affirmed for her with a warm smile. But a moment later, his smile had faded as he stepped back, and let forth a low whistle to the deer.

Before any of them could say a word, the deer set off toward the trees at a run, so swiftly that at first it was a struggle to hold on. Soon, they were riding more steadily, but just as they had grown used to the pounding of the hooves on the ground, there came a strange braying noise from one of the deer. At once, the deer vaulted into the sky. Having taken flight, the astonished riders held on even tighter with wide eyes and open mouths. Rendan smiled and began to laugh.

"This is amazing!" he called out.

"Glad dey know where the're goin!" Tog shouted, holding on to the antlers.

"I still fail to see how I can face the black magic of three witches," Onrozul said from a few feet away. "I am but one man."

"You are not alone," Tanaska said. "I bring with me the power of my goddess, and you have your magic. Rendan and Tog have their own skills. We will be victorious."

"Your confidence is refreshing," Onrozul said. "I wish that I had it."

"I just hope that we are in time," Rendan added and looked ahead at the mountains.

* * *

Arvulia had been waiting alongside Iyrgalla at the entrance to the temple. They knew the others were returning soon. Arvulia was a thousand years old, at least, and so infused with the powers of hell that she would be favored upon her eventual arrival there. The hells had advised her of the girl's creation and that she was a source of such magic it was possible Arvulia could be young again. With renewed life and energy, she could plague the mortal world even longer.

But the magic was not held to her longevity alone—there was so much power within the girl that the Drach could make their return to power. The king and his paladins—the force which had banished them—would pay, and then the three witches could begin to recruit more. This thought brought a smirk to her face as she heard the approach of the wolves and goblins. Arvulia turned to Iyrgalla.

"Make the chamber ready," she ordered with a croaking voice. "We mustn't delay."

"Yes, coven mother," Iyrgalla acknowledged and hurried inside with all speed.

The wolves rode into view and at the head of them was the horse carrying the witch called Pelyx. The riders dismounted at the entrance to the coven's temple,

Pelyx approached and presented the crying infant to Arvulia, who took it and smiled at it from under her hood. A dry, terrifying laugh escaped the coven's mother, and she dragged a warty, twisted finger gently across the girl's angelic face.

"We will repair to the sacrificial chamber and ensure our swift return to power with her blood," Arvulia said.

"Yes..." Pelyx agreed.

"Worlyx," Arvulia said. "Ensure we are not disturbed."

"Who would come here?" the goblin asked. "We were not followed."

"Of course you were followed," Arvulia snapped. "This girl is far too important to have just been left to our clutches. Kill any who arrive."

"As you command," Worlyx acknowledged and turned to his underlings while the witches disappeared into the temple. "Spread out! Kill anyone who appears!"

Deep inside the temple, the infant was placed on the altar in a large chamber meant for sacrifices. Incantations were read, while outside the goblins waited with spears and swords, bows and arrows in the cold. Fire swelled in the sacrificial chamber in a large pit, and the girl began to cry. The preparation for the sacrifice had taken most of the day, as the ways of magic were often a time-consuming affair that required precision and timing. Arvulia looked down at the infant while a dagger of ebony was brought forth by Pelyx.

"The hells will see us release the magic in your silver blood," Arvulia said. "Silver blood of magic to fill us with the means to impose the wills of our masters here...everywhere!"

* * *

Outside, the goblins became puzzled as four large deer strayed into view, digging around in the snow some fifty yards from the temple. Worlyx had been expecting men or elves, but deer? These were no invaders. He thought to tell his goblins to slay the deer for meat, but Tanaska emerged from hiding, and she swiftly approached with her sword, a holy blade given to her by the Order. She was rushed by the goblins, but her left palm extended toward them and a blessed flash of light flashed, blinding the goblins.

Rendan's ears were filled with the goblins' screams as he moved in to engage the enemy with his own blade. The creatures reached up to cover their eyes, but Tanaska gave them no quarter. She was quick to engage them, and Rendan joined her while Worlyx shouted orders for more goblins to join. He had not moved far, however, when a crushing impact from his left struck him, and he realized that the dwarf was there. Worlyx shrieked as he toppled over a ridge, and Tog rushed after other goblins.

Several goblins closed in on Tog from atop another ridge while he engaged others. They were preparing to descend upon him with spears when very suddenly, the ridge they were on erupted with flame. The goblins were incinerated as the spell exploded, crumbling the ridge and attracting the attention of all in the melee. Onrozul remained nearby, his hands still outstretched as he gaped in amazement at what his magic had done.

Arvulia's eyes darted left at the sound of the explosion. Without looking, she lifted her left hand.

"Iyrgalla. Pelyx. See to it," she said. "I will complete the sacrifice."

The two witches hurried away while Arvulia looked down at the infant.

"Now... My precious," she sneered. "It is time."

Outside, the goblins had begun to flee as the four rescuers looked at the entrance to the temple.

"All right, now we must pray we are not too late," Tanaska said.

A green, glowing orb of energy raced from the darkness and struck Tanaska, while Rendan dove away. Tanaska cried out as she went down, but Tog quickly lay himself over her to protect her from further attack. Rendan and Onrozul stared into the darkness, both ready for another attack. A cackle issued forth from the gloom, and a moment later Iyrgalla strode into view, closing in on the dwarf huddled over the quivering paladin. She let the green energy flair in her palms again as she leered at them. Tog eyed the holy blade next to Tanaska.

"You will burn for your intrusion," she said.

"Witch!" came a shout. She turned her attention to her left as Onrozul approached. He extended his hands toward her, and rays of light jetted at her, only to be blocked by her green energy.

She laughed.

"You fool!" she blurted with a laugh. "Your magic is no match for the Drach! Your feeble light show cannot harm me."

"How 'bout dis?" Tog snarled from behind her, and thrust Tanaska's holy blade forward.

It burst through the front of her and she howled in horror and pain as the blessed blade sent its energy through her. Pelyx had staggered from the dark. Her ancient eyes were wide as she took in the sight of black blood spreading underneath Iyrgalla while light erupted from the wound. Her eyes hardened with rage at the dwarf, and she closed in with red lightning spiraling around her hands and up her arms.

"You...filthy...dirt mover!" she seethed, approaching the dwarf.

Tog's face tightened, and his eyes narrowed while his teeth clenched.

"Not been called that in more'n two hundred year, yeh foul thing," Tog growled at her.

She unleashed her lightning, but Rendan stepped between them quickly, lifting the enchanted blade. The magic of the blade seemed to absorb the power, and Pelyx screamed with frustration as Tog helped Tanaska up. Pelyx unleashed more of the red lightning to the same effect as Rendan stood his ground.

"Your terror is at its end," Rendan said.

"You think you will destroy the Drach with this pitiful band of rabble?" Pelyx asked. "Do not dare to believe that this world will ever escape evil's shadow."

"Evil's shadow...but not yours," Onrozul uttered, drawing her attention.

She was in time to see the blast of fire come forth, but not in time to block it. Flames struck her and sent her reeling backwards. By the time she had struck the outer wall of the temple, she had been reduced to ashes.

Onrozul quivered, and soon collapsed to one knee. The others gathered around him.

"Are you all right?" Rendan asked.

"I will be," Onrozul answered. "Magic can be draining."

"We must find the girl," Tanaska said resolutely, and looked to the entrance to the temple as Rendan helped Onrozul to his feet.

Rendan led them inside, listening for any sounds to give away the location of the girl. The sound of the crying guided them through the corridors to the sacrificial chamber.

Arvulia looked up from the infant on the altar, watching as Rendan led the others into the chamber. As they spread out and readied weapons, the scowl on her face turned into a grin and she laughed.

"How adorable," she said. "As though you stand a chance."

"Your other witches are dead," Tanaska said. "You are all that is left of the Drach. Give us the girl."

Again, the witch laughed.

"Don't be daft," she said. "This fight is about to be over."

Rendan walked toward her and shook his head. "I don't think so," he said. "Your magic here has faded, hasn't it? That's why you need the girl, and that's why you haven't attacked us."

"I'll show you why this girl is so powerful," Arvulia said, and lifted the dagger.

Onrozul lifted his left hand toward the witch, directing his palm at her. She gasped as the dagger flew from her grasp and struck the wall nearby. Her eyes darkened, and she turned from the crying baby.

She lifted her hands. Black energy flared out, striking them all. The searing hot pain brought them all to their knees. Rendan looked around at the others to see that they were writhing in agony of the black magic. He looked down at his sword as Arvulia looked them over and lowered her hands.

"So, you see? That was but a small taste of what awaits you if you tangle with me." She turned her back to the group, picked up the dagger, and looked down at the infant. Her crooked smile of blackened teeth spread across her face.

Rendan returned to his feet, tightening his grip on the sword.

"I haven't finished...yet..." he snarled through the pain.

She wheeled about, her eyes fixating on him as she brought her hands up again. He concentrated on the girl, his family, and all of Clainsmyth.

She shrieked and unleashed her black magic.

The sword glowed a bright, brilliant blue as the black magic struck it and was cast back, spreading the dark energy through the walls, the ceiling, the floor, but mostly, back into Arvulia herself.

She was blasted back as though she'd been launched from a catapult, and was hurled into the flaming pit behind her. Briefly, the flames turned black, then red, and with a howling scream, the coven was no more.

Rendan rushed to the baby.

She cooed at him, and he smiled down at her as he ran a gentle hand over her head. The others were returning to their feet and approached. Tanaska put a hand on Rendan while he gently picked up the infant and cradled her against his chest.

"That was amazing," she said.

"It was the sword," he assured her.

"It was no sword that stood up to that witch," she said. "Now, we've a baby to deliver to some spirits."

He smiled at her.

The temple shook and rumbled around them as they ran for the exit. Tog halted Tanaska at a junction of corridors as a large piece of stone fell. Dust and smoke filled the air as they pushed on, and moved quickly with Tog now in the lead. As the archway of the main entrance began to collapse, the four of them had to dive to reach safety. Rendan cradled the infant so that as he struck the ground and rolled, she was not hurt. Rendan grinned at the little face with the wide eyes.

"Is everyone all right?" Tanaska asked as the four of them returned to their feet. "The girl?"

"She's absolutely perfect," Rendan said with a smile. "Now let's get out of here."

"I pray we can make this cathedral, or at least find Maratouken before it is too late," Oronzul said.

There came a shriek as Worlyx rushed them from where he had been hiding. He drew back his blade, but before he could bring it around, a mighty hoof stomped down, crushing the goblin and his armor against the stone of the mountains. The group looked up to see one of the deer looking down at them. Rendan smiled.

"I wager he knows the way to the cathedral," he said.

* * *

Indeed, the flight upon the deer had been a rush, traveling down in the cold air with the blessed girl in their hands now. Finally, in the darkness, the group found themselves on a different, snow-covered mesa where a stone cathedral of magnificence stood. Numerous ghostly figures floated and flitted about the area as the deer delivered them right to the archway leading into the cathedral. Maratouken stood there, beaming as he waited, flanked by Theraylyxus and Gyth.

"Close, but just in time," he said to the group as they dismounted from the deer and brought the girl to him.

"Here she is," Rendan said, presenting the bundled child. Theraylyxus took the sword from Rendan.

"Ah, Mehloria," Maratouken said as he took the infant. The other spirits looked at her. "Welcome home. We will make sure the four of you are taken home as well, but for now..."

The group went into the cathedral to find that many more ghostly figures waited, and a stone table stood. They made their way to it and placed the infant there. Prayers were said, welcoming Mehloria to the world and her place amongst the spirits. Light began to cover her as the prayers and procession went on. Maratouken held her up, blessing her as the light grew in intensity. Rendan looked over at Tanaska as the light beamed skyward, and then...the spirits were gone.

"It is midnight," Rendan said. "It is Clainsmyth."

"It was good to stand beside you," Tanaska said. "With you all, but I feel we must all return home."

"Yes," Maratouken agreed, appearing as a ghostly form now. "From now, our magic, Mehloria's magic, will make your world a better place. You are to be commended and rewarded."

"Clainsmyth's preservation and strengthening is my reward," Tanaska said with a smile.

"I just want to get home," Onrozul said. "It has been a most trying night. A very safe and relaxing Clainsmyth to you all."

"Come," Maratouken said, and led them outside. They were back on the deer, and Onrozul was the first to sail away into the sky.

Tog bid them farewell and promised to visit Rendan in the future, and then also flew off. Rendan and Tanaska shook hands once more.

"You are good, and brave," she said. "Come and see me in the castle. Perhaps you should join the Order."

"I'll be happy to visit," he said. "I'll leave the Order to far more capable people."

She smiled again, and they flew their separate ways.

The next thing he remembered, he had awakened before the warmth of Kandrek's fire. He recalled the journey he'd just made and smiled. Shortly after, was back on Hawlice, riding home. After returning to town, he received his four Shrochs, and set out to feast with his family. Upon arrival, he stepped into the home where his family was glad to see him, but seemed somewhat surprised at his disheveled appearance. He attributed it to the ride, but then noticed something—the feast was grand and bountiful.

"We were set to do our cooking, and messengers said they had been sent by you to deliver this bounty," Rendan's mother explained. "Said you had asked for it to be delivered because you'd been away, working."

He smiled. The abundant feast was inviting, and he realized how hungry he was. He lifted his eyes skyward.

"Maratouken be praised," he said. "All the spirits of Clainsmyth and Mehloria be blessed."

"Mehloria?" his mother asked.

He laughed.

"You'll know soon," he said. "A very happy and merry Clainsmyth."

ABOUT THE AUTHOR

JOSHUA A. BROWN

Joshua A. Brown is a child of the blockbuster era of films.
His imagination was stoked by exposure to many works of
literature,
film, and music from an early age. A former police officer,
Joshua is now a musician, film maker and published author.
He lives in the country in central Iowa and is a graduate of
Iowa State University. Tending to horses, chickens, cats, and
dogs, his life is a busy one.
For more information on Josh and his many projects,
check out www.3b-entertainment.com

🅕 facebook.com/Josh3b

🅐 amazon.com/-/B01N9T8KMG

THE FADED PHOTOGRAPH

R. A. DARLINGE

White.
    Innocence.
Peace.

I stood at the window, looking out at the falling snow. The soft glow of the streetlamp before me was like an ethereal presence. The snow was unblemished. The wind blew puffs of the powder into wisps of sparkle. To most, I assume, the scene would be tranquil, romantic even. In my mind, however, I saw only the ash and destruction of the machines of war.

It was winter solstice and though the events that brought this mood had transpired over one hundred and fifty years ago, the ache had never once diminished. The ghost of my reflection looked back at me with hollow eyes, morphing from the chiseled features of the lead singer of Siren's Kiss, to the younger siren I had been then. Twin brother of a god, confidence radiating from every scale. My mind painted the picture further; my golden hair and voice drawing the masses, the showers of roses and trinkets falling at my feet at the end of every performance. Handsome and well built, I wanted for nothing, foolishly became an eager servant of the god of Gluttony, taking on the task of paying attentive court to a madman. How naive I was...

I returned to the present, banishing the thoughts that would take me further into depression, focusing on the sounds coming from the nearby parlor. My beloved Oliver, a thirty-seven-year-old human giant of a water mage, had allowed Mi'khalea and Finnegan to descend upon my home. All three of them were determined to bring a bit of Christmas spirit to my 'dreary' existence. They couldn't know that this was not a night for festivities. It was forever a night of memory and mourning. This... and the rest of the month of December.

To be fair, it was my fault. I had never told them the reason I didn't celebrate Christmas or New Years. It was something personal, too painful to share. Though I felt guilty that I hadn't at least shared it with Oliver, my husband and lover.

Finnegan, a newly turned werewolf, had scars so vivid that streaks of red were vibrant against his pale skin and russet hair. He arrived with his mate, Mi'khaela, a maned wolf nature spirit, earlier in the evening. Finn toted a fine spruce tree on one shoulder, a mischievous glint in his green eyes as he pushed his bulk past me through the open door, growling. "It's for your own good, Fish Sticks."

Miki, her violet eyes dancing with amusement and arms full with bags of frippery had grinned. "That's right, Scrooge McDuck. Oliver deserves more than a mausoleum for Christmas, and since we've been invited for Christmas dinner, you get no say in the matter."

She had been right. No matter what I said, they ignored my protests. In a way, I was glad they were doing all the work. I'd make them take it all down too. *Damn interfering pests*, I thought with hidden amusement, my lips twitching as I cloistered myself away from the lights, the scents and sounds of merrymaking.

Glancing to my right, I caught a glimpse of the small photograph on the bookshelf. The faded black and white portrait of a steadfast and honest being, Rolf. Soldier, pilot and research subject, and my soulmate. I reached for the gilded frame, pulling it closer. Even in the gray, black and white tones, his forceful personality was evident. I could easily see through the image to the day it was taken.

December 21, 1940. Eight days before the assault on London that would take his life.

I was drawn back into the past as I gazed at the photograph. The sounds of the others faded to be replaced with the sounds of the train I had ridden into Salsburg that winter. I had gotten leave from my duties attending to the Fuhrer, that sick and demented personality. Only in fellow demons had I seen such a nature, twisted and zealous to his own ends. I had come to hate the orders I had received. The god of Gluttony, my master, made it clear that I was to use the power of my voice to ensure the ever-increasing desires of Adolf Hitler until it led to his downfall.

My eyes lifted from the photo to the falling snow taking me further into memory. It had been snowing then as I exited the train in Salzburg, Austria, the bustling crowd chattering about the upcoming festivities as if there weren't a war going on. As if there weren't hundreds -no, thousands of men dying to the west and south and in the hidden camps in the east. I had turned the fur collar of my coat up shielding my neck against the wind. Within moments, I had collected my single bag before heading toward the hotel where I would spend the Christmas holiday. In my pocket resided the letter. I caressed the well-worn envelope, the letter written in Rolf's handwriting warming me from within. I must have read it a hundred times, only half believing he had actually gotten leave. It was too bad we couldn't spend more than a few days together before he had to return for a mission. But at least I'd have him for Christmas.

Had I known what would be the outcome of that mission, I would have never let him go.

Or would I have?

Pinching the bridge of my nose, I looked at the photograph again. The smiling face looking up at me told me the answer. Rolf would have laughed at my insistence and kissed me before telling me that the gods of air were on his side and to stop my worrying.

I sighed, turning slightly as the sound of laughter came from the parlor. I felt a small tug, an ache, as someone decided to play a carol from that era on the piano. My eyes began burning and I found I couldn't bear to hear the sounds any longer. I wasn't fast enough to escape though. Oliver stuck his head in the open door of my study. "Nic, I know it's not your favorite holiday, but do you have to be such an Ebenezer Scrooge?" He inched further into the room, "Come on, I've got eggnog. I can spike it for you." He tempted me, his eyes glinting and tone smooth as fifty-year-old bourbon.

I couldn't face him. I couldn't let him see me like this. He'd want to know why, and I wasn't ready to tell him. Nor anyone else. "Go have fun, my love. I will join you in a while." My voice cracked slightly and I hoped he didn't notice.

I heard soft footsteps behind me, the presence of my mate both soothing and harsh in my current state. His fingers brushed my neck. "What's that you got there?" His voice was low, concerned.

I realized belatedly, that I was still holding Rolf's picture. "A memory." I replied, cooly.

Oliver's cheek rested against my shoulder. "I know that. Who was he," he murmured, his breath warm against my ear. "You've never wanted to talk about him. Was he your lover?" His arms slid around my waist. I felt a knot of tears forming in my throat.

"Leave it alone, Oliver. Go back to decorating." I was harsh and mean. I didn't want to be, but... I couldn't talk about it. I couldn't speak the words. I knew if I did, the memory would come alive, smothering me further. Those last days were so precious.

Oliver didn't move, only hugged me tighter. "Want me to send them home, Nicholai? I didn't realize it would hurt you this way."

Refusing to answer, I tried to pull away, but he held me firmly. "Nope. Sorry, babe, you're not getting out of this. You're my mate and you're in pain. Tell me. I can't help you if I don't know."

I looked up into his face, the pale green of his eyes almost silver in the dim light. I looked back at the photo, my fingers wrapped around the frame as if I were afraid to let it go. Perhaps I was. Perhaps I was afraid that Rolf's memory would fade like the photograph. Dissolving into the mists of Time, taking Rolf with them. No one remembered him. Only I cherished his memory. If I forgot, he would cease to exist.

"Alright." I murmured, looking back up into his face. "But I wish to go outside, where there is silence. I..." Glancing at the open door, I heard music and murmurs from the parlor softly filtering in.

Oliver caught my chin, lifting it so he could brush his lips against mine. "Let me go excuse myself for a little while," he said, his eyes conveying a slight hurt at my attitude. "I'm coming right back, so no disappearing acts Nicholai Vaschenko."

I gave him a half-smile. He knew me all too well. "I promise," I replied, meeting his gaze.

The photo drew my gaze again as Oliver left the room. I stared into Rolf's face as I overheard Oliver speak and the softer more muted replies of Mi'khalea and Finnegan. He was back in mere moments, closing the study door behind him, and moving to my side. "I brought your coat," he said quietly, draping the heavy fabric over my shoulders.

I placed the photo back in its niche on the bookshelf and slid my arms through the sleeves, reaching into the pocket to find my gloves. Looking up at him again, I nodded and reached for the door handle. The cold chilled my face as I stepped out onto the veranda, the sounds of the ocean mingling with the crunching snow as we walked toward the stone railing.

Oliver brushed the railing clear, then turned to rest against it, his hands tucked warmly his coat's pockets. I took out my cigarette case, pulling a clove from within before tucking the case back into my pocket. Placing the clove between my lips, I lit it, inhaling deeply as I tried to collect my thoughts. "First, as you know, when demonkind or celestials take up residence here on earth, they live many lifetimes." I took another pull from my clove, anxiety making my stomach churn.

Oliver was quiet, letting me speak at my own pace, for which I was grateful. "When I arrived here from Hakkah, I was not known as Nicholai Vaschenko." I sighed, my gaze shifting from the oceanscape to Oliver's face. He remained silent, only indicating with a nod that I should continue. I returned to looking out over the churning waves. "I have been known by many names throughout the ages, but we will only deal with one."

"I can think of a few names for you, Nic. Starting with asshole."

I started at the sound of his voice, choking on the smoke I had just inhaled. My eyes met his, and I saw that while his tone was acidic, his eyes were filled with amusement. "I'm sure Mik'haela would agree." I replied, fighting the nausea his tone had induced.

Oliver snorted, "Oh, I know she would. Seriously, Nic, I know all this. What's so important about the name you're dancing around but not mentioning? I mean, I know your true name, not just the moniker you go by now. What did you do? 'Cause I'm drawing blanks."

I sighed, averting my eyes before answering. "You know I was given charge of the Gluttony of this world. Mostly monitoring it and keeping it balanced. But when necessary, I use my voice to tip that balance." I swallowed, feeling the bile rise in my throat. Had it not been for that tipping of the balance... Rolf...

I shook myself, taking another drag from the clove. "The name I went by when I met Rolf was Viktor Pfeiffer. And I was the one responsible for his death." The tears froze on my lashes. "You see, had there been no war, Rolf would never have received the orders that led to his death."

Oliver pushed off from his perch and came to stand in front of me. "Nic, why would you say such an untrue thing? I've known you since I was five. You protect your lovers, not lead them to their death."

I closed my eyes. "They're not untrue. I was called to Zakhar, where my twin, Nathaniel, rules his kingdom. The great council had decreed this planet needed some adjustments. It was agreed that Nate, as a god of War, could have free rein once again. I was told to take up a place at the side of a man named Adolf Hitler. To ensure his desire for supreme dominance was fed so the war would encompass the world."

Memories flowed through my mind, each bringing another prick to my already wounded heart. "At the time, I took those orders with confidence in the council that I had always had. Confidence in my twin that this was the right thing to do. How could I have known? How could I have possibly guessed how horrifying that particular human truly was."

Oliver plucked the smoldering end of my cigarette from my limp fingers and tossed it aside. He pulled me into his arms, holding me tightly. "Nic, you never cease to amaze me. You're a demon, brother to a god of war and you detest demonic ways. Well... most of them at any rate."

I reached to clutch the back of his coat, my face buried in his shoulder. I gave him a pain-filled, ironic chuckle. "And you, my beloved human, are more demonic than I sometimes. We are quite the pair." My mind whirled with thought, my heart aching as I reluctantly pulled away.

Looking down, he lifted one hand up to cup my face. "You are my one and only love, Nic. I would do anything for you. Tell me about Rolf. What was he like?"

I leaned into the warmth of his hand. "Rolf was bigger than life. Tall, but nowhere near as tall as you, my water giant." That earned me a snort, but I went on before he could reply. "He was beautiful, golden hair that shone like burnished metal in the sun. His eyes were the color of blue topaz, and there was always a glint of mischief sparkling within their depths. He was a bit too smart for his own good too. A mind like a steel trap and when he was focused, he was intense. A bit like you, actually, but his strengths were military and flying. He was a destroyer, while you're a builder." I smiled softly as I realized how similar yet opposite they were. "I could never get him to relinquish his beliefs that this war was just. He'd had his head filled with the strength of the Third Reich from a young age. It's amusing now, after all the chaos and evil of that war. I wasn't German, and this should have made him disdain my company, but from the moment we met... Well... you know very well how a connection like that works."

Chuckling, Oliver squeezed me. "Indeed. I do know. Is that why you never talk about him? Are you afraid I'll be jealous?"

I cocked my head, eyeing his serene face. "One of the reasons. He was my soulmate in that lifetime. Just as you are in this one, and that kind of mating is fragile. One tiny thing can shatter it, irrevocably."

"Not likely with us. We've had most of my life to build this

179

bond. From the day we met. Do you remember? The aquarium when I was five?"

I smiled, "I remember. I was shocked that you could see me in that form. Not many humans can see true demonic or celestial forms. You were so curious, nose pressed against the glass of the tank I was hiding in. And then, I was shocked again, when I saw the amount of power you held in that tiny body."

He laughed. "I guess it was the fertilizer that made me grow so tall. I remember how fascinated I was. You had a fish's tail. You looked like one of the lion fish swimming in the reef, except your colors were wrong. All blues and grays. And your hair... Nic, your hair is amazing. But I tell you that all the time." He shook his head, giving me a wink before returning to his perch on the railing. "Those days were the happiest of my childhood. Learning magic, making friends with my element and its fellows. Having you there to praise me."

I scoffed, "I did not praise you, Oliver. I pushed you to learn. To gain control before someone took notice of you and twisted your soul."

Oliver was silent for a long moment, turning to look out over the ocean himself. "You did praise me, Nic. You smiled at me. You showed me new and even greater things. You fed the fire within me. Maybe you don't consider that praise, but I did. You saw the potential I couldn't see at such a young age. The confidence you had in my abilities kept me going, even after you left."

I fidgeted, the old guilt of leaving him returning. I'd gone as far away from him as possible, never dreaming we would meet again thirty years later. "You know I had to leave, even if you didn't understand then. She would have noticed had I stayed. I pushed it staying for the two years I did. I couldn't risk it any longer. She has done enough to those I care about."

"Was she there too? With Rolf I mean." He turned his head to look at me.

The cold I felt now had nothing to do with the snow. "She was. She and her...lover. Together, they ripped the fabric of your world apart. Taking this world to the brink and almost dooming its very existence. Rolf got sucked into their machinations. He was bred to many demons, and was a stud in the service of the Master Race that was being developed."

"The blond, blue-eyed Nazi Master Race?" His voice held doubt, and I knew he guessed the truth.

"No. The real Master Race involved blending Hitler's Aryians with demons and creating the ultimate fusion of demon and human. She's still trying after all these years. The Wulf Meister we saved Finnegan from is proof of that. I just don't know how far reaching it is. He cannot be the only one she employed. So many of the scientists and doctors escaped when all was said and done. We can only hope to find and eradicate them."

Sighing, Oliver replied with some force. "We will find them, Nic. And we will destroy them and that bitch."

Glancing up at him, I saw an anger that reminded me of Rolf. The intensity of a hound on the scent or the hawk sighting its prey. I couldn't agree with him, though. She had evaded every attempt to assassinate her.

Ymene held my pearl— half of my soul.

Lifting a hand, I touched the three scars that marred the left side of my face from my forehead to the corner of my mouth, slicing over my eye. People say the eyes are the window to the soul. For demons that is even more accurate. Souls can be stolen through the eyes, and Ymene had stolen half of mine. She held it in a pendant cage that hung around her neck. She used it to call me, to draw me out of hiding to try to reclaim it, hoping to force me to hand over my twin. Which I would never do.

It was this loss of my pearl that made it impossible to fully soul-bond to Oliver, though Mi'khaela claimed ours was the strongest bond she had seen in a long time. Other than hers, of course. Thinking of the nature spirit calmed my nerves slightly, her snarky attitude at life always made me wish I could be more like her. Not that I would ever admit that to anyone. And spirits forbid she found out.

Instead of getting into an argument, and before Oliver could prompt me, I chose to shift the subject back to Rolf. "The time Rolf and I had was short, but we tried to make every occasion seem like a lifetime. A summer holiday on the Rhine. Winter skiing in the Alps. Secluded hideaways when we never left our rooms. High society balls at grand hotels. We had the means. We were treated like royalty everywhere we went because of our rank and with whom we had close associations. We used it. We were careful, however. No one could ever know that we were lovers."

"Why not?" Oliver's voice held incredulity, but also curiosity.

"At that time, it was illegal to be gay, Oliver. We could have been jailed or, because of who we were associated with, killed outright. It made it hard in the more public places we stayed. I remember one time almost getting caught and Rolf insisting that I start yelling at him for giving himself to some cheap floozy instead of saving it for his stud duties. Since I hated the fact he had to do this, my anger at him was real when I began yelling." I snorted, a small smile appearing on my lips.

"Damn, I forget how hard it was for people like us back then." He winked at me. "So glad I don't have to hide my love for you." I smirked at him, but Oliver chuckled and went on. "I'd probably like Rolf, even if I think Hitler and his regime were...well...you know, insane and disgusting."

I nodded. "Yes. I agree with you on both counts. Rolf and I didn't speak of politics for that reason. We were just a couple who tried to live outside the war. We doted on each other, made love every chance we got. We made silly promises and challenged one another to fulfill them without being detected."

"So that's why you're so good at surprises." Oliver burst out laughing. "The espionage of gift giving. Spirits, Nic. You're like that old spy character 007. Do you know that one? It's really old, still in the 1900s and early 2000s."

I gave him a look, shaking my head with amusement. "Oliver, I was alive back then, remember?"

He gave me a sheepish grin and scratched the back of his head. "Oh yeah. Anyway. Punchline ruined."

I chuckled, "No...I get it. We were like that, I suppose. At one point, Hitler asked me if I was wooing the lady that sent me the gifts or if she was just hopeful." Shaking my head, I snorted. "I had to look him straight in the eye and say that she was hopeful with way too much time and money on her hands. It was one of the hardest lies I ever told him. I know I was shaking when I offered him a candy from the box that had arrived with twenty-four roses and a card. I was even more terrified when he picked up the note and read it." I got lost in the memory for a moment, reliving the panic I'd felt thinking that we would be discovered. I shook myself, coming back to present, seeing that Oliver was looking at me with concern.

"It really was hard wasn't it," he murmured sympathetically.

I nodded and continued the story. "Rolf had sent the presents and note as a thank you gift for our time in a small cabin hidden away in the Alps. The note had read;

Thank you for bringing the sun into a very dreary winter. -R.

Hitler had laughed, looked at me and said, 'She's definitely hooked. Is she blonde?' When I said yes, he had told me to breed her and see if my voice bred true. I'd wanted to vomit, but I forced a laugh and told him I would consider it."

Oliver shivered, his lips twisting. "Well, that took the glamor out of it. Ugh, was he always that vulgar?" At my nod, his lips pursed even further. "Disgusting."

I looked at my mate and lover, the fear of sharing Rolf fading slowly, until he asked, "So why now, Nic? What happened on this day that makes you so melancholy?"

I shivered again. He stood, assuming I was cold, and reached for my hand. "Come on. The kitchen is empty and we can warm up. We shouldn't be able to hear Miki and Finn from there either."

I let him lead me around the side of the house and in the kitchen door. Oliver stomped and shook the snow from himself before taking his coat off and hanging it on a peg next to the door. I slowly copied him, straightening my suit jacket and retrieving another clove as Oliver began to bustle around the kitchen.

"Hot chocolate?" he asked hopefully. I snorted but acquiesced.

He happily busied himself at the stove while I sat on a stool at the counter. I lit my clove and silently watched him, smoking over half before I spoke. "You asked why today?" I began playing with the edge of the placemat. "It's really the last ten days before New Years Eve that affect me the most. December 19, 1940, I arrived in Salzburg Austria to meet Rolf for Christmas. His train was supposed to arrive that evening so I went to the hotel and got settled into my rooms, the anticipation at seeing him high. I had a letter with his promise to be there. We hadn't seen each other in almost a year. He was stationed with the Herrenmensch, and I remained with the Fuhrer as he moved around."

Oliver slowly stirred the milk, his back to me, but I could tell he was listening. I took another long drag of the clove, exhaling the spicy smoke and watching it curl upward. "I arrived in the morning, so I rested, bathed and dressed for dinner. We never met at the stations. It was too risky and if talk should arise, well, we've already discussed that." I looked down, dropping the slightly fraying corner of the placemat.

"We always met by 'accident.' Usually at a party, on the sidewalk outside a hotel, or at dinner. It depended on what city we were in. I was going to be 'the seated party' this time, him encountering me as I enjoyed dinner alone. Except he didn't arrive. I must have sat in that dining room for three hours, enjoying dessert much longer than necessary." I crushed the end of my clove and pulled out another, lighting it, the feelings that I had felt that night just as painful now. My heart never stopped clenching.

Oliver silently poured the hot liquid into two mugs and placed one in front of me. He stood on the other side of the counter, leaning on his elbows. "He showed up though, right?"

I nodded, remembering. "He did. Late in the afternoon of the twentieth. There was something wrong with him. He could never hide things from me. But I saw the sparkle in his eyes had gone out." My throat tightened, the clove shaking between my fingers. "The meeting," -I swallowed, forcing myself to continue- "had been casual. He was checking into the hotel as I was leaving to go shopping. We exchanged pleasantries and agreed to meet for dinner. I left, but my chest was so tight with worry that I couldn't help but look over my shoulder at him. I saw he was making his way to the lift, his shoulders slumped and eyes hollow. I didn't find out what was bothering him until later that night. I was in my room and he'd knocked softly on my door. I opened it, checking for eyes and ears before letting him inside. When I closed the door, he collapsed into my arms, sobbing." My own throat tightened. Even now, the agony of his weeping never left me.

Oliver reached out and took my hand, squeezing it. I couldn't speak, only squeeze his hand in return, holding onto it like a lifeline as I silently smoked. He waited quite a while before prompting. "Why was he so upset?"

I jumped, focusing on his face. I swallowed. "I'd mentioned he was, for all intents and purposes, a stud. Well, apparently, he had grown attached to a particular girl. Her name was Irene. She, of all the girls he performed with, was one he enjoyed. He told me that she had gotten pregnant the previous November. He sobbed as he told me how much she had been looking forward to the baby. I held him, stroking his hair, sitting on the floor. I thought he was getting ready to confess his love for her and leave me." I snorted, pain radiating through me. "But no. He clung to me, begging me not to ever let go. I promised I would always be there and to tell me what had happened. Finally, his voice a mere whisper and hoarse from all the crying, he did. Irene died in childbirth. He had been given leave to see the child of their union. When he arrived, he held the baby girl and named her Victoria. The doctor told him she was not to be entered into the breeding program because her mother had died in her first childbirth. I knew Rolf had been happy about that. He dreamt about the war ending. When we could find somewhere to live together. When we could take in an orphan and have a family."

I put the clove in the ashtray and ran a shaking hand over my face. "Suddenly, I knew what he had done. And I knew the outcome. The doctors and scientists were callous. They only saw the mothers and babies as subjects."

A soft noise caused me to look up into Oliver's face. I could see he'd guessed the truth. His eyes shimmered with echoes of my own pain. He didn't speak, but the hold on my hand tightened further. I took a deep, shuddering breath and went on. "It wasn't long before I had it from him. He'd asked to take the child to a wet nurse and to raise it himself. They had told him that this was impossible. That the child, though Aryian, was considered a cull and would be destroyed.

An innocent baby, an Aryian...bastards." My voice caught, and I closed my eyes against the tears that wanted to come. "He had to hand his daughter over to them and walk away. That had been right before he boarded the train to Salzburg. He'd wanted to gift me with a daughter named after me." My heart shattered again, tears finally slipping down my cheeks to fall on the counter as I bowed my head. Oliver was around the counter in seconds, pulling me off the stool and into his arms.

I sobbed into his shoulder as he picked me up like a child and carried me up the servant's stairs to our room. He kicked the door closed, crossing to the fireplace to sink down and cradle me in his arms as I cried. He let me cry, rocking and soothing me until I had finished and was numbly staring into the flames. "Nic, do you want children?"

I blinked, looking up. He was watching the flames as well, his expression worried. "No." I shook my head. "No, I do not, Oliver."

He frowned. "Then, why?"

I looked into the fire. The flames curled and danced as they rose and fell. "He thought they killed her, his child, his dreams for the future. It ripped me apart."

"Oh." Oliver shifted me, settling me more comfortably in his lap. "Wait... Are you telling me she wasn't killed?" he murmured, understanding dawning on his features.

"No, she wasn't killed. One of her nurses, a close friend of Irene's smuggled her out. I later learned she was granted permission to incinerate the child. She was witnessed to have thrown the bundle into the fire, and stand there to watch as it burned to nothing in the furnace. She then carried the baby out of the compound in a basket full of yarn and took it to her family in a remote Swiss village. Rolf never knew. He was dead before the month was out."

I absently felt my vest pocket for my handkerchief, my nose and eyes flowing as the agony tore at my heart. "I only found out after he was dead a year, when Hitler went further into the occult and began confiding in me. That is when I met her. Little did I know she already knew me. Ymene lusted after my soul, something about payback and restitution. I never have figured out what she truly wants other than Nate."

I gave up searching for the handkerchief and was quiet as I thought about the demoness a moment before shaking my head. "Anyway, the real reason Rolf was denied keeping his daughter, was that Irene was a demon and funnily enough she was a lesser siren. It shouldn't have surprised me since I am a greater siren and Rolf and I connected easily enough. I was angry, and torn when I realized why Irene had died in childbirth."

A growl escaped my mate, his face was dark with anger. "She wasn't in water, was she? Fools. Beasts!" Oliver shifted, jaw tight, the muscles of his jaw twitching with his anger. "How hard is it to realize that merfolk of any type need to give birth in water? Damn them." He leaned to one of the tables, grabbing a square of cotton from inside one of the drawers. He handed the handkerchief to me, obviously trying to control his anger. "What happened after he told you?"

I wiped my face and blew my nose, also trying to get ahold of myself. The ache made it hard to speak. "I held him all night as he alternately cried and slept. I'd never seen him so upset, so broken and lost." I swallowed, looking at Oliver. "I promised him that when the war was over, we would have our family, that I loved him, and I would never betray him. That promise...is the reason I don't want children. It was our dream,his and mine, and it was shattered in less than two weeks after that promise was made. I can't...give that promise to anyone else. The memories would be too great."

Oliver finally relaxed enough to smile at me. "I can respect that. I don't want children either, Nic. I'm not meant to be a father. I think it would change me in ways I wouldn't be happy with. So...I guess what I'm saying is that I understand. I love you so very much." He cupped my face. "What happened after that? Finish the story, give me your grief. Share with me."

The emotion behind his words filled me with warmth. He wanted to know. To be there for me as I had been for him. I smiled, covering his hand with my own. "We had a subdued Christmas, though the presents we had bought for each other were exclaimed over and the dinner we shared included laughter and festive spirit. We spent most of our time making love or just within each other's arms. We said goodbye at midnight on the twenty-fifth because Rolf had to be on the train back to the air base for an all out assault on the Allied Forces."

I clenched my fists in my lap, tears forming once more. "On December twenty-ninth, his squadron left on the largest aerial strike on London. They called it the Blitzkrieg."

Oliver sucked in his breath, but he said nothing. There was nothing to say really. I nodded. "He was an incredible pilot, used to flying guard for the bombers. He had accumulated quite a kill list by that time, taking out many Allied aircraft. This time, however, he didn't return from his mission. His body and plane were never located. But I knew... the moment his life ended. I'm lucky I was still in Salzburg. I was incoherent for days. I couldn't eat. Couldn't sleep. I lived in some sort of half-dream state where I could see Rolf, but I could never get to him. When I came out of it, it was already 1941, and I was alone." Tears dripped from my chin, falling onto my clenched hands. I watched them roll from their impact spot down to dampen my slacks.

Oliver was silent. I didn't want to look up at him. I went on, my voice a monotone. "I returned to my duties, and was able to find out what had happened or at least what had been reported. He was seen by several of his squadron being hit by an anti-aircraft barrage and going down. Something he should never have fallen prey to. His name was added to the list of the 'glorious dead.' The world moved on. No one ever spoke of Rolf Adler again. Sometimes I wonder if his grief was just too great. If my love wasn't enough..."

I finally looked up to see Oliver's cheeks shimmered wetly in the firelight. He reached for me again, pulling me into his arms. "Oh Nic how'd you survive losing your soulmate like that?" he murmured hoarsely into my hair.

I wrapped my arms around him. "I..." Oliver soothed me, his fingers combing my hair and lips against my neck.

"You don't have to explain," he whispered. "Even if it was horrible, I'm so glad you did. I wouldn't want to be alive without you."

My heart flipped and I could feel his love filling me. I returned that love and more, as I turned to kiss him with intense passion and a need so deep. He responded, understanding and meeting my need with his own passion.

We finally made it back downstairs to find a note from Mi'khaela attached to the undecorated tree.

We'll be back tomorrow.
Figured you two lovebirds needed the space since Oliver never
*   returned. (rude by the way)*
Anyway. See you for breakfast. It had better be good too.
You owe me, Fish Sticks.

With love,
Miki

I looked at Oliver, tired amusement sliding through me. "Call that woman and let them know breakfast will be at eleven sharp." I yawned, drained from the sharing and emotional upheaval. "I am going to swim in my tank for a bit."

Oliver kissed me as I turned to go. "I'll be up in a while. I love you, Nicholai."

I met his gaze, a soft smile on my lips. "And I love you, Oliver."

The next few days passed without the heaviness that usually hung over my home and self. Mi'khaela and Finnegan were prompt for breakfast and they stayed until late that night. After finishing the decorations, they moved from the parlor into the kitchen where the three of them amused me by making cookies. The old adage 'only one chef in the kitchen' became rather clear as they bickered over spices and recipes. As the kitchen filled with the aroma of confections, I even unbent enough to help them decorate a dozen or so, much to the irritating delight of all three of them.

I was able to have some quiet the following day as the trio left the house early to go shopping. I sighed happily, sipping tea as I gazed at the tree. I couldn't openly admire it while Miki was in the house. She would make the most absurd comments and foul my slowly budding festive spirit.

The fir was about nine feet tall. Its base swelled beneath it like a belle at a ball, its needles thick and deep green. Mi'khaela had chosen silver, white and blue as the theme and I had to admit the baubles, lights and ribbons looked quite lovely. I wondered what their tree at home looked like. Probably decorated with shamrocks and beer bottle lights. I grinned to myself, I adored Mi'khaela, and the feeling was mutual, though to the casual outsider, it appeared that we hated each other. And we both liked it that way.

When Christmas Eve rolled around, Finn and Miki came with overnight bags and secretive smiles that they shared with Oliver. I even caught Oliver and Miki whispering about something as I rounded a corner, but neither would spill. Whatever it was, they had identical diabolical grins painting their faces. I wasn't sure if I should be only afraid or very afraid. If Miki was involved, probably the latter.

We spent the day together. I was rather glad they were all there. The camaraderie was exactly what I needed, though I would never admit it. I sat watching as they played in the snow. They had an impromptu snowman building contest and cajoled me into being the judge. I gave the award to Finnegan. He grinned widely as the other two, who had rather nice normal snowmen, gaped at me. Finnegan on the other hand, had made a life-size replica of me in all my glory. Actually, it was more like an enormous glob of snow with a vaguely recognizable fish tail and sticks poking out in a reasonable approximation of my spines. He grinned broadly at Miki and Oliver as I presented the award; a gingerbread man decorated by my hand. I watched as Miki narrowed her eyes at her mate, "Suck up," she stated as Finn and Oliver dissolved into laughter. I even chuckled a bit. She was right. Feeding my vanity would always gain you points in my book.

Dinner was served promptly at eight, and we all talked of plans for the future as we enjoyed the beef wellington, new potatoes and crisp green beans. Rolf still lingered in my mind. The pocket watch he had given me that fateful Christmas proudly hung on my vest. The inscription within read:

You have my love for all time. -R.

It was still painful but after sharing my sorrow with Oliver, I was able to wear it without fear. I would always love Rolf, and Oliver knew this. Thankfully, he understood.

We adjourned to the parlor after dinner for dessert and coffee. Finnegan sat at the piano and began playing caroles. Soon we were all singing along. Oliver requested that I sing, I'll Be Home for Christmas, and I gave in, feeling more festive than I had since that painful Christmas so long ago.

I was in the middle of the song when the bell rang at the door. I turned slightly as John, my butler, passed the parlor door on his way to answer it. I kept singing, my audience rapt as the meaningful song washed over them.

Just as the last note filled the air, John appeared at the doorway, beside him was an older woman. I looked at her, then stared at her as John announced, "Ms. Victoria Pheiffer, sir. She says she has an appointment."

Oliver was on his feet, crossing the room quickly. "Thank you, John. Hello, Ms. Pheiffer, please come in."

She glanced at Oliver but her gaze returned immediately to my face. "Thank you," she said in a heavy Swiss accent, stepping through the doorway, but not toward the chair that Oliver had indicated. She instead walked toward me. I was frozen in place, taking in the graying, burnished gold hair and blue eyes. The softly angular features, the bright inner light that shone in her eyes. "You must be Viktor. You still look the same as your picture." She held out a photograph, the edges worn by much handling.

I looked down, taking the photo from her small hand. Looking up from that picture was Rolf and I. It had been taken at a ball in Berlin, shortly after we met. We were both laughing, but neither of us were looking at the camera. Our eyes were on each other. I looked up, back into the blue eyes that were so familiar. "I am, or was, Viktor Pheiffer." My voice sounded tight, choked as we regarded each other.

"Hello, Vater." Victoria said, tears welling in her eyes.

My heart exploded, and tears began to fall down my cheeks as I reached for her. She moved into my arms, her own winding tightly around my waist as we cried and held each other. I breathed in her scent, and there he was, muted but still there. This was the child

Rolf had wanted to present me with that Christmas so long ago. The one he thought was dead. The one who I had thought unfindable.

I released her after some time, and led her to the small loveseat. I sat next to her, her hand in mine as I looked down at the picture again. "How?" I looked up, my gaze finding and locking first with Oliver and then Mi'khaela. Oliver had his hand over his mouth, though I could see he was smiling as tears traced down his face. Miki was being held by Finnegan who was grinning from ear to ear as well. Miki, though her eyes were shadowed, smiled at me and blew a small kiss. I swallowed thickly. "You three...You did this? You found her?"

At their tearful, laughing nods, I turned back to my sweet Victoria. "Let me just look at you. You look so much like Rolf... How did you end up with Pheiffer as a last name, rather than Adler?" I asked, reaching out to cup her cheek.

She leaned into my touch, her eyes spending as much time examining me as I was her. "Nana Ingrid thought it vould be safer if I used my other vater's name, since I vas supposed to be dead."

I smiled, just hearing the word father directed toward me made my heart do somersaults in my chest. "How did she even know about Rolf and I? We kept silent about our relationship."

She chuckled, and I about fell over. The sound was rich and so much like Rolf's it was scary. It seemed as if she inherited all of him and nothing of Irene, the siren who gave birth to her. "Rolf told my mother many things. They loved each other in a vay. They wrote letters to each other, smuggled in and out by my Nana Ingrid. He told her about you, how he loved you so much. How you both vanted a family after the var." She opened her purse, pulling out a ribbon wrapped packet of letters. She placed them in my hands. "Here. These are the letters Papa wrote to my Mother. They are filled with you. These are vhat let me survive, knowing that my mother and both my fathers' loved me, even vhen they couldn't keep me."

Her eyes shone with tears, and I leaned across the space to kiss her forehead, my hand stroking her hair. "Oh, my sweet girl, your

Papa loved you. He died not knowing you were alive. And the thought of your death almost broke him."

She smiled sadly. "Nana told me he died in a plane crash during the var. She believed you thought I was dead too."

"He died on December twenty-ninth, 1940, and I didn't know how to find you. I eventually discovered you were smuggled out. Ingrid was able to tell me that much the one time she saw me. I was with a group of officials who had come to see the compound where your mother lived. She had only enough time to tell me that you were safe and then she had to leave. I never got her name, until now, and she was gone from the compound when I came back to find her. I had to carry that with me, that you were safe and cared for. I figured you didn't even know who I was. So, I left you to grow and live your life. I never stopped loving you, for you were the pride and joy of your Papa. You were supposed to be our little girl, and that..." I clenched my teeth, grinding them.

She placed her hand along my face, the skin cool, much like my own. "The juggernaut of var stole our family from us. Nana told me that she couldn't get the whole message to you, Vater. It's ok. Your Oliver and the lady Miki found me. He's my stepfather isn't he?" The amusement in her voice was evident, the ages of human and demonic relationships so often skewed to the extreme.

I caught her hand, kissing the palm before looking over to where Oliver had been standing. All three of them had disappeared. "Oliver?" I called, my voice booming into the hall. "Mi'khalea? Finnegan?"

I heard voices, footsteps and Oliver appeared in the doorway, followed by the couple. "We wanted to give you two some privacy," Oliver said, coming directly to me. He leaned down to brush his lips against mine. "Merry Christmas, Nicholai."

Tears sprang to my eyes again. "You... I love you. And thank you." I paused, looking at all three of them in turn. "You three did this for me, for us."

Miki gave me a watery smile. "Yeah, Fish Sticks. We did. You owe me so much right now."

I grinned through my own tears. "Look Sprite, I owe you anything you want."

She snickered, rubbing her hands together. "OOOOH... Hey Wolf-man, want to go on an all expenses paid trip somewhere?"

Finnegan snorted. "Tease later, sexy. This is his moment."

They both took seats across from us as Oliver pulled a cushion next to me and sat cross-legged on it. I looked at Victoria. "This is Oliver, and yes, he is your stepfather." I glanced at Oliver and winked.

Oliver grinned up at me before he looked at my daughter. "Well, now that's how to have a child. And to think, I'm younger than you." He giggled. "Demons..." They shared a moment, each looking at each other with laughter dancing in their eyes. Finally, Oliver asked, "Was your trip satisfactory, Victoria?"

She laughed, and again I was forcefully reminded of Rolf. "A First-Class ticket and met at the airport by a limousine? Of course it vas satisfactory, you silly goose."

Oliver grinned. "Well, you were a very special present that should have been delivered on December ninteenth, 1940. I had to see that my Nic finally got the gift Rolf wanted so much to give him."

I couldn't speak. My throat closed and my eyes filled with tears. Another man loved me so much that he fulfilled the promise my dead mate had made me. "Oliver..." I whispered around the lump in my throat.

He looked at me, "I just want you to be happy, Nicholai. I love you more than life itself." He took my hand, kissing the knuckles as the last of the old pain was released from my heart.

I looked over at Finn and Miki who were cuddled together, smiling at the three of us. The clock on the mantle began to chime. Oliver glanced over at it. "Oh look! It's Christmas everyone! Merry Christmas!" He exclaimed as all of us rose.

Everyone, including Victoria, received a hug, welcoming her into our weird little family. I stepped away for a moment, the photo Victoria had given me in my hand as I went to the window. I looked down into Rolf's laughing face then up into the dark night sky. It was snowing again, but the glow of the streetlamp was now warm and inviting as I said, "Merry Christmas, Rolf. She's finally home. Our family is complete. I love you. I'll always miss you."

I could almost hear his laughter in the soft swishing of the snow, but as I turned I saw that it was Victoria, my daughter, who was laughing at something Mi'khaela said. I stepped back toward my family, a new and warm feeling filling my heart.

Christmas.

And family.

ABOUT THE AUTHOR

R.A. DARLINGE

One half of a dynamic writing team, R.A. Darlinge has been writing her whole life. Her goal is to bring readers character driven stories they will love, cry and read again and again. This is her first published story, but stay tuned, there are many more to come. She lives with her writing partner, Aörali Eden and her pup, Mia, in Florida. Be sure to follow them on Facebook, Twitter and Instagram for updates and extras.

facebook.com/elvenbloodhound

twitter.com/elvenbloodhound

instagram.com/elvenbloodhound

amazon.com/-/B0826BJT1X

HALF CHAINED, ENTIRELY UNWANTED

EZRA RAIKES

To be free as the winter lights.
Neither cold nor clouds dethroned the true king of Night-crown. With no moon to fade them, purple and blue ribbons of light waved in unhindered arcs despite the tufts of buoyed snow.

The solstice festival had begun. Darkness swept over the vast sea of ruby leaves that was the Red Forest of Nordan, and Zara watched auroras dance atop the peaks of the mountains in the distance.

She yearned for the same liberation, but the formidable walls of Thorne Manor had been both home and prison for her ten years of life. Only her younger brother, Zaiyel, kept her company in this prison of pointed arches, vaulted ceilings, and stained glass.

But mortared stone was only the first and least frightening barrier between them and felicity.

The Sentinels patrolled the surrounding forest. Under the scarlet leaves, none escaped the horrors of bone shrouded in black. Sustained by forgotten magic, the towering, silent behemoths indiscriminately slaughtered whatever wasn't Zarr.

They called them guardians, but they were prison guards to her and Zaiyel.

Zara worried she and Zaiyel didn't have enough Zarr in them to make it past to safety. *Halfbloods don't last long in Nordan,* she quieted her rebellious yearning.

Dozens of sharp jolts wrenched the back of Zara's head and she staggered.

"Akeza!" Zara's neck and shoulders seized up, bracing against the pain. "Stop it!" She dug in her heels as her half sister yanked her about.

"What's wrong, dirty-blood?" Akeza yanked the plethora of tight black braids again, dragging Zara's head to the level of her waist. Her half sister twisted her wrist and the hair she clung to. "You shouldn't look up. This is where you belong."

Unwanted tears of pain and hurt—but mostly of hate— threatened Zara.

"I said stop!" Zara headbutted Akeza's side.

Energy skittered down the older girl's arm and into Zara's scalp. Zara shrieked as the fire of electricity burned through her whole body in an instant. With a scalding laugh, Akeza shoved her to the snow-dusted floor of the courtyard.

Zara curled against the chill of winter's embrace while the tremors of shock faded in her nervous system. She unclamped her eyes as her father's legitimate daughter knelt in the snow.

She flinched as Akeza took her wrist and held it aloft. Two years Zara's elder, the Thorne heiress pursed her lips in scorn, judging the difference between Zara's amber skin and her own ivory complexion.

"If I were Dad, I would have abandoned you in the forest when you were born. You're not a pureblood. You don't belong anywhere but under a mound of dirt just as unclean as you. The Sentinels killing you would be a mercy." The disdainful look on Akeza's otherwise pretty face filled Zara with revilement as bitter as vomit.

"Just wait..." Zara hissed through clenched teeth and ripped her wrist from Akeza's hold. She sat upright, at eye level with her half half-sister, and stared her down. Pale grey eyes to pale grey eyes, they murdered each other. It was the only trait their shared father had given them both. Not even their black hair was of the same shade or texture. "When I get my magic—"

Akeza stood and leered. "If you inherit any magic, it will be at best half as grand as mine." Her amusement faded. Loathing replaced it. "You're half of what I am. You will never be better than me in any way."

Zara's blood boiled. She tasted bile at the back of her throat. Her soul wanted to cry. How could family, even if they were only half related, torture one another? Zara's body ached from the years of torment, though she refused to show Akeza the damage. The chill stung her eyes, but she didn't care. She would never cry in front of Akeza.

The heiress witch strutted away, flicking her silky raven hair over her shoulder, but she paused and turned. She jerked her head to the firewood stacked against the wall of the courtyard.

"Bring more inside, but leave after. You and your wretched brother aren't welcome for dinner—and I'm sure you don't want Zaiyel to cry when he doesn't get any presents." Akeza gave a snort of derision for her half-brother's hurt.

Zara clenched snow in her fists while she watched Akeza stride through the wide entrance and into the Thorne Manor proper. Heat and candlelight escaped from inside, but the slamming of the doors closed Zara off from comfort.

Zaiyel's soft face and warm smile flashed in her mind, and her wrath faded. He was so pure, trusting, and stupid. He hadn't yet learned they would never be accepted in Nordan, much less wanted.

Everyone said he looked just like her, but she knew they didn't mean well by that. Their dark complexion and tight-coiling hair divided them from the Zarr purebloods with their skin white as death and hair sleek as raven's wings.

Akeza's younger, full brother, Nazir, abused Zaiyel in much the same manner. Nazir would ridicule or taunt him, but little Zaiyel would cry and stay for another beating, desperately pleading for affection never given.

Zara hurled the compacted snowballs with all her strength, but they didn't fly far, symbolic of her lack of might. Years of torment and abuse had sapped her spirit. Only desperation fueled her protest.

I'm pathetic. I can't protect him. Zara stared into the night sky and the aurora. What had previously seemed like dancing ribbons of freedom revealed themselves as mocking, luminescent chains. *Saints watching over us, if you have any compassion, please—please send us an angel. I can't protect Zaiyel. I can't!* Tears unleashed and she didn't hold them back.

"Don't cry, Zara," Nazir's smooth voice cooed from behind. It caught in between tones both comforting and mocking.

She swiveled about and wiped her eyes on her sleeve. He crouched before her with his forearms on his knees, watching her with eyes as reflective as mirrors. Sniffling, she turned away. He was too pretty to ignore, yet, but his cute face hid a temperament perhaps crueler than his older sister's. His methods ran opposite to Akeza's. Where the Thorne heiress was loud and rampaging, Nazir waited in ambush like a scorpion, silent until the poison of his sting set in.

Reaching into his pocket, Nazir retrieved a silvery handkerchief and handed it to her. She took it and dried her tears before her self-worth revived soon enough to stop her.

He was the same age as her, and she hated that she liked him. Nazir was the closest thing she had to a friend in Nordan. He was never mean to her, but he bullied Zaiyel.

Little, defenseless Zaiyel. He didn't stand a chance against Nazir and definitely not Akeza now that her magic had awoken.

"One day I'll kill her," Zara blurted. She scrunched the borrowed handkerchief in her fingers, arms shaking in barely restrained rage.

Nazir smiled and gave a short laugh. "I hope you do."

She bit her lip and fought a smile. Such wicked words from Akeza's own blood brother, but Zara loved hearing him say them.

Nazir took her wrist in a much different manner than Akeza. He bounced to his feet, pulling her up after him. She was taller, but she knew it wouldn't stay that way for long.

"You won't defend her?" Zara held out his handkerchief for him to take back, but he tapped her hand away.

"Why would I?" Nazir squinted, like the concept was entirely foreign.

"You're family—full family. You stick up for one another. Isn't that what Nightcrown is all about—staying together to survive the longest night?"

Nazir snorted a laugh, giving a deceptive, innocent smile which should have belonged to an angel and not this demon of a boy.

"I'll bury her alive myself if you don't get to it first."

Zara giggled and he grinned, noticeably pleased with himself. She regretted his heartlessness amused her when directed at Akeza, but she wouldn't take back her laugh.

Nazir walked backward toward the firewood with a smug grin plastered in place. He turned and stacked the split logs in his arms. Zara hurried to his side and did the same.

"You're wicked," she said, unable to withhold the smile from her lips.

"And you like it. So it's okay."

But not all the time, she wanted to say, but he already headed for the manor. Zara jogged after him.

Nazir kicked the door, and it opened to the warmth and glow beyond.

Zaiyel heaved the oversized handle, lugging the heavy door with his scant body weight. A bright smile stretched from ear to ear.

"Finally," Nazir snapped. "We were only banging on the door for ages. I thought I told you to open it as soon as I knocked," his voice turned scathing in an instant.

Zaiyel ducked his head into his shoulders, joy stolen, replaced with a crushed look of failure.

Zara stepped forward. "Nazir, we just—"

"Saints, Zaiyel, you can't do anything right. No wonder Mom beat you earlier. You want me to tell her you're acting out again? Should I summon the bluebirds?"

"No—I promise, please, Nazir—I'll be better! Don't call them!" Tears already clouded Zaiyel's crystal grey irises and Zara's heart collapsed from the hurt he felt. Zaiyel tugged at Nazir's sleeve, staring up at him with huge eyes.

Nazir scowled, his lips twisting in disgust. "They'll come for you if you continue to disobey." For reasons known only to The Great Necromancer, bluebirds always preceded his monstrous cadaver servants.

"Nazir, stop, please," Zara pleaded. The rest of the world considered the birds heralds of hope and good times, but the azure plumes struck a different chord in Nordan. Bluebirds, symbols of the Zarrs' persecutors, were harbingers of doom.

Zaiyel saw them in his dreams, bluebirds all about, luring the Sentinels to him. In the dark of night, he had crawled into her bed often enough for her to know his fright.

Nazir's eyes flashed Zara's way, cruel and playful all at once.

"I want to help. Don't call The Sentinels!" Zaiyel's bottom lip pushed out.

"Alright," Nazir answered, and a breath of relief escaped Zara. The corner of Nazir's mouth twitched upward. "You want to help?"

Zaiyel nodded enthusiastically, a smile returning to him despite his wet lashes.

Nazir dropped the firewood. The logs clattered to the floor on top of Zaiyel's feet, banging against his skinny legs.

"Ow!" Zaiyel scrambled back and fell, clutching his shins and rocking. He whimpered, trying not to make a sound, though tears streamed down his cheeks. The pain proved too much, and he cried.

"Nazir!" Zara lowered her own load to the floor and rushed to Zaiyel. She wrapped her arms about him as a shield and cradled the sheared sides of his head to her chest.

"You, boy, silence!" Father roared from across the great hall where a table overflowing with festival delights awaited the legitimate Thornes. A mountain of presents loomed in the corner where hanging lights representing an aurora swayed, blinking with a dozen colors.

Zaiyel fought her to stand and obey their father, but she held him down. Father never used Zaiyel's name, as if he couldn't even remember it. If Zaiyel wouldn't refuse, she would for him. She would teach him to rebel.

Boy was no one. If Malef Thorne demanded something of his youngest son, he would use his name!

A shadow passed over Zara and Indira Thorne slinked by. Hateful pleasure at Zaiyel's suffering revealed her for the matriarch witch she was. She reached her own son, Nazir, and stroked his cheek. She beamed at him with the false smile her son had inherited.

"You're cold, my angel," her voice was just as smooth as his. "Come closer to the fire with your family." She pressed on his back, separating him from his foul half siblings.

Nazir caught Zara's eyes but didn't protest his mother's request.

Indira cut off her son's gaze with her body and glared Zara down.

"Leave." The sudden coldness cut Zara worse than the sharp winter winds. "If I see you again before the morning, you'll spend the rest of the week sleeping on the doorstep."

Indira made her point without saying it. Even the pigs slept inside a barn. She and Zaiyel were beneath them.

Zara glared back and smashed her teeth together, jaw muscles twitching. She wouldn't react. Indira wanted her to. She wanted an excuse to beat them bloody. Zara wouldn't give it to her. Not now. Not ever.

"Perhaps The Sentinels won't smell your polluted blood, but that risk lies on your shoulders. I eagerly await." Indira's eyes raked over the unwanted siblings.

Zaiyel shivered against Zara's embrace. The mention of The Great Necromancer's unholy animations was enough to ensure the undead haunted his dreams.

A shallow, taut nod was all Zara managed. The Thorne matriarch sneered before sauntering away to the end of the vaulted hall. Nazir walked at his mother's side. His expressionless cursory glance ripped Zara to her core. Tears wet her lashes, but she buried the vulnerability beneath resentment.

"Zaiyel," Zara spoke as softly and quietly as she could, "We'll be okay. You have me." He stared up at her. "And I have you," she added.

His bottom lip trembled, but he nodded.

I won't let them treat you like this. She wiped his cheek with her finger. *You deserve better.*

"The fire's not going to feed itself!" Akeza barked from the end of the great hall.

Her half sister's coarse tone repulsed her. Zara's insides twisted, and she bit her tongue as the noise grated her eardrums. She clamped her eyes shut to withstand the visceral reaction.

"Go wait in the courtyard," Zara told her brother, offering the biggest smile she could manage, though she knew it was a sorry one.

Zaiyel sniffled and nodded again. The heavy door shut after him.

Zara's muscles strained as she heaved all the wood she and Nazir had both collected into her arms. Her biceps and forearms ached as she hurried across the length of the cathedral-like hall.

The wood clunked as she set it down. Indira glared at her. The woman's downturned mouth twisted in an incorrigible sneer as she joined her husband and children around the mountain of gifts.

Boxes heaped upon boxes in a stack taller than Zara, taller even than Father. Red paper shimmered in a dozen shades and patterns with shiny black and silver ribbons. Hanging snowflake and star ornaments made of crystal glistened with mesmerizing sparkle.

Akeza tore marvelous, reflective scarlet paper to pieces and shrieked with joy at the contents. Squealing, she threw her arms around their father. He returned her full embrace and gave a pleased laugh.

"Only for my little girl!" He lifted her off her feet in a tight squeeze.

Though she stood next to the fire, cold riddled Zara's aching muscles and settled far into her bones. The frigid grasp of Nightcrown seized her heart in its skeletal hands, wrenching the wounds which never healed.

That's what Nightcrown was to her and Zaiyel, as merciless and damned as The Sentinels beyond the walls.

Bruises of neglect throbbed from within her spirit. Eyelashes clung together, wet with tears which wouldn't fall.

Indira freed Akeza from her father's embrace and held a black lace dress to her daughter's shoulders.

Zara gasped. It was the most beautiful dress she had ever seen. Indira and Akeza *oo*-ed at the delicate rose pattern.

A dress fitting for a Thorne heiress. Malef beamed at his eldest with eyes full of pride.

A tremor rippled through Zara and jealousy stabbed inward, cold and murderous as icicles in her frozen heart.

"Father?" she spoke with the barest of sounds. He inclined his head as if to peer over his shoulder and the heat of hope flickered inside her, but his gaze never crossed the plane of his back.

Tears streamed down her cheeks, and she could barely see through the river of hurt. Zara spun on her heel and darted for the doors.

I just want a family. It's the only present I want!

Her palms pressed against the massive wooden doors of Thorne Manor, and she froze in place.

Zaiyel can't see you like this, she told herself. Drying her tears, she steadied her breath. *Don't look back,* she commanded herself as she swung open the door and slipped through.

Her eyes betrayed her and flicked to the happy family. Not one of them returned her gaze. Not one of them cared what happened to two unloved children on Nightcrown's Eve.

She shut them out with the door. Light, warmth, and family snuffed out.

Clear, treble bells chimed in the family chapel, signaling the true beginning of the festivities. Like stars twinkling and snowflakes falling, the crisp ringing of little bells celebrated in chorus, praising the saints for their gift of the nighttime lights during the long dark.

She stood with her face to the door and back to the world. Each chime thrust like a needle into her skin. Her body numbed more with every piercing.

"Zara, are you okay?" Zaiyel's shaky voice was another high-pitched chime, but this one didn't hurt.

She turned and watched a tuft of snow land on his nose. Her gaze drifted further. The front gate wasn't latched. The complex locks proved useless. Zara's eyes darted to every corner of the courtyard. The gate guard was nowhere to be seen.

They didn't have long.

It was now or never. Zara grasped Zaiyel's hand and broke for the gate.

"Zara! Where are we going?" he said, fear in his voice.

"Away from here—and we're never coming back."

"But The Sentinels!" Eyes huge in terror, Zaiyel dug in his heels, but she pulled harder.

"You! Halfbloods, where are you going?" The gate guard hurried across the courtyard, breaking into a dash when Zara clasped the gate with her free hand.

"Go!" She shoved Zaiyel to the other side and slammed the gate after them.

Iron-wrought vines covered in metal thorns burst from the hinges. They weaved like metal serpents through the parallel bars, growing denser with every passing moment.

The guard cursed as the enchanted gate hid them from his view.

"Run, Zaiyel!" She seized her brother's wrist and bolted into the Red Forest beyond the safety of Thorne Manor.

"Zara!" Zaiyel cried, but still he ran, his trust in her proving greater than his fear.

Already, she could hear the magical iron vines untangling from the gate. She abandoned the path.

Crisp snow and crimson leaves crunched beneath their boots, but the dense canopy of ever-flourishing, red-leafed maples hid aurora and starlight alike. Her eyes hadn't yet adjusted to the dim.

"You're not getting away, filth!" The guardsman roared, and Zaiyel sobbed.

Faster. Zara ran with all the strength her legs could give, nearly dragging her brother through the leaves.

The trees grew dense. Thick and slender trunks clustered close, their near-black bark and branches twisting and coiling. The spindly limbs reached and clawed for them.

Zaiyel tripped over a root and fell. His hand slipped out of hers.

"Don't leave me, Zara!" he screamed, and she slid to a stop.

The guard laughed, and his voice neared. "I've got you now!"

Zara cast her eyes about. There! A hollow beneath a tree's ancient roots was their only chance. She heaved Zaiyel up and pressed him into the hiding hole, squeezing in after.

Zaiyel whimpered as she held him close.

The guard raced through the wooded maze, his colorless skin and the silver piping of his coat the only tell of his presence in the dark of the forest. He skidded to a halt in the spot the two of them had just abandoned. He panted, chest heaving, and his grey eyes darted between each void between the trees.

He cocked his head and listened. Zara held her breath.

"I know you're still here, little half Zarrs." He came closer one slow, quiet step at a time. Snow crunched as heavy boots compacted it. Leaves crackled beneath his tread. "I don't hear your tiny feet anymore." He lowered his voice and shoulders as he sneaked nearer their hideout. His sight focused on the ancient trunk, first at the branches, then downward.

A knowing smile stretched his face when he caught sight of the hollow.

"Here, little boy," the guard crept closer. "I've got candy from the mistress saved just for you."

Zaiyel twitched against her and Zara squeezed him tighter. The guard stopped, boot buckles clinking no longer. He crouched and stared straight into the hole beneath the trunk.

"Boo."

He lunged forward, seizing Zaiyel from Zara's hold. Black leather gloves scrunched as they tightened around Zaiyel's arm.

"No!" she screamed, launching herself after him.

"Zara!" Zaiyel kicked and squirmed in the guard's arms, but the man held him tight, twice her brother's height and many times stronger.

"Quit struggling!" He shook Zaiyel, and the boy cried.

Zara rammed into the man's legs, and he staggered but regained sure footing. "Zaiyel!" She punched at the guard's abdomen. He grunted in pain but swatted her away with a heady smack to the side of her face.

A mouthful of snow and leaves met her when she reeled into the ground. *We won't go back. You can't make us go!* Scrambling to her feet, Zara spat out bits of stem.

The flash of metal beckoned her eye. At the guard's hip, a dagger reflected the scarce aurora light filtering through the canopy.

Zara charged him. She wrested the weapon from the scabbard and plunged the pointy end into his stomach.

The guardsman cried out in shock as blood spurted from the wound and splattered onto the pure snow beneath. He grabbed for her, but Zara ducked his desperate attempt. She stabbed him again, this time higher. The Zarr crumpled with another cry of pain.

Zaiyel crashed into the ground as the man fell. Zara pointed the dagger out with both hands on the hilt. Her brother scurried behind her and clung to her arm.

"You shouldn't have..." The guard writhed, moaning as he bled out. "The Sentinels will..." He dragged himself a short way, leaving a red trail in his wake. With one final whimper, he lay still and didn't move again.

"Is he dead?" Zaiyel's eyes bulged.

Zara's breaths evened and the panicked pang in her lungs subsided to a dull ache at the bottom of her ribcage. "Yes. We're okay." Her hands trembled, jittering the dagger in the frostbitten air. Zara's breath clouded in front of her face.

The crack of a twig snapping surged renewed adrenaline. Her insides burned. She whipped around, and Zaiyel held fast to the back of her twill coat. Her gaze darted between tree trunks.

The Sentinels—they couldn't have come so fast. Could they?

A solitary reindeer raised its antler-crowned head and observed them. Its jaw worked up and down as it chewed on the scant under-brush. Disturbed, the animal bounded along, and Zara watched it disappear behind towering trunks. Relief crashed over her, and she lowered the apprehended weapon. Wildlife. Nothing more.

"Are they going to kill us because we killed a Zarr?" Zaiyel whispered, as if the normal level of his voice was far too loud. He didn't have to explain who he meant for Zara to understand. For too many years, Nazir had terrorized Zaiyel with stories of the skeletal guardians.

"We're Zarrs, too," she enforced, bolder in voice than in spirit. *Yes*, she wanted to say, but her brother wasn't old enough—or even strong enough—for the truth.

If they find us, we won't stand a chance.

But they hadn't been sighted yet.

"Unmagical children aren't threats. To them, we're nothing more than animals, just like the reindeer." She didn't believe her own argument. She had just killed a pure Zarr. The guard's blood cried out to the watchers. Without a doubt, The Sentinels would come.

Cold wind howled through the trees, stirring leaves which didn't stick to the snow into short-lived twisters. Scarlet, five-point leaves from the miniature whirlwinds stuck in her braids, and she brushed them out. Zara's eyes darted to and fro.

Gentle chirping pulled her from the haunting embrace of the silent forest. The canopy shook in the breeze, raining leaves forever stained red with the blood of the Zarrs' enemies.

A little bird fluttered to a lower branch.

It's just a bird.

Its feathers gleamed brilliantly in the light reflected from the snow. Bolder than the sky and brighter than sapphires. Zara looked closer. She couldn't avert her gaze from the most beautiful blue she had ever laid eyes upon. Warm and peaceful, she gaped at the vivid feather coat she couldn't have imagined.

Like the high treble bells of Nightcrown carols, the bird sang. Transfixed, Zara stepped towards it. The bluebird bounced on its perch and departed into the lofty branches at her approach.

Zara's gaze drifted to the ground, sinking into the dense fog rolling in at the feet of the trees. Voiceless terror filled her as fast as a crack splitting glass. Her blood froze, flowing through her veins at glacial speed. Fright paralyzed her limbs.

The air tasted of dust and decay.

She clasped her hand around her brother's—her fingers clenched into a fist with nothing between them.

"Zaiyel!" She whirled about, breaking fear's immobilizing hold. The foul curtain of cloud swirled and thickened, reaching higher and filling every nook and cranny. "Zaiyel!" Zara hurled herself around the nearest black trunks, clinging to the rough bark so they wouldn't disappear.

"Zara! ZARA!" Zaiyel sobbed, his voice a ghost's, lost in a kingdom of mist. She heard the fast patter of his feet in a panicked run, branches cracking and snapping but fading.

"Stop running. I'll find you!" She charged blindly ahead, both arms in front to guide her. Branches whipped her body and face as she bolted through whatever stood in her path. Blood trickled down her cheek.

Her brother's crying ceased. He shrieked and fell silent.

"Zaiyel!" Zara tripped in haste and crashed into the snow face first. She scurried on her hands and knees, scrambling to her feet at the base of another blackened, weathered tree. Low-hanging, pointed branches swayed gently in the breeze at the level of her face.

Zara pushed them out of her view and leaned against the still, ancient trunk.

Her shoulder sank into muslin.

The sharp branches curled around her hand.

Breath forsook her. Lungs strained with no relief.

Tarnished bone fingers without muscle or sinew wrapped her own flesh covered ones.

The loose, shredded ends of a fraying black shroud danced as the repugnant wind siphoned inward. The hoarse, rasping breath of a long-dead, towering humanoid lifted the ends of her braids.

Her eyes raced along the folds of the tattered sable cloak, peeking into a bared skeletal thorax with looping strands of dull black beads stuck between yellowed ribs. Darkness made its home where a heart and lungs should have. Up her eyes rose. Beneath the hood awaited a mouth with a pointed chin and four rows of stained teeth wicked as thorns.

Zara screeched and lurched free. She tore through the Red Forest with reckless abandon. Her legs didn't give up and neither did her voice, screaming in terror.

She barreled into something low and tumbled, rolling fast into a glade.

"Zara!" Zaiyel wailed. His cheeks and pants alike were cold and wet.

"Hurry!" She pried herself from the ground and him after her. Holding his hand tight she turned and stepped directly in front of the mouth of hell.

A Sentinel crouched to her level, tendrils of fog twisting about bone and cloth. Sewn into the mantle, raven feathers and the teeth of a dozen different creatures sprouted from its shoulders.

Tugged by the curling wind, wooden beads clinked against exposed ribs.

Death hunched over and the maw that consumed life hung open and waiting.

Zaiyel shrieked.

The abomination's arm rose swiftly, ancient skeleton clanking. Its mighty palm of bones smashed into Zara's chest and she soared. She crashed into the earth at the other end of the glade.

Zaiyel! Her voice didn't work out of weakness. She couldn't move. She could hardly feel anything.

The clawed fingers of The Sentinel enclosed Zaiyel's neck. His cries yielded no response.

Feeling returned and every part of her body screamed in agony, but she could make no move or sound of her own. She could only watch in horror as The Sentinel stood to its massive height, lifting tiny Zaiyel up with it.

He kicked and flailed, swinging wildly by the neck to no avail. Zaiyel's little fingers strained at the skeletal grasp as his airways clamped.

Tears flooded Zara's eyes and everything blurred. Already, her brother's erratic movements slowed, jerking in strenuous twitches.

Night Angel—save Zaiyel. He's the only one who matters—please!

Zaiyel's limbs stilled. His entire body sagged in the undead's grasp.

The Sentinel tilted back its head, spreading wide the jaws of the final night. The king of Nightcrown prepared to feast.

Sobs wracked her body. The anguished tremors sunk her further into the carpet of snow.

A warm breeze whipped into the glade as a scarlet sail unfurled, banishing the fog in a wide circle like the eye of a storm. A red cape hung in the air like the wings of a great bird—or, no, an angel!

The base of scarlet cloth clasped tight about the shoulders of a man dressed in black. His short hair was black like a crow's feathers and his skin glowed as white as the moon that should have shone.

Crouched beneath Zaiyel's hanging form, their night angel was a Zarr.

With one hand on the ground and the other stretched behind

him, the Zarr in Red glared down the shrouded wight. The angel's eyes glinted like stolen diamonds while his cape at last settled.

Light came first. Heat came after, rippling through the circle of dark trees and drying her tears. Fallen leaves burst into flames, shooting in all directions like fireworks. What once was fog became white smoke.

Golden fire surged to the tops of the trees forming the glade, and the canopy burst into radiance like that of a sun encircling them.

Zara clamped her eyelids shut, but still she saw the blinding glow. She hid herself behind her arms. All cold and agony vanished.

Death screamed, but she was not afraid. The howl of The Sentinel, faded with the golden light and was no more.

Stars blinked in the clear night sky when she opened her eyes. The aurora's ribbons stretched over them like paths to heaven guiding them at the end of it all.

Zara pushed herself upright.

The Zarr in Red knelt on the ground with Zaiyel draped lifeless in his arms. The boy's closed eyes would never open again.

She hurried to the center of the glade and collapsed on her knees beside the Zarr. Cold tears rushed to her eyelashes and her lips trembled. She stared into the diamond eyes of the guardian angel come too late.

Zara begged him in silence. All the sorrow in her gaze channeled streams down her face.

If only I hadn't dragged him out. Zaiyel, the only person she had loved was gone forever. If only we had stayed!

The Zarr pulled off a glove with his teeth and let it fall. He wiped her tears, softly sliding his thumb across her cheeks.

"What's your name?"

"Zara," she choked on a sob.

"Don't cry, Zara." No hidden mocking laced his tone like that of Nazir's. Though the words were the same, they comforted her so much more than her half-brother's.

"But that's all I can do!" She hid her face in her hands, the sorrow more than she could endure. "It's all my fault. Zaiyel never would have died—if I hadn't killed him!"

The Zarr's firm hand gripped her shoulder, giving it a single shake. "No." It wasn't a threat, but he allowed no room for disagreement. "Look at me."

Zara peeked through her fingers, sniffling behind the shield of her hands. The faintest of black stubble shadowed his square chin and defined jaw, but it was by far his eyes that were the most beautiful. Like stars, she stared at them and they stared back. If she dared to wish on them, would it come true?

Zaiyel, come back!

"Never suffer blame that isn't yours. You have enough hurt already," he said.

Zara's tears shut off and she dropped her hands to her lap, her defenses against him lowered. She nodded, slowly at first, but then with small assurance.

The Zarr in Red switched his sights to her brother and cradled him closer. He let go of Zara's shoulder and pressed his ungloved hand to her little brother's unmoving chest.

Golden fire glowed from his palm, briefly illuminating the glade once more.

"Zaiyel," he said in a clear voice. "Wake up."

Her brother's darkened eyelids fluttered open, and he stared, wide-eyed, at their savior.

Zara gasped and covered her mouth.

"Dad?" Zaiyel's little voice squeaked.

Warmth overflowed Zara, burning from her heart and melting the ice which had taken over. Different tears spilled this time, tears she welcomed.

The Zarr gave a crooked smile, and Zaiyel tried to mirror it. "No, I am not." He shook his head and let her brother down softly.

"I think you are," Zaiyel refused. The man's smile transformed from amusement to apology.

"I'll take you home."

"No!" Zaiyel burst to his feet, and Zara stood with him.

"We can't go back." She hugged her brother close.

"It's where you belong." The man didn't stand and let them look down at him.

215

"We don't belong anywhere! No one will accept us!" Zara shot back, but regretted her words at the Zarr in Red's frown.

"Make them." He returned her insistence.

Zaiyel crossed his arms, pouting. "I don't want to." The night angel ended his stare with Zara and smiled at Zaiyel. "I want to go with you," her brother fell forward and wrapped his arms around the Zarr in Red's neck, burying his face in the scarlet cape.

The Zarr hesitated, but hugged her little brother back, closing his eyes as he did so. "I can't take you,"—his voice was low, almost a whisper—"as much as I would like to." He released Zaiyel and pressed the boy's shoulders back to make him a proud figure. "There are some things you need to do yourself."

The Zarr in Red took Zara's free hand in his and Zaiyel's in his other. He looked at each of them in turn. "You have each other—and that is by far the best present you could receive."

ABOUT THE AUTHOR

EZRA RAIKES

A lover of crows, coffee, and wine; a connoisseur of villains, and pluviophile; some might consider Ezra as a strange bird. A Master's graduate from University of North Carolina, in Architecture, Ezra designs community oriented spaces with as much care and finesse as he gives the arcs of his stories. When he's not in his field of study, he enjoys writing and painting. Having done both for nearly as long as he can remember, his greatest joy comes from creating stories. He truly can't remember a time when he didn't have a cast of characters in his mind itching to come to life on paper, be it through words or images.

His debut novel The Harvest Ring is set to release Autumn 2020.

How to find Ezra:

Sarifael.wixsite.com/ezraraikes

facebook.com/ezraraikes

twitter.com/EzraRaikes

instagram.com/sarifael

amazon.com/B0825N1W54

A SOLSTICE PROMISE

DRAGONNESS WYVERNA

Vermifiut Academy was the only one of its kind and, therefore, elite. The royalty and nobility of all the kingdoms of the five continents sent their children to fill its grand stone halls in the name of peace and friendship. Elves mingled with centaurs, selarthins befriended nymphs and satyrs, and dragons walked humbly in human form to talk face to face with the smaller beings. They would learn of each other's cultures, their politics, their beliefs, and so come to understand each other.

At least, that had been the plan.

Scota, a selarthin of the La'Qoari tribe, stood in the center of the hall, making herself as small as possible as bodies swarmed around her. Her large, doe-brown eyes flicked from side to side as she pulled her arms close to her chest, making her already thin body smaller to avoid being swept away. The other students walked in groups of their own kind: elves of Fin Gambol making snide remarks about the satyrs of Kierakiel River, the centaurs of Mardaga pushing their way through the cluster of Othrakin selarthin, and the nymphs and dryads of Joh'Ritten calling snide remarks to each other from opposite ends of the hall. Scota shoved her fists into her elongated ears. She had been at the Academy for four months and the backbiting and spite had been nonstop. It made her want to run back to the safety of her home, Ragyeth Forest. It didn't help that the Winter Solstice was quickly approaching, bringing with it the memories of all the holiday traditions she was fated to miss.

A pair of hands slid around her waist as a chin rested on her bony shoulders. "I've got you," a voice said through her knuckles.

Scota lowered her hands and let herself relax.

The body moved from behind her, taking her hand as it moved into her view. She knew who it was, of course; it was Shyftin, the albino dragon prince of the Versain Realms. He was in his human form, dressed in the purple and green robes of his station. His violet eyes twinkled as he began pulling her down the hall. "Agrona and Chroniclus are waiting for us."

Scota hurried to keep up with him, pressing her face into his arm to avoid the looks of disgust thrown at them by the other students. Interspecies peace had been the goal, but very few were for interspecies romance. Thankfully, she and Shyftin hadn't been the only ones who had taken peace "too far". The other couple was Agrona and Chroniclus. Agrona was a fire dragon from Charfias, the youngest daughter of the volcanic ruler. Chroniclus was an elf from another world entirely, though his mother hailed from the courts of Fin Gambol.

Shyftin took Scota to the central hall of the academy—a massive, multipurpose room that was mostly used as a common room. The room had seven fireplaces, each crackling and roaring against the winter chill that somehow pervaded the academy. Couches, chairs, and tables were arranged around the room as well, encouraging groups to meet and socialize. Most of the chairs held the varying cliques such as the elves of Fin Gambol, the satyrs of Kierakiel River, and the nymphs of Joh'Ritten. The room was loud with conversation, covering even the sound of the centaurs galloping across the room and nickering to their friends.

Agrona and Chroniclus were sitting in front of one of the fires, Agrona crouching so close to the flames she was practically kneeling on the ashes. Her vibrant red hair spilled over her shoulders, her pale fingers caressing the flames. Chroniclus sat on the couch behind her, his long silver hair tied back with a black ribbon.

Agrona's royal colors were red and yellow, but she had chosen to wear the colors of Chroniclus's home—red and black—stubbornly and loudly declaring their relationship to the entire academy. Scota admired their courage, but she still wore her tribal colors of green and brown.

Shyftin grinned as he sat next to the elf, pulling Scota down with him as he said, "Think you can get any closer to the fire, Aggie?"

The dragon cast a scathing look back at him. "I could sit in the fire, Shyftin, but then the rest of you would freeze."

Chroniclus held out his arms, his blue eyes catching a brief flash of light from the fire. "I'm freezing now. Keep me warm?"

Agrona pounced into the elf's lap, tucking her head against his shoulder as he wrapped his arms around her. Scota heard a few snide comments from the Fin Gambol elves behind them and ducked her head. There was no way the dragon or the elf had missed the cruel remarks, but neither seemed to care.

Scota wished she had their strength. Shyftin had brought her to the Academy, made clear his own feelings for her, but as much as she loved him, she had a hard time being as free as the fire dragon. She thought of home, the approaching solstice, and the romantic festivities of her tribe. She dreamed of kissing Shyftin in the shelter of a selarthin home while the trees filtered a snowstorm, and she became all-too-aware of the arm around her. She looked down and bit her lip, hoping he hadn't noticed her sudden discomfort.

He had. One white hand slid over hers. "Are you okay?" he asked, drawing her eyes to his.

She nodded. "Yes. Just homesick."

Chroniclus cocked his head thoughtfully and said, "I've never been to The Versain Realms during the solstice. What's it like there?"

Scota shifted, glancing at the night sky beyond the window. "This is about the time the cold winds would be coming down the mountains, and the warriors would be coming in from the Long Hunt. The kalkaa would send the nursery home, and we would spend the fortnight with our parents for the Amorast Festivals."

"The Amorast," Agrona cast a teasing grin at the girl. "Isn't that the Selarthin mating ritual?"

Scota blushed. "The Amorast Trials are before the festival, they are not the festival itself. The Amorast Festival is a celebration of love, romantic and familial. While new families are being established,"—the tips of her ears turned red and she avoided looking at Shyftin—"old families play games and get to know each other."

"What kind of games?" Shyftin prompted.

"My father hid new toys around the hut and had us find them, while my mother created puzzles and challenges for us. Then, at night, we would tell each other riddles, and whoever guessed the most answers correctly got to wear the family skalli." Seeing her friends' blank expressions, Scota spread her arms and explained, "A skalli is a crown carved from the antlers of a stag. My mother carved ours from the stag my father hunted during the Amorast Trials." She cast a pointed look at Agrona, who laughed.

"We have our 'Amorast Trials' in the spring, like sane beings," Shyftin teased, pulling her close. "Though we call ours the Damsha Gra, and it's not so much a trial as it is a dance." He spun off the couch, twirling expertly despite his human form. "It's an aerial display of grace, beauty, and stamina, all to impress the lady of our desire." He knelt in front of Scota and kissed her hand, grinning as her blush deepened.

"Then how do you stave off the winter's chill?" she asked, tripping over her own tongue.

"We dance." He laughed and settled back into his seat beside her. "It's not as gaudy of a show, but it is fun. Of course, my favorite of the winter dances takes place on the longest night: the Damsha Blailyn. We retreat to the Blailyn Cavern in the deepest part of the mountain, which is a massive, empty space filled with fungus and rocks that glow blue, purple, and green. Then, the royal family perform the Kohrdyra Dahm, weaving in and out of the columns and stalactites, bending the air with our wings and tails. If we do the Kohrdyra Dahm right, the wind will bend through the cave and the rocks will sing while the rest of the court begin their own dance, keeping the music flowing until dawn. Then we'll all fly up to the mountain's peak and watch the sun rise on a thawing world."

"That sounds beautiful," Scota sighed.

"That sounds cold," Agrona complained, shivering deeper into

Chroniclus's chest. "You should come to Charfias during the winter months. It's warm all year 'round."

"And miss out on the Amorast and the Damsha Gra?" Shyftin laughed. "Not likely!"

"Just because it doesn't get cold on Charfias doesn't mean we don't have reason to come together and celebrate," Agrona huffed. "While you all are staving off frostbite and death, we're celebrating life. The Fias dance, too, wind-boy, and our dance is fueled by heat!" She breathed fire into her hands, leaning forward to avoid burning her elf boyfriend. "Watch the flames. See how they dance? That's life. Warm, erratic, pulsing. That's how the Fias dance—flying with the wild call of the flames, creating our own fires to dance with. It's the Saorteine." She snuffed the flames, frowning at her empty hands as she leaned back into Chroniclus. "Of course, my favorite part of Saorteine is the drink. Your winter is the harvest season for cacao and peaberry. The Selarthins of Charfias grind both into powder, boil them in water with cane, and when you drink it, you feel as though you can dance for days. I like peaberry a little better than the cacao, but when it comes down to it, I'm not that picky." She sighed. "I would kill for a drop of warm peaberry right now. It not sweet like the cacao, but a good peaberry is rich and revitalizing."

Scota looked to Chroniclus. "What about you, Chroniclus? I'm sure you must be missing your family right now. After all, you're from a different world entirely!"

Chroniclus smiled good-naturedly. "I may be from Mid-Realm, but my mother is from the court of Fin Gambol. She liked to tell me of the old king, Movale, who loved the night of the solstice. Every year of his reign, he would build a massive bonfire in the palace courtyard and invite every citizen of Fin Gambol to come to the castle. He would lay out a feast for them, and insist that the rich eat with the poor, to learn of what the less fortunate have suffered. The next night would be a masquerade, and everyone that had come to the solstice celebration the night before would return, this time wearing a costume and bearing a gift for someone they had met at the solstice. The poor would receive something of greater splendor than they could have ever dreamed, and the rich would receive something more beautiful and humble than they had ever seen.

King Movale ruled for two millennia, but his celebration continues. They called it Movale's Blessing."

"I like that," Agrona said.

"So do I."

The four friends turned in surprise, completely unaware that the centaur headmaster, Atleus, had been listening to their stories.

Atleus pawed at the stone floor, his brown eyes trailing out of the frosted windows to the whitening world beyond. He then looked to the segregated students feasting in the warm halls. "There are few days that can bring people together like the solstice," the centaur mused. "I'm sure you aren't the only ones who feel homesick. The solstice is still five days away. Do you suppose you could help me arrange a solstice celebration that incorporates traditions from across the continents?"

"Are you sure you want us to help you?" Agrona looked first at her friends, then at the oblivious assembly. "They don't exactly like us."

Atleus bent over, rubbing his chin as he looked her in the eye. "When has that ever stopped you?"

"He has a point," Chroniclus said, tugging on her hair.

"Yes, but I'm lazy."

Shyftin chuckled and nodded at the centaur. "We'll help you. Her, too." He gestured at Agrona, who made a face at him.

Atleus beamed. "Excellent. You will be excused from your classes until the day after the Solstice. Agrona, you and Shyftin will fly to Charfias to retrieve the peaberry and cacao you spoke of, and Chroniclus and Scota will remain here and prepare the other festivities."

"I'd much rather take Chroniclus, Headmaster," Agrona protested.

Atleus flicked his tail smugly. "I'm sure you would, but you and Shyftin will make better travel companions, and you won't have to worry about carrying Chroniclus and the fruit. Having Shyftin with you will make the journey much easier."

"As you say, Headmaster," Shyftin agreed. "We will leave in the morning."

Scota grabbed Shyftin's hand as the centaur trotted away. "It will take two days of nonstop flight to reach the nearest island. You'll never make it!"

"Don't worry, Scota. If Agrona can cross the Arien Sea, then so can I."

"It's easy," Agrona added. "Trade ships cross the sea in droves. We'll fly as far as we can, pay a ship's captain to let us sleep on the deck, then finish the trip the next day. I'm sure a wind dragon like Shyftin can create a few gusty breezes to boost our speed." She nudged Shyftin, who grinned.

He gave Scota a quick kiss on the cheek. "It will be fine. You'll see." He stood and moved toward the door, signaling for Agrona to follow. "We should take advantage of the night, though. We'll need to be properly rested for our trip."

Agrona nodded. "I could sleep." She reluctantly pried herself from Chroniclus's lap to follow Shyftin to the cavernous dragon dormitories beneath the academy.

Scota watched them go, feeling a pit form in her stomach. "The Headmaster wants them to fall in love, that's why he's sending them together."

Chroniclus turned to face her, considering her expression thoughtfully. "You don't think Shyftin can remain faithful for four days?"

"Agrona is beautiful and amazing."

"She is, and so are you." He smiled and reached out, tugging her golden red hair playfully. "You have nothing to worry about. Shyftin loves you."

Scota smiled, but her eyes wandered back to the hall where Shyftin and Agrona had disappeared together.

Shyftin left with Agrona the next morning without waking Scota. Chroniclus kept Scota distracted by decorating the banquet halls with candles, evergreens, and berries. Atleus, the teachers, and the servants helped gather decorations and prepare presents for the other students. It was busy work, but the nights were too quiet. Scota would lie sleepless in her bed for hours, staring at the stars through her windows before finally giving up and leaving her room to continue her work.

Four and a half days later, Shyftin and Agrona returned. Chroniclus and Scota dropped the evergreen crowns they had been weaving and ran out into the cold afternoon to meet them. Agrona practically dropped out of the sky, the red scales of her chest catching the sunlight and casting red spots on the white snow as they heaved with exhaustion. Shyftin landed more gracefully beside her, folding his wings so that the servants could reach the saddlebags draped across his back.

"Aggie!" Chroniclus slid into the snow by her nose, peering into her fluttering blue eye. "Are you alright? Were you attacked? What happened?"

"She's being dramatic again," Shyftin replied with a shake of his head.

Agrona's eyes snapped open and she grinned, baring her draconic teeth at the smaller, white dragon. "Don't be sour just because you lost. We raced the last twelve miles." She sighed and settled back into the snow, which was rapidly melting under the fire dragon's burning belly. "This is the first time that the cold has actually felt good."

"No resting on your laurels, princess," Shyftin said, shaking himself as his draconic body began to shrink. Within moments, he was adjusting the hem of a vest across his human waist, and wrapping his arms around Scota's twiggish frame. He kissed the selarthin in quick greeting, then grabbed a saddlebag from Agrona's back and shook it in her face. "You're the only one who knows how to turn beans into something delicious."

"It's not like it's hard," Agrona replied. "You just need boiling water and lots and lots of cane."

Shyftin grinned then took Scota's hand and led her back inside, ducking into a shadowy corner just past the central hall. He brushed her hair behind her ears, cupping his hands under her chin as he kissed her. Scota felt the paranoid worry of the last few days melt away, and she let herself sink into his embrace.

"I missed you," he whispered, lowering his hands to pull her into a tender embrace.

"I missed you, too," she murmured against his collar. She ran her hands along his back, pulling him tighter against her. "I was a little worried that the Headmaster's plan would work."

"Plan? What plan?" He pulled away to look at her, his pale lips twitching into a smile. He laughed suddenly and kissed her again. "I would never choose Agrona over you. Never."

Scota felt her face split with an ever-widening grin. She pulled him back to her and kissed him again and again. They didn't stop kissing until Chroniclus tapped her on the shoulder and loudly cleared his throat.

"If I don't get mine, you don't get yours," Chroniclus teased.

Shyftin held up a finger and stole a final kiss. "I love you," he said, squeezing her hand before jogging down the hall toward the kitchens.

Chroniclus grinned as they watched the dragon leave, then he jerked his thumb toward their unfinished wreaths. "The sooner we finish, the sooner we can get back to our dragons."

Scota couldn't meet his gaze; she could feel the heat spreading from her cheeks to her ears. "Then I suppose we'd better get it over with. The solstice is tomorrow you know."

They raced back to the wreaths, laughing and teasing each other as the wreaths fell into place.

That last night was the longest. Chroniclus and Scota worked through the night, their fingers getting tangled in an endless line of evergreen crowns. They twisted and tied, braided and tucked, and finally finished the last crown as the rosy fingers of dawn cast its light over the fresh blanket of snow. The servants came in to refresh the fires and quietly clean up the stray berries, twigs, and twine that hadn't made it into the final product while the pair unknowingly slipped into an exhausted sleep. They didn't disturb the two, but one maid stopped to drape a blanket around their shoulders.

Shyftin found them at breakfast the next morning. He signaled to Agrona to be gentle, and they carefully woke their significant others.

Scota groaned and swayed as she blinked at the dragon prince. He kissed her forehead. "Come on. Let's get you to bed so you can actually enjoy the party tonight."

She clutched at his hand. "Are you coming with me?"

"Yes, but I can't stay. You sleep, I'll see you tonight." He tucked her into bed, kissed her one last time, and then slipped out.

Chroniclus and Scota slept. When they woke, night had fallen, and familiar music was drifting on the evening breeze. Rooms apart, they leapt to their feet and simultaneously began cleaning and primping. Chroniclus pulled out his best suit, lacing his jacket up with expert speed, while Scota piled her hair up in a fancy bun wrapped with glass beads, and then smoothed out her new dress. They bumped into each other on the way to the great hall, smiling and chuckling nervously.

"You look nice," Chroniclus said. He bowed and held out his hand. "Do you think our partners would mind if we escorted each other to the feast?"

She accepted his hand and tucked her arm in his. "I think they'll survive."

Arm in arm, they entered the great hall. The lights flared, the music swelled, and dancers suddenly swirled around them. Scota clung to Chroniclus's arms, eyes wide as they absorbed the scene. There were evergreens glittering with gold and silver baubles that twined around the gothic arches, dripped from the fireplaces, and snaked across the tables around roasted delicacies of every kind. In the center of the room was a massive bonfire, and two dragons, one white, one red, flew around its glittering peak in a rehearsed dance that could only be the Kohrdyra Dahm. Chroniclus and Scota stopped a few feet away from the blaze, their necks craned upward, mouths open in wondrous awe as white and red scales caught the firelight and cast a reflection across the room.

Agrona and Shyftin dipped, the tip of Agrona's wing catching the tallest peak of flame. The fire curled around the leather of her wings, following her movements as she spun, then burst out as she spread her wings, catching the cold wicks of the candles hidden throughout the room. The great hall seemed to burst as hundreds of candles lit, causing the dancers to stop and watch the display. The fires turned colors: green, blue, and purple, then they leapt from the wicks and danced in choreographed arcs around the dragons caught in the finale. Red wing met white, tails entwined, and the two dragons spiraled down into the heart of the bonfire.

Scota stifled a gasp. "Shyftin?"

Chroniclus squeezed her shoulder. "It's okay. He's with Agrona."

"But he's a wind dragon! He's not immune to fire like she is!"

"Aggie knows that. Trust her."

Seconds later, the bonfire opened like a daffodil, bent to Agrona's will. The two dragons stepped from its center, dressed in the resplendent robes that befit their current human stature and rank. Their hands were clasped and raised as one in triumph. The great hall erupted in applause, and there was even the echo of a nicker of approval from the headmaster. Agrona and Shyftin waved gracefully to the crowd then found their true partners.

"That was amazing," Chroniclus said as soon as Agrona was within reach.

"I know." She tapped his nose and flashed a smile. "And that was just the last five minutes. Can you imagine what the first hour was like?"

"Absolutely stunning?" Scota guessed. She rested her head against Shyftin's shoulder. "I wish I had gotten to see all of it."

"You needed your rest," Shyftin replied, tucking a stray hair under a string of beads. "And there's always next year, when we'll have more time to prepare."

"And to practice!" Agrona laughed. "If you think we were amazing with that rushed bit of practice we had on our journey to and from Charfias, just imagine what we could have pulled off with a month!" She fanned herself, feigning sudden exhaustion as she dipped dramatically, forcing Chroniclus to catch her. "That wore me out!" she simpered. She bolted upright and grabbed the elf's hand, dragging him back across the hall. "Let's get a drink to refresh ourselves!"

Shyftin smiled after them then bowed to Scota, offering his hand to her. "May I have this dance, my lady?"

She blushed and glanced around at the twirling dancers—the majority of whom were elves. "I—I'm not very good at dancing. We were so busy getting ready, I didn't have a chance to practice."

He took her hand and pulled her close to him. "Follow my lead and sway with the music."

"Okay." She clung to him, moving her body with his as the music carried them across the floor with a romantic croon. They swayed at the edge of the dancers, foreheads pressed together, eyes closed. She took in his heartbeat, the smell of mint on his breath, and the warmth of his arm around her waist. The music ended too soon, and in the breath between songs, Shyftin had guided her to their couch by the fire. She sighed as she fell into that familiar crook in his arms, comfortable now that she knew what to do and how she fit.

He nuzzled her hair. "Are you still homesick?"

She thought of her warm home in the forests a continent away. Her father had hidden the presents by now—or had her brothers and sister already found the gifts? "A little," she admitted. "Though, honestly, the solstice hasn't been the same since my mother died. I think—I think I like this better, though... Being with you. You keep the cold away."

"I like this, too." Shyftin smiled and pulled away, resting his arms on his knees as he considered her. "But maybe, after we've finished with this school and can go back to our homes, I could come see you... For the Amorast Trials?"

She sucked in a breath and sat up straight. "The Amorast Trials are for establishing new families."

He chuckled. "Yes, we've established that. And maybe that's what I want to do. If that's what you want, too?"

"Shyftin, I—of course it's what I want to do! But will your father allow it?"

"My mother has already given her approval, so my father has to allow it. What about your father?"

"My father is a mere chieftain of a selarthin tribe. He would never go against his prince." She took his hand. "And he likes you. You brought me here, didn't you? You opened this whole new world for me. He loves you for that; I love you for that." She went to kiss him, but he dropped to one knee and fumbled a small wooden box from his pocket.

"This isn't a draconic tradition," he admitted. "And I know it isn't a selarthin tradition, but Chroniclus told me about it, and I liked it. We're breaking all of the other traditions, so why not?" He opened the box and held up a ring carved from mother-of-pearl and crested with an amethyst. "This is a promise. A promise of my undying love for you. A promise that you are mine, and only mine, and I am yours, and only yours. A promise that will be fulfilled and sealed for eternity once we leave Vermifiut Academy. A promise that we are one."

Scota slid from the couch and into his arms, ignoring the ring and going straight for a kiss. "It's a promise."

Shyftin slid the ring on her finger and kissed her again. Once. Twice. Four times.

Agrona slung herself over the couch, a cup of steaming brown liquid in each hand as she cooed at the kissing couple. "Congratulations!" she said, right before thrusting the cups between their faces. "Drink up! I absolutely nailed the recipe, and it tastes amazing! Drink! Then it's time for presents and riddles. The party isn't over yet!"

Shyftin and Scota laughed as they obliged and accepted the drinks. One was sweet and chocolatey, the other was bitter and revitalizing, but both were as delicious as promised. They downed the cups, the hot liquid reaching to their toes and pulling them to their feet—or was that just Agrona dragging them back onto the dance floor?

ABOUT THE AUTHOR

DRAGONNESS WYVERNA

Dragonness Wyverna lives in Maryland with her family and her dog, Pippin. When she's not writing, you can find her curled up, devouring books or drawing dragons on any surface she can find. Dragonness runs Blotted Ink, a short story blog frequently starring Scota, Shyftin, Chroniclus, and Agrona.

https://blottedinksite.wordpress.com/

facebook.com/Dragonness-Wyverna-1941403912851290

twitter.com/DragonnessRawr

instagram.com/dragonnessw

FOLLY AMONG THE HOLLY

L. R. HUSEBOE

"Come on, Myrah, do you really want to spend Christmas with your aunt and uncle again? It's going to be packed with their five kids and two grandkids, isn't it?" Charlotte asked, plopping onto the overstuffed loveseat beside me and snatching the bag of Cheetos straight out of my hands.

"It's always loud." I sighed. "But that doesn't mean it isn't fun."

Char huffed in annoyance. "I know you well enough to see how much you don't want to go." She took a large handful of Cheetos, orange staining her palm, and nibbled one. "My parents are expecting you," she added mildly.

I glared at her. "You seriously didn't tell them I was coming over without even asking, did you?"

She grinned, her fingers and lips already stained cheesy orange. "Of course." She shrugged a shoulder. "How else was I to get you to come over, Myrah?"

I opened my mouth to protest, then shut it again. It was impossible to win an argument with her. Ethan would also be there and months have passed since I saw him last. I wasn't mentally prepared.

"They're coming to pick us up in thirty minutes, by the way," Char stated, studying an interesting Cheeto.

My body went rigid. "What!" I shouted, jumping up. "What?" She still didn't look at me.

"Thirty minutes." She laughed. "Better start packing."

I stormed to my room, the pressure of only thirty minutes to pack making me panic. Glad my three roommates had already left for their own homes for the holidays and weren't here to see me run about, I frantically stuffed my overnight bag. I was sure to forget something.

Charlotte finally came into my room, watching me pack, licking her fingers clean of cheese. She leaned against the doorframe, smirking at my effort to get ready.

"You couldn't tell me this when you got here?" I demanded.

"And miss seeing you freak out? Of course not!" She snickered, licking her pinky clean before reaching into my sock drawer to toss a few onto my ever-growing pile of stuff to pack.

"Really, I can't say I missed you picking on me all the time," I muttered.

I ripped my bag open and started stuffing things into it, not caring how it was arranged. Grumbling, I shoved a lock of wavy brown hair from my cheek, wishing I had kept it in its usual ponytail.

"So, you've enjoyed your semester without me," Char said, sounding disgruntled. "Why didn't you go to university with me? I thought we planned that ever since elementary," she whispered.

I froze, unwilling to meet her gaze. A warm hand to my shoulder brought me out of my panic.

"I know Ethan was an idiot, but it was——" she started.

"No, Charlotte. I don't want to talk about this. He made his decision. I've made mine. I'm only coming over because your parents are expecting me," I snapped, pulling out from under her touch. "I'll be civil, as long as he is, too," I added.

"All right, Myrah. I won't pressure you to tell me what happened. I don't want to argue with you. It's Christmas Eve after all." She took some of the things off the bed and helped me pack.

"Thank you," I whispered, looking up and seeing the concern in her green eyes.

"You're welcome. Just know I'm only looking out for my best friend," she said with a bright smile.

I pulled the zipper shut, grinning back. "I know. Now let's go. Your mom will be here soon, right?"

Charlotte's phone buzzed, startling me. She didn't even seem to notice it going off. "We have like ten minutes, I'm sure. Do you have everything?"

"Yeah. I think she's here now. I can hear your phone," I stated.

Snatching her phone out, Char smiled. "I don't know how you always hear it when I don't," she muttered. "Hey, Mom. Yeah, we're leaving now. Yes. Okay. See you shortly."

I wet my lips, still not wanting to do this. "Let me guess, she's in the parking lot."

"Yup. With the engine running," Char chirped.

I sighed audibly this time, heaving my bag onto my shoulders. "Let's get this over with."

"Is it really that bad to spend Christmas with me?" she asked, stopping in my doorway and blocking my path. She turned to face me, her green eyes dark with hurt.

"No! No, Charlotte, of course not. It's just been so long since I've last been over." I felt my cheeks heat with a blush.

"Oh, well, I guess that is true." Char smiled. "Remember the first time you came over and Ethan teased you relentlessly because you'd never seen a Gameboy?" Her giggle lightened the mood in the room.

"Don't remind me!" I walked toward her about to shove her playfully when my phone vibrated. I jumped, not used to it going off. I tore my bag off, quickly taking it out of the hidden inner pocket. My heart sank at the name displayed on the screen.

"Your uncle?"

I nodded silently, my heart sinking through the floor. "Hello?" I said meekly.

"Myrah, your ride will be there in an hour. Dinner will be at seven," my uncle's voice said, sounding tired.

"Um...Uncle Allen—" I started but he cut me off.

"Speak clearly, Myrah. You know I hate when you stutter," he snapped.

I flinched, wishing Char wasn't here to see. At least she couldn't hear his harsh words. "I'm not coming," I stated, my voice cracking slightly in apprehension.

"What? Why?" he demanded.

"I'm going to Charlotte's this year," I said.

"You know we have dinner on Christmas Eve every year. It is a time for family, not friends. You will return here and spend it with your aunt and I." There was the tone of finality I hated hearing in his voice. He used it with me whenever I tried to ask for something, acting as though I never deserved to have things go my way.

"But I already promised—" I began.

"No buts about it, Myrah. You are a part of this family, and I will not have you missing out on dinner. Where would you have been if I didn't take you in after your father died? Foster care," he growled.

Tears quickly welled in my eyes, and I turned away from Charlotte further, ashamed. "Charlotte's mother is..." I tried again knowing it was pointless to argue.

"I don't care. I expect you to be here in an hour," Uncle Allen said.

Before I could say anything else, Char wrenched the phone from my hand, a dark look on her face as she caught the tears in my eyes. "Hi, Mr. Stone. This is Charlotte, Myrah's friend. We've made plans to spend the holidays together." She shook her head angrily, her jaw tightening as she listened to his rebuttal. "No." She snorted. "I see." She was silent for a moment, her eyes staring at the wall, a look of murder on her face.

I wanted to take the phone back and push her away. She knew how overbearing my uncle could be. He'd never let me go anywhere while growing up, and I was only attending this school because I'd lied about where I was going to get away from him. Char wasn't going to be able to change his mind.

I watched in shocked silence as the air in the room changed, the lights dimming. A roaring filled my ears as the look on Charlotte's face grew angrier. "Now, see here, Mr. Stone. Myrah is an adult. You have no say over what she does and doesn't do, or even how or what she decides. She will not be going to your place today nor will she come tomorrow," Char growled, her green eyes taking on a hint of yellow.

"No!" I shouted, reaching for my phone. I could barely hear my uncle scream when it was replaced with a crack. The sound shattered the silence in the room. I squeaked, staring at Char.

My phone fell from Char's hand in two pieces, completely broken in half.

"Oopsie," she said, glancing at me with a meek grin. "My bad."

"What? How?" I whispered, taking an involuntary step back from her, my mind reeling.

"Um, my grip?" she stated, shaking her hands in front of her face, shards of glass falling onto the carpet.

A bang at the door made both of us jump.

"There's my mom!" Char exclaimed, seemingly trying to draw my attention away from the broken phone.

I opened my mouth to ask again how she'd done that, when Char grabbed my bag and right arm with her free one and dragged me toward the door. I wanted to press the matter, but didn't even know what to say. Had it been one of those things I thought I saw, but hadn't? A shadow that was never there? A flicker of light only I seemed able to see?

It's just my imagination, I thought. Like usual. I let her drag me away as I kept staring at my phone.

"Don't want to keep my mom waiting any longer, right?" she pressed, pulling my door open.

"About time!" Char's mom said. "I was starting to worry I'd have to send Ethan up here to get you two." An annoyed look crossed her face before relief replaced it.

"Hey, Mrs. Moore," I greeted, doing my best to give a smile but failing. "Sorry about the wait. Charlotte was talking to my uncle." It wasn't a lie, yet it wasn't the full truth either.

"Is everything all right?"

I wanted to tell Mrs. Moore about my phone, but Char spoke up first. "Yeah, it is now," she answered, carrying my bag on her shoulder, her gray coat already on, as well as her hat and gloves. "Coming?" she asked me.

I tried not to glare at her. Glancing back at my room and the mess I'd left, I turned to go grab my phone at least.

"Leave it," Char muttered.

"And have someone get hurt?" I snap.

"Who's been hurt?" Mrs. Moore demanded, worry making her tone sharp.

"It's nothing, Mom. Myrah's just worried her roommates will get hurt in this bad snowstorm," Char lied smoothly.

Before I could refute her words, she set my bag down and snatched my coat and hat and threw them at me. I glowered for a moment before giving in. "You better explain this to me later," I whispered.

She grinned. "You know I will," she said, grabbing my bag again.

"Are you sure no one was hurt?" Mrs. Moore asked, looking us both over in concern.

"Mom, please, let's just go. Ethan is waiting, and it's cold out," Char said.

Let him freeze, I thought.

Char pulled the front door open and chilly wind hit my face, instantly freezing my cheeks and nose. Snow fell in a heavy curtain, a thick white blanket covering everything, even the road.

When we got to Mrs. Moore's car, I took my bag from Char, meeting her gaze. I smiled, trying to convey that I wasn't mad at her for yelling at my uncle. He deserved it, that is, if I was being honest with myself. As I reached for the door handle, it swung open. I blinked the snow out of my eyes and met Ethan's dark green ones.

"Ethan," I murmured. My heart felt as though it were trying to beat its way out of my chest. I turned from him, slipping into the car, as Char and her mom were already in and buckled.

"Myrah, it's been a while. How's your first semester going?" Ethan asked, trying to take my bag. I shoved it between my legs, out of his reach. I didn't want to be near him.

"It's been good. Tiring, but that's no surprise." I laughed. My voice sounded strained even to my ears. I could never control myself around him.

"Well, my husband has dinner almost ready for us," Mrs. Moore said brightly. "I hope you're hungry!"

Char talked the entire trip to their house, not giving me the silence I would have preferred. I let her prattle on, using the time to settle my thoughts and feelings. I did my best not to think about my broken phone and Charlotte's eyes turning yellow. I've seen stranger things in my lifetime. I thought. Have caused much worse things to happen. What's a broken phone to my parent's car crash? My feelings about Ethan were harder to suppress. Even with nearly seven months to get over him, they were still raw.

We arrived at the Moore residence as I gained some semblance of control over my emotions. I got out before Ethan could try to be a gentleman, hurrying to Char's side, leaving him behind.

"It's about time you three got here," an elderly woman said from the open door, gray hair billowing in a sudden gust of frigid air.

"Grandma!" Char squealed. "I didn't think you'd be able to make it." Hurrying to the woman, she hugged her fiercely.

"Of course I'd make it. This is an important day after all," she said, smiling brightly. She pulled back and saw me, her eyes growing wide with surprise. "And who's this?"

"Hi," I said, extending a hand, shaking hers. "I'm Myrah."

"Nice to meet you, Myrah. Have you told her the wonderful news yet, Charlotte, Ethan?" she asked, continuing to hold my hand in hers. I nearly pulled away from her grip, but I didn't want to be rude.

Something in the air changed. I felt the tension from Char and her twin, Ethan. Glancing over at them as their grandma let me go, I waited for Charlotte to answer.

"No." She shook her head. "I haven't told her. Maybe we should head in and get warm. This blizzard is only going to get worse."

"Huh. I thought that would have been the first thing you told your best friend," Ethan muttered. He pushed his way forward into the house, leading the rest of us inside and out of the snow.

"Well, I'm sure she knew it was happening as it's your nineteenth birthdays tomorrow. It's common knowledge, even for a changeling like you," their grandma said, smiling sweetly at me.

I froze in the doorway, Char beside me. "What?" I blinked, my mind going blank. Surely I hadn't heard the older woman correctly.

"Oh, I guess you haven't been told yet," Grandma murmured, sounding sad. "Sorry to be the one to break the news to you my dear. You're a changeling, all right."

"How can you be certain, Mom?" Mr. Moore asked, coming from out of the kitchen set at the back of the house. The smell of ham followed him out of the room, reminding a part of my dazed mind that I was hungry. I pushed the thought from my head, concentrating on this strange conversation.

Grandma turned to me. "You see odd things happen all the time, don't you?" she asked, her green eyes so like Char's yet dark with age and wisdom.

I'm not going to say yes to that. Everyone will think I'm crazy! I thought, trying to focus my mind.

"I'll take your silence as a yes," she said before I could answer properly.

"Myrah... Why didn't you ever tell us?" Char said, hurt in her eyes.

I twisted the gloves in my hands as I took them off, giving myself time to answer. There were several things I wanted to ask and to say. "I... I didn't want you to think I was crazy," I whispered. I'd let slip to friends in the past, back in elementary before I met her, that I could see strange things. They ostracized and bullied me for it, calling me insane.

"I'd never think you were crazy, Myrah," Char said, taking my hand in hers and pulling me into a hug.

I laughed. "I know." But it doesn't mean you won't later, I thought. If I told you everything. I blinked quickly, forcing the tears not to fall.

"Well, come in, come in!" Grandma said, taking my bag from me as Char let go. "Make yourself at home."

"So, what is a changeling anyway?" I said. The smell of dinner returned to me as I looked around, admiring the large and open feel of Char's home.

"It means someone who has been switched at birth with a human child," Grandma answered, smiling gently at me.

I didn't know what to say to that. I had heard of changelings before as I adored reading fantasy.

"Who are her real parents then?" Char wondered.

"I couldn't say. Changelings aren't very common. I've only met two others aside from you Myrah," Grandma said.

Following behind Char and her grandma into the living room, the Christmas tree caught my attention. There were a few presents under the tree, and a little train ran endless circles on its track. I smiled sadly at the scene, overwhelmed by so many decorations everywhere. My uncle never had more than a tiny tree in his house during the holidays. He always said it distracted from family time.

"You like it?" Ethan said, startling me as he stood by my side.

I whipped around, trying to smile. "Yeah, it looks great," I exclaimed a little too shrilly.

"I'm glad you like it," Char said, taking my hand, pulling me to follow her into the dining room.

I was glad for the sudden shift in conversation away from me. "Of course I do." I looked over my shoulder and back at the tree, wanting to get a better look at it. It was something to keep my mind off what Charlotte's grandma had said. I didn't want to admit that it felt like she was telling the truth.

Something in the corner of my eye caught my attention, making me refocus on the tree. The lights were blinking oddly. At first, I thought they were on a timer, but after letting go of Char's hand to move closer, I realized there was no electricity to them. There were no wires connecting them together. Instead, the tiny glowing lights moved within the small globes.

I squinted, trying to wrap my mind around what I was seeing. They looked like multicolored lightning bugs.

"What are these?" I asked, pointing to the lights. Everyone looked at me, including Mr. Moore and Ethan who had entered the kitchen while I was admiring the decor.

"What things?" Mrs. Moore inquired sweetly.

I pointed toward the tree, wondering why I just couldn't keep my big mouth shut for five minutes about things that would never be there in the first place. But maybe they could see these things too.

Grandma had called me a changeling. They'd never made fun of me before, why would they start now?

"Oh, it's just the aerials keeping the lights glowing. It's an important day for Ethan and Charlotte after all," Grandma answered into the silence.

I looked between her and the aerials, which hadn't disappeared like most of the strange things I'd seen in my life. "Aerials." The name sounded familiar. "So...fairies then?" I whispered.

"You really can see them, can't you?" Char murmured.

I looked to her, surprised by her words. "Well, since we're admitting to things, yeah." I nodded. "I can see them. They're pretty." I stared back at the tree, watching the aerials bat against the glass, their tiny wings fluttering. "Are they wanting to be in those globes?"

Char giggled. "Of course." She brought me closer to them so I could see them better. "They're like insects. Not very smart. They live for only a few months and are so numerous in the Fae realm you're likely to maim a few just walking through a field."

"Fae realm?" I asked, my attention drawn back to her. I raised a brow. "What's that?"

"It's where I'm from," Grandma answered.

I turned to face the older woman. "There's a whole other world out there?" I guess that makes sense.

Grandma nodded. "There are pockets that overlap with the Mortal realm. Many of the things you've seen is the overlapping. This house is a hotbed for it."

I remembered the times I'd seen the shadows and heard the tinkling laughter while staying over in the last few years I'd known the Moores. Why does everything this woman say make so much sense? I wondered. Why am I willing to believe her so quickly? I don't even know her.

"Why don't we continue this conversation over dinner?" Mrs. Moore inquired before I could muster up the courage to ask more questions. "Dinner's going to get cold if we don't start eating soon."

I nodded. "All right." I followed behind them, ignoring the aerials as they buzzed around their globes. I wanted to talk more, but I was also hungry. The smell of food was impossible to resist any longer.

We passed through the kitchen and into the dining area where a large table set for six waited, burdened with more food than we could finish in one sitting. Char sat on my right, while Ethan took the chair across from me. I wasn't going to be able to ignore him if he wanted to talk with me. I focused on his grandma instead, hoping she would start talking if no one else was going to. Silence reigned as we started our meal, but that wasn't anything new to me. My uncle hated idle chatter while he ate.

"So, Myrah, how long have you had to hide you could see strange things?" Grandma suddenly asked.

I almost dropped my fork and the ham speared there. "Why do you ask?" I said, wanting to change the subject. Why does she want to know something like that? "A long time," I finally answered, setting my fork down.

"No wonder you barely reacted to your phone," Char muttered.

I noticed she'd hardly touched her food. Was she so worried about breaking my phone she wasn't eating? She never passed up the chance to eat.

"That was an accident," I said, touching her arm in reassurance. "You were mad at him."

"What happened?" Ethan inquired.

"She broke my phone while telling my uncle off," I answered with a grin. A part of me wondered how I was going to explain my broken phone to my uncle. Another part worried about my uncle's wrath after the Christmas season when I would have to face him. Having him get told off by my best friend was amazing. I was glad she'd done it.

"Why'd you do that?" Ethan said.

"Now Mr. and Mrs. Stone will be even less likely to let Myrah over." Mrs. Moore said sharply, facing her daughter. Her lips were tight with a frown.

"They aren't my guardians anymore. I can do as I like. I wouldn't be here now if Char hadn't done that. Of course, I don't really understand how you snapped my phone in half," I stated, looking to her for an explanation.

"Charlotte! You know better than to use your telekinetic powers outside this household," Mrs. Moore stated sharply.

My mouth dropped open. Do her powers have some sort of connections to the Fae? I wondered.

"I didn't mean to do it Mom. I'm sorry." Char's shoulders slumped. "I know it's no excuse, but I was angry with Mr. Stone and what he said about Myrah,"

"I'm sure it was awful," I muttered. He rarely said anything good about me, telling me I would never amount to anything and was a waste of his time.

"It really was," Char agreed, her green eyes flashing yellow for an instant. The dishes rattled as the table shook in response to her feelings.

I shoved away from the table in surprise, glancing at everyone else to gauge their reactions. They stared at Charlotte. I could feel the pressure in the room change, which made the small hairs on my arm rise. The Moores seemed completely used to this sort of thing.

"Now, now. Let's not get angry at a foolish human," Grandma gently admonished.

"But he shouldn't have said those things about Myrah!" Char growled, her eyes glowing brighter.

"He's nothing more than a fool who doesn't know how to handle a Fae," she replied, her voice still calm and collected.

I blinked at Grandma's words, not sure if I liked being called a Fae. Wanting to comfort my friend, I pushed the thought aside. "Char, it's fine. He's never been the best person, and I'm fine with that. I no longer live with him and he has no control over me," I stated.

"Well said, dear," Grandma said, smiling warmly at me. I blushed, not used to getting compliments from someone older than me. She turned to Ethan. "You should have chosen her," she said. Everyone grimaced in shock at her words.

I felt my jaw go slack as I met Ethan's embarrassed gaze.

"I...I tried to," he slowly said, looking away. "Things just never seemed like they'd work out," he muttered.

I blinked, the silence thickening. Anger sparked in my chest at his words. Finally, I found my tongue. "Excuse me? I asked you point blank how you felt about me after telling you my feelings, and you said you didn't see me as anything but a sister," I hissed, ashamed as tears filled my eyes. All this strange talk about Fae and Char's sudden powers and my reunion with Ethan was too much to handle after hearing his admission.

"Are you a complete idiot, Ethan?" Charlotte gasped, clasping a hand over her mouth.

"He's an idiot," Mrs. Moore muttered.

"Grandson, you really have been a fool. Why would you lie?" She took a large bite of food, shaking her head.

"I was afraid to commit to a relationship. I was young, okay?" he protested weakly.

If his parents and grandma weren't here, I would have jumped up and smashed his face into his food. "It was seven months and two weeks ago," I said, gritting my teeth, nostrils flaring. "I told you how I felt. And you laughed at me. And went out with Jennifer the next day." I let the tears continue to fall. He'd crushed my soul and left me half the person I was.

"Okay, look, I'm sorry!" Ethan said. "I was a moron. I didn't know how to go about telling you how I really felt. So I just ended up pushing you away and hurting you."

I looked away from him, wiping the tears from my cheek furiously. "It doesn't matter, Ethan. I'm over it."

"I highly doubt that," Grandma said sharply.

Her words caught me by surprise.

"I can see it in the way you act toward him, and what you're saying now. You still love him, don't you?" She set her fork down and gave me her full attention. "We Fae talk about our feelings, even when we don't want to. Everything is open among us. It's one of the many things that set us apart from the humans." She smiled gently. "And why I can read the emotions you're trying to hide on your face."

I gulped, my lips quivering. "I... Of course I do!" I cried, the tears trying to fall faster.

Ethan reached across the table and took my hands into his. "I'm sorry, Myrah. I never meant to hurt you. I was a fool to let you go. Forgive me?" he asked.

I nearly pulled my hands from his grasp. I wasn't sure what to make of this turn. I love him. But am I ready to forgive him? I asked myself. His green eyes were full of hope. And I saw a future there I wanted to share with him. I wanted to be happy, and this was my way to that life.

"I can forgive you," I finally said.

The largest grin I'd seen appeared on his face, pulling the dimple I loved on his cheek. "Thank you." He pulled my hands to his lips and gently kissed the back of my left hand.

"Wait! Everyone's—" I began, trying and failing to pull away slightly, my cheeks red with surprise and embarrassment.

His smile grew wider. "I love you too," he said.

I returned his smile, feeling lighter than I had in years.

Grandma clapped her hands together, giggling with glee. "Excellent!" she exclaimed as Ethan and I pulled apart slightly. "I think it's time then."

"What do you mean?" Charlotte inquired, a stupid smirk on her lips as our eyes met. I couldn't glare at her as I was happy.

"It's time for your Christmas and birthday presents. What better time to give you these than now?" Grandma said. She got to her feet, hurrying to the living room, practically skipping out of sight.

"Where did I put those again...?" she muttered just loud enough for me to hear. "Ah! There they are." She came back to the dining room carrying two small boxes in one hand.

"You're going to give them now?" Mr. Moore questioned, sounding surprised.

"And why not?" she demanded, putting a hand on her hip and raising one brow. "I am the Elder of our clan which makes it my right to gift them when I feel the time is right."

I stared between the two of them, wondering what could possibly be in those little boxes. They were wrapped in silver and gold with a tight bow tying them shut. What is she going to give them?

"I thought we were waiting for Christmas day. That is the—" Mr. Moore said before Grandma cut him off.

"Son, I decide when to give them to the twins. And that time is now. You'll have the right once I have passed on. Besides, it's close enough to midnight," she said, a bright smile lightening her tone.

I shifted in my seat, eyeing the front room. "Even with me here?" I asked.

Everyone looked to me with surprise clearly evident on their faces. I blinked, having assumed that was why Mr. Moore was so hesitant for his mother to give the gifts to Char and Ethan.

"My dear, you're a part of this family," Grandma said. "Ethan has told you his feelings, and you obviously return them. And this is something that affects you too."

I didn't know what to say. The last person to tell me they loved me, before I met the Moores, had been my father. He was the last person I considered family. I covered my mouth with a hand, doing my best to keep all my emotions in.

"I was going to tell you about this anyway," Ethan stated, taking the gold box from his grandma.

"And this is one of the reasons I asked you to come over," Char said, also taking a box.

I blinked again, startled by my friend's admission. "What do you mean?"

"You'll see in a moment," she answered.

I sat back in my chair, watching as Ethan nodded to his sister and they both opened their gifts at the same time. A part of me was expecting something to pop out at them. Nothing exciting happened. The twins reached in, pulling out identical silver keys. I stared at Ethan's face, my heartbeat accelerating at the look on his face. Why doesn't he seem happy?

"Oh, Grandma! Thank you," Char cried, launching herself into the woman's embrace.

"Yes, thank you," Ethan said, his words soft. He met my gaze, forcing a smile.

"They're very pretty," I said, admiring the intricate design.

Grandma chuckled. "They're not just pretty, my dear."

"Uhm...you've lost me. What's so special about these keys? Did you give them their own place?" I inquired, growing tired of being in the dark.

Grandma looked at me with confusion mirroring my own. "Oh, that's right. I guess you wouldn't know about portal keys."

"Portal key? To where?" I said. My mind reeled at the implications of her new revelation.

"To the Fae realm," Mrs. Moore answered.

I glanced to her, surprised she'd been the one to answer. "Fae realm? Like, fairyland?"

Char laughed. "Yeah, you could call it that too. Though there aren't as many little people with wings like you're thinking. Most are like Ethan and I."

"Really?" I said, hoping she'd elaborate.

"Half human," she added.

I blinked, taken aback by Char's admission. It makes sense, of course. I bet her Grandma isn't human, I thought.

"Grandma, is everyone waiting for us already?" Char inquired, changing the conversation faster than I could keep up with.

"Of course, Charlotte," she answered. She turned to Char, her eyes twinkling. "Preparations are complete for your arrival."

Char smiled widely. Then her face fell. Her eyes met mine and I saw a deep sadness there. I unconsciously reached for her hand taking it in mine, hating to see her upset and not knowing why. "Char, what's wrong?"

"I'm glad I found out you are one of us," she whispered. Her eyes brimmed with tears. "I always knew there was something special about you. But I don't know what's going to happen now, and it scares me."

My tears returned in empathy with hers even though I didn't completely understand why she was crying. "Why are you afraid?" I asked.

"Charlotte, it's okay," Ethan stated before his sister could answer. He reached across the table again and took her hand. "I haven't made my decision yet either," he added.

"Hey now, I can't help if you don't tell me why you're scared," I said.

"These keys open the portal," she managed to choke out, rubbing her eyes and sniffling.

"Yeah," I said gently. "I got that."

"It's a one-way path," she whispered.

The world around me seemed abnormally silent. Rushing filled my ears. The room darkened. I felt light headed and realized I had stopped breathing. I sucked in a shaky breath. "A one-way trip," I clarified.

"It is," Grandma confirmed softly.

My eyes travelled to her, not wanting to believe her. "How did you all get here then?" I demanded.

She lifted a crystal key hanging from around her neck. "I'm the Elder. We're given diamond keys to visit our family in the Mortal realm. I'm here both to see my grandchildren and to offer them the chance to live with me in the Fae realm, if they so wish it."

I turned to Ethan and Char. "Do you want to go there?" I asked quietly, looking to Ethan first.

He shrugged. "What I want is here right now," he stated, gazing at me pointedly.

A stray tear stuck to my eyelash, making me blink. "I see. And you?" I murmured to Char.

"What I want is both here and there," she whispered. "Paul is there, waiting for me."

I'd heard her mention Paul before. He was her childhood friend and her secret crush. She hadn't mentioned him in years. "Then you should go and see him," I said, smiling as wide as I could.

"But we'd never see each other!" Char shouted.

I kept smiling. "This is a chance to meet with your childhood crush. Don't let me stop you from going," I admonished softly. Turning to Ethan, I met his gaze. "I'd understand if you went with her. She's your twin and family," I continued, my smile faltering.

"Why are you children being so emotional?" Grandma sighed, coming to stand behind my chair and touching my back. I turned to face her, releasing Char's hand, thinking the older woman wanted to comfort her granddaughter. Instead, she took my hand and gently squeezed it. "I already explained this to you, Myrah. You're a part of this family," she said.

"That's right!" Mrs. Moore exclaimed, hurrying over to hug my shoulders.

"Would I be able to get my own key?" I asked, staring up at Grandma. "I only have Char and Ethan in this realm."

Grandma nodded. "I came to collect my wayward son," she

said, shifting her weight to her other foot as she glowered at Mr. Moore. "It's high time I retired as the Elder of our clan. And there's always room for more in our family."

My heart burst with joy at the thought of going with Ethan to another world, a place where there would be people who loved and cared for me. I would never have to see or speak to my uncle again, and I didn't feel remorseful in the slightest. I smiled at Ethan, seeing the happiness reflected in his own expression. I looked to Char whose tears had stopped falling and were replaced with a grin.

"Wait until you meet Paul," she squealed with glee, clapping her hands together. "I know you'll love him."

"I'm sure I will," I said. "When do we leave?" I asked Grandma.

"First thing in the morning," she said. She walked around the table and sat down to finish eating. "Finish up, everyone. There's apple pie for dessert with plenty of whipped cream."

ABOUT THE AUTHOR

LAURA HUSEBOE

Laura Huseboe lives in the United States in South Dakota with her loving husband and lap-cat Yuki. She has spent her life dreaming and telling stories to appease her overactive imagination while living the mundane life of a retail worker. When she's not working, she can be found in her lair creating new worlds or visiting old ones in her written works.

facebook.com/laura.huseboe

twitter.com/LauraHuseboe

instagram.com/laurahuseboe

amazon.com/-/B0825N1NWK

HUNTER'S MOON

E. S. FURLÁN

"If they don't shut up, I'm going out there to make them shut up."
Cassia shot a dark look out the high window of their apart-
ment. In the street below, a group of children chattered and
laughed. Joyous calls of 'join the hunt!' and 'feast!' filtered through
the gaps in the rickety walls Cassia shared with her debtor, Aldert.
Muttering, she shifted on her chair and turned to find him grinning
at her frustration. The handsome giant had his feet up on their
table, tossing hazelnuts one at a time into his mouth.

"Let them be, mistress." Aldert's charcoal eyes didn't waver from
her face. "Surely you were just as rowdy on the Hunter's Moon as a
child, no?"

Cassia rolled her eyes. When she was a child, the attendants in
the orphanage encouraged such behaviour, but she couldn't recall
ever joining in on it. She preferred the sombre religious ceremonies
for the holiday that she got to partake in once she was accepted to
the Acolytes of Erwyn. Rather than give Aldert the satisfaction of a
rebuttal, she cast another glance out the window before trying to
focus on the task at hand.

Soon the priestess would choose the next Acolytes to go forth
into their Isolation. Only the best would secure a place. And she had
no intention of waiting another year before starting on the path to

being blooded and accepted as an Acolyte in the temple. To be selected, she needed to master the delicate art of the death whisper. With it, she would be able to commune with the dead without divination tools. Any common conjurer could seek guidance reading bones or casting lots. The chosen Acolytes of Erwyn were expected to be in a league all their own, and so tuning in to the voices of the dead without external aid was a vital aspect of serving the goddess of death and rebirth.

"Are you not looking forward to the Hunt?" Aldert had no intention of letting her study. "I am. The food is always amazing."

"There's more to life than food." Cassia's tone was terse. Closing her eyes, she sought the state of mind required to tune in to the voices of the dead. But Aldert didn't take the hint.

"Of course." He chuckled. "Fighting is good, too. And bedding people—men and women, ideally both at once. Eh?"

Cassia opened her eyes to shoot Aldert a dark look. He met her gaze with a puzzled one of his own. Between the raucous children and her enthusiastic companion, she had no peace.

"I'm trying to concentrate." She suppressed a frustrated sigh. "I have until the Hunter's Feast to prepare, and I have yet to hear so much as a filthy word from a dishonoured dead. Aldert. Please."

"Why would you want to hear from a dishonoured one?"

"Aldert—"

"The priestess says you need to start with someone you know. Who do you know who was—" "Aldert!" Finally, her tone silenced him. "Please, I need peace to practice. Don't you have anything better to do than hang around here?"

A crafty look flashed over Aldert's handsome face. She narrowed her eyes at him. He shrugged and gave a nonchalant look at their table.

"I might," he admitted. "If we were going to host a Hunter's Feast of our own."

Eyes still narrowed, Cassia held his impertinent stare for several moments. She didn't even know why she was so resistant to the idea. And if it meant getting some peace from her debtor's antics, even if only for a few hours...

"Fine." She held up a warning finger. "But just the two of us. Nothing extravagant. We can't afford to feed the whole block."

"Got it." Aldert's infectious grin drew a reluctant quirk from Cassia's lips. "Just us—and Saffron. Nothing big."

"Alright, but no one else."

Cassia could tell he wasn't listening anymore. He'd already pulled on his furs and reached for the handle, nodding and waving a hand at her. Deciding to take her victories as they were, she let him leave. The children below in the street scattered, screaming, as his giant form careened through them, intent on his mission. Cassia allowed herself a small smirk before returning to her training.

Aldert bounded through the streets of Anukthar. His furs flapped in the breeze. His feet slipped over the icy streets. Snow gathered in small drifts against buildings, and the sky above was clear and crisp. All around him, people shopped for food and small gifts for their loved ones. Aldert joined them eagerly. He earned a small wage lifting heavy things from various warehouses and crafts-men, and he had no problem spending it all on the Hunter's Moon feast. At each new addition to his haul, his grin widened and his heart swelled, tucking them into the blessed burden he bore on his shoulders.

Then there was the issue of where to stash it. He could have taken it back to the tenement, but Aldert wanted it to be a surprise. Cassia was dour and focused far too often. Given she was the only reason he, a foreigner, was allowed in the ancient, sacred city, Aldert was desperate to give her a break.

He was on his way to a fishmonger he often helped with crates when a familiar voice cut through the air. Saffron. She sounded irate, sending a shiver of unease down Aldert's spine.

"...you can't just do whatever you like, you're a Harte," she was saying. "We have a name to live up to."

Aldert breathed a sigh of relief that her ire was not directed at him and stopped to eavesdrop with no shame. She was standing in an alleyway off the main square. The target of her irritation was Bay, her younger brother.

"Mother had no complaints," he shot back. Saffron sighed.

"No, she did not," came her terse reply. "But you know better, and you shouldn't have done it. Now we'll have to pay for it."

The sounds of boots scuffing against uneven cobblestones met Aldert's ear. He smirked. Bay's exploits were well-known, but the young noble still had too much remorse to be a true terror. The next moment, Bay was shuffling out of the alleyway with a scowl on his face. Deciding he'd best ask Saffron while he could, Aldert gathered his nerve and stepped out into the alley. Saffron's pale face and cold, dark eyes almost froze him in place. He swallowed and stood his ground.

"Saffron, how are you?" he tried. She smirked at him. He could never shake the feeling she enjoyed toying with him, which only added to his unease.

"Feeling festive, of course." The conversation Aldert had overheard was far from that, but he didn't mention it.

"Festive enough to come for Hunter's Moon at the tenement?"

Saffron's features shifted for just a moment before her usual mask of calm was in place once more, but Aldert was sure he had shocked her.

"Did Cassia agree to that?" she asked.

Aldert nodded, though he hoped Saffron would give him an answer soon so he could leave. The noblewoman gave him a suspicious squint.

"Is that what all that's for?" She glanced at the bundles on his shoulders and raised her eyebrows. Aldert nodded again. Saffron pursed her lips. "I'm supposed to spend the feast night with my family. It's tradition."

"They can come too." Aldert knew Cassia would go to bed early if it was just the two of them. "The more the merrier."

Saffron gave him an amused look. Aldert realised too late that for a family of Saffron's standing to share a meal with paupers like him and Cassia, in a tenement no less, would be highly improper. He had little regard for social norms. But Saffron could not afford to ignore them—not without good reason, at least. Aldert thought back on all he knew of Anukthar's political landscape.

"Isn't Willow Pen spending part of the Hunter's Moon feast in the temple orphanage this year?"

"She's working there." Saffron rolled her eyes. "She hopes it will win her the common vote in the new year's lots."

"Do you think the 'common vote' really believes she's there because she cares about them though?"

Saffron gave him a shrewd look. Her thin lips widened into a smirk as she quirked an eyebrow at him.

"Whereas you actually do have lowborn friends," Aldert continued. "It's common knowledge already. Seeing your mother accept Cassia and me at her Hunter's table could only be a good thing."

Saffron gave him an appraising look. Aldert could see the pieces all falling into place behind those coal black eyes, and he knew he'd got her even before she grinned.

"You're not as dumb as you seem," she acknowledged. "Very well. My family will join you in the tenement."

Aldert grinned in return, unphased by the not-so-subtle insult. It suited his purposes for people to believe him a simpleton.

"Excellent." He adjusted his bundle of supplies on his shoulder. "You know what to bring."

She gave a curt nod before turning on her heel. Aldert continued on to the fishmonger, trying to clear a chill from his bones that had nothing to do with the season.

"Why does it irk you so, child?" Sofien's croaky voice broke Cassia's train of thought. "You and Cuinn used to love the Hunter's Moon feast."

Cassia shifted on the low stone bench under the roofed colonnade in the orphanage courtyard. Braziers around her and Sofien, her old tutor and mentor, kept the cold at bay. Sofien's watery blue eyes still carried a shrewd glint despite closing in on ninety summers.

"I don't know," Cassia admitted. "But I didn't come here to talk about that. I wanted to see how you are. You look well. Better, at least."

Sofien smiled, tucking a stray strand of silver hair behind her ear before reaching her withered terracotta hand out to clasp Cassia's knee.

"We never were the family you needed, were we?" she mused.

259

"Not after he left. We tried, but it's always harder to lose blood you've grown with."

"Sofien…"

"No, I'm not saying you hold it against us, dear, far from it. Just that I wish we'd been able to do more."

Pursing her lips, Cassia gave her mentor a frustrated look. The old woman grinned, eyes dancing merrily.

"Please, Sofien."

"Oh, you are so serious!" The crone chuckled, though it brought phlegm up, drawing a wracking cough from her.

Cassia watched with tears pricking her eyes and handed her a handkerchief.

"Thank you," Sofien wheezed between breaths. "Well, I'm still dying, in case that wasn't obvious. I doubt I'll last the season."

The old woman sat back on the bench, eyes serene as she watched a flurry of snow whip up and then dissipate in the courtyard. Cassia sat rigid on the stone beside her, following her gaze.

"There must be something," she said at length. "Some remedy, some treatment we haven't tried yet. I'll go to the archives—"

"There's nothing." Sofien smiled, though her eyes became distant. "And you should be practicing for the Isolation exam, not cooped up indoors, poring over books on my account. Or if not that, then feasting with your friends for the Moon."

Cassia suppressed a grimace and glanced away. Of all the things for people to care about, the Hunter's Moon feast was not one she anticipated needing to defend against.

"It just doesn't feel that special." Her tone was curt. "Our Lady Erwyn doesn't care. It's not a rite in the temple. And it's just another day. If only people would stop pretending it isn't."

Sofien laughed at that, her voice cracking over the throaty sounds. She took Cassia's hand in her own and patted it.

"You're so serious," she said again. "Do you remember the feast days here? You loved them! You were up before dawn, tearing around the place like a consort of Erwyn, waking us all up. And decorating the halls—oh, my, I have never seen a child climb as you did to hang the wreaths! But you did."

Cassia closed her mouth to swallow her interjection.

"You only stopped in your eighth year." Sofien gave her a shrewd look. "After he left. And then you always seemed to be somewhere else in your mind."

Cassia sighed. She turned her dark eyes on her mentor and brought her hand to rest on top of Sofien's.

"It hardly matters now. He's never coming back."

Even now, the admission stung more than it should. It had been nearly a decade. She was under no illusions that he would reappear, no longer hopeful that one day she would look up and see his face in her window or open her door to find him there. Those were the fancies of a child. She was no longer a child.

"No, I suspect not," Sofien agreed. "But family is more than just blood. Do I not think of every child in this place as my son or daughter? Do you not dote on me now as though I were your mother?"

"Who but you is my family, then?" Cassia scoffed. "Aldert? He is my debtor. Once his debt is paid, he will be on his way."

"Pish-posh. His debt was paid many moons ago, and you know it." Sofien scoffed in return. "He is a lord in his homeland. Do you think he would stay if he didn't want to? And not just him. Saffron, too. Is she not your friend despite the pressure on her to only mix in lofty circles?"

Cassia rolled her eyes, earning her a light smack across the back of the head from the old woman. She knew what Sofien was saying. All that flew through her keen mind were retorts and caveats. But she knew it was no use to voice them. Hunter's Moon had such a strange effect on people.

"I want to give you a gift," Sofien continued. "Never tell this to the others, but you were always my favourite. If I'm to die before spring's first blooms—which I am—then I want to leave you with something meaningful before I go."

"Sofien, please, you don't have to," Cassia murmured. "If all goes well, I will be leaving for my Isolation. I cannot take anything with me."

"No, nothing so tawdry as a trinket or bauble." Sofien fixed her student with a steady gaze, and a chill ran down Cassia's spine. "I have already arranged it at the temple."

Tears rose in Cassia's eyes. The sting of them subsided as they rolled down her cheeks, knowing what her mentor intended. She reached out instinctively and clutched at the old woman. Beneath her clothes, Sofien's body had withered further than Cassia realised. Terror gripped her, and she clung tighter to the closest person to a mother she'd ever known.

"No—no, please, I can't... I can't do that to you. What if you survive? What if the healers are wrong—"

"And what if they are? Am I to live like this a hundred years? I ache all over, Cassia. I wake bruised and breathless. I cannot walk without a cane and two people to catch me if I should fall. No." Sofien's mouth set in a hard line. "I will not live like this. It's more than just my body; it's my soul. I am tired in places sleep cannot reach. I'm ready. And I want my death to mean something."

She wrapped her bony arms around Cassia's shoulders as the young woman sobbed. Clucking her tongue, soothing as best she could, Sofien waited until Cassia's tears had run their course before placing her wizened hands on either side of the young woman's face.

"The only thing I would regret is leaving you without people to call your own." Her tone was so soft and tender, and it only stung Cassia's heart all the more. "Sacrifice is our way, child, you know that. Perhaps mine can bring back that which you feel you lack."

A thousand protests hovered on the tip of Cassia's tongue. But the determined glint in Sofien's eye silenced them, as did the tight squeeze on her hand. The authority of her mentor's wishes bore down on Cassia until she broke, nodding and sniffling even as her heart railed against it.

Saffron kept the pain from her face as she looked at her mother's writhing form in their peristyle. Three healers attended the noble in distress, one administering the elixirs while the other two held her down. By Saffron's side, Jade, the family's steward, watched in silence. Those who knew of Anise's illness were all in the room with her.

Finally, she stilled, the elixirs replacing the twisted anguish with sleep too peaceful to be natural. Saffron sighed. Jade pressed a hand gently into her shoulder, then pushed to draw her away.

"It's getting worse." Saffron made sure to keep the anxiety from her tone. "Might it be poison? The symptoms came on so suddenly."

"If it was, would the poisoner not have waited until you left for your Isolation?" Jade pursed her lips. "Unless their aim is to prevent you going."

Saffron considered it. The problem with living in a city where the entire upper echelons of society either were assassins or were related to them was that every minor illness needed close scrutiny for treachery.

"Perhaps." She found she had little energy for contemplation. Her mother's illness had now lasted months, worsening each time it seemed to have passed. "Have the fetcher look into the pantry stores. Perhaps someone has found a way to interfere with the grains."

Jade bowed and went to do as she was bidden, leaving Saffron to watch as the healers arranged her mother on the bed and checked her pulse. She was about to speak when something crashed elsewhere in the house. Turning on her heel, Saffron hurried to the atrium. Her brothers were red-faced and breathless, eyes alight. Both were covered in egg and mud.

"Bay! Yarrow! What on earth have you been up to?"

Both boys turned to face her. Yarrow had the grace to let his smile falter but Bay glared up, unabashed.

"One of the vendors in the market called us vagabonds." Bay shrugged. "We couldn't let the insult stand."

Quelling the rage rising in her as best she could, Saffron stalked closer to them. Her dark eyes were cold as she surveyed the pair.

"I'm not surprised he called you that," she hissed. "Given how you look, vagabonds is a compliment."

"We can't let the commoners get away with such insolence!"

"No, you shouldn't be giving them reason to insult you in the first place! You do realise we hold our position by election, right?"

"Mother is an expert at elections," Bay retorted. "She'll sort it out."

At that, Saffron almost lost her cool. Their mother was in no state to manipulate a ball of wool, let alone the changeable crowds of Anukthar. But Bay and Yarrow had never witnessed the strange illness afflicting her. In health, they would be correct. The matriarch would smooth over every indiscretion and turn her sons' irreverence into an advantage. But, were she in such a state, she would certainly not allow the boys to run amok in town without severe consequences. Saffron

tried to think what punishment her mother might dole out for their behaviour. But even as she went over options, she knew it was useless. They had no respect for her authority. As though reading her mind, Bay stepped forward with a jaunty gait and flashed her a grin.

"Come, sister, don't ruin the Hunter's Moon mood with unpleasantness."

He continued on into the house while Saffron seethed. Yarrow watched his older brother leave with wide eyes, then looked at Saffron. She glowered at him. He shuffled past her with a muttered 'sorry.' As her brothers left, Saffron had to fight the overwhelming urge to slide to the floor and sob.

Nuts, meats, a variety of root vegetables... Aldert gave a satisfied nod as he tallied the feast. Very little was fresh this time of year, but he was sure they would eat well. Perhaps not as well as Saffron's family was used to, but there was nothing he could do about that. The fishmonger chewed a stick of liquorice and watched the pile grow as Aldert added to it.

"Expectin' visitors for the Moon?" the woman asked. "That's quite the stash."

"Oh yes." The thought occurred to him that Saffron would stay all the longer if there was an audience, and thus prolong their evening. "Nobility, in fact."

"No!" The fishmonger scuttled closer, her beady eyes gleaming. "Who is it, then? Willow Pen? Her family are such a blessing on this city, Lady love them."

Aldert shook his head, leaning in closer with a conspiratorial smile. The woman mirrored his movement.

"I've heard the Pens skim from the tributes they collect," he told her. "But it goes no further than between us, yes?"

The woman nodded, her braids bouncing, and Aldert knew the rumour would spread through the city by nightfall.

"So who, then?" the fishmonger persisted.

"Ah, I cannot say—I've said too much already." Aldert gave a regretful look. "But I can say it is a most ancient and powerful family. One my mistress is bonded to by choice, not by debt. But, again—"

"Not a word." The fishmonger tapped the side of her nose and gave a wink. "Not to a single soul."

Aldert smiled as though glad of her silence, then turned back to his stash and let the smile become a crafty grin. Now all he needed was a Hunter's gift for Cassia.

Smoke from censers borne by novitiates swirled thick between Cassia and Sofien. The priestess guided them both to carved wooden divans, linked by a thin silver chain. Cassia barely registered the hands tying the chain around her neck. Her gaze flitted to Sofien. The crone's face was serene as she caught her student's eye. A novitiate offered Cassia a bronze cup of dark liquid, pressing it into her hand before helping her raise it to her lips. The room spun. The contents of Cassia's stomach churned. Sofien accepted her own cup and drained it in one gulp. Her throat constricted under the chain as she swallowed.

Then the priestess was speaking, the novitiates murmuring their parts, and the rest passed in a blur before Cassia's befuddled eyes. She felt heavy; she felt sick; she could feel cold, disembodied fingers running over her ankles and plucking at her clothes. No matter how hard she tried, she could not close her eyes. The voices around her faded in and out of her comprehension. She wasn't aware of falling unconscious, but the realisation that the room was empty, the voices gone, hit her in a rush.

Sitting up, her gaze was drawn to Sofien. The old woman was lying on the divan. Her eyes were closed, her face expressionless. She might have been sleeping if not for the lack of breath stirring in her chest. Cassia stumbled to her feet and reached out to clasp her mentor's hand. It was cold. Sofien wasn't there anymore.

She placed the dead woman's hand back beside her and made

her way out of the room as though underwater. Shaking in the temple atrium, she tried to console herself as shock battled against her usually steely nerves. It had been quick. It had been painless. But the realisation that Sofien was gone hit her in waves. The ancient woman, the constant source of comfort and security in Cassia's life, would never again be sitting in the orphanage courtyard weaving, nor keeping the children in line with her firm authority.

A novitiate, returned only a few months earlier from his own Isolation, approached and cleared his throat.

"The body is ready," he told her. "I pray her sacrifice brings you luck in the examinations."

Cassia nodded and rose. The novitiate's words barely filtered to her at first, but then she frowned. The examinations...? He thought Sofien would give up her life for some petty status symbol? A flicker of anger rose in her, but she quelled it, making do with a hard look at the novitiate. From the cut of his robes, he was a noble. It figured.

"I will fetch her other kin," Cassia said. "We will be here within the hour."

Tears blurred Cassia's vision as she walked. The slippery streets, alive with festive joy and off-key song, closed in on her from every side. Sofien had sacrificed all she had, all she was, for Cassia to find her family once more. But she had never felt so alone.

She was so caught up in her misery that she ran headlong into Aldert. Taken off guard, she rebounded and almost hit the floor, but his strong hands caught her arms and righted her.

"Sorry, mistress, sorry. I was not watching where I walked, clearly. Are you alright?"

Despite knowing that he referred to their collision, Cassia couldn't help the fresh tide of sorrow overtaking her. And then her tears began in earnest. Once they started, they would not stop. Even when Aldert wrapped his giant arms around her, she still could not quell the sobs racking through her body.

Endless moments passed before she became aware of Aldert still holding her. His deep voice shushing and soothing her. She pulled away, drying her tears with her sleeve.

"Sofien is dead." After the depth of emotion she'd felt, her voice was strangely flat. "She's... I left her—her body—at the temple. She died to...to bring Cuinn back to me."

Aldert's mouth twisted in sympathy. He placed one giant paw on her shoulder and squeezed. Cassia accepted the gesture, though it barely registered.

"May Lady Erwyn grant her a blessed rest," the giant said.

Cassia nodded, fresh tears welling in her eyes. The sting of them stirred her to action. She

stiffened her spine and looked away, already on the move.

"I must go. I must fetch the other tutors from the orphanage—her former students, too—I don't

know how long I'll be gone."

"I will come with you." Aldert surveyed her, his expression unreadable. "The work will be

quicker with two instead of one."

Cassia opened her mouth to protest. This was her job, her responsibility—only now, when it

was already done, did she realise that she had taken Sofien from more people than just herself. And for what? Cuinn was likely dead already. She had no family and yet had let her mentor die for the false hope. But her objections died on her lips. Aldert's gaze, soft and tender and devoid of its usual mischief, persuaded her to nod and allow him to lead her on their mournful path.

The Harte household was full of bustle on the morning of the Hunter's Moon. Bay alternated between the exuberance of a boy half his age at the overflowing chests of gifts and disdain for the excitement Yarrow expressed. For once, Yarrow abandoned his blind acceptance of his brother's attitude. He bounced from Saffron to Jade with giddy enthusiasm, showing off each gift in turn. Saffron gave and received with good humour, though she kept a cautious eye on her mother. The matriarch looked older than her years. Still, she was lucid enough to partake in their joy.

"A dagger! My, such gorgeous engraving," the matriarch commented as Yarrow showed off a gift. "Fitting for a future lord in the Guild's Councils."

Saffron smiled, though she made no move to claim it as coming from her. It went against tradition. Each person knew only that they were cherished enough to receive, not who might cherish them so.

"What time shall we head to the lower town, Mother?" she asked once the gifts were all given. "Aldert gave me no fixed appointment."

Anise pursed her lips. Saffron had expected the reluctance but was glad that her mother had relented. The power of the gesture— and with elections so soon—could not be denied.

"We will rest for an hour, then depart," Anise decided. "Be sure the servants know not to pack the best silverware. I'm sure your friends have plates and cups of their own."

"I'm sure they do."

Saffron excused herself and went to check on preparations for the feast. She didn't know how much food Aldert and Cassia would have available. She didn't want to burden them, not when they were doing her a favour by improving their public image with the commoners.

In the kitchens, the servants had packed two baskets of food and small gifts for each Harte to carry. Most would be handed out to the crowd, if there was one. Saffron hoped there would be. But she paid special attention to the basket destined for her friends. Nothing too extravagant—if all went well, the three of them would soon leave Anukthar, and she knew Cassia would sell everything she owned to fund the trip—but something she hoped would be meaningful. Her pale, slender fingers ghosted over the carefully wrought iron necklace. The metal was cheap but the craftsmanship was exquisite. More than that, though, embedded into the pendant was a stone saffron hoped her friend would recognise.

"We're ready when you are, my lady."

Saffron startled and replaced the pendant in its box. She turned to the servant and nodded. "Fetch the litter," she ordered. "And ensure my brothers are presentable."

"Open it."

Cassia couldn't resist the childlike delight etched into her debtor's face as he handed her a small wooden box. She smiled and thanked him, rough fingers working over the stiff clasp until it came loose. Inside, a pile of red dirt, dry and fine, met her eyes. She frowned and gave Aldert a quizzical look.

"It's dirt," she said.

"It is dirt," he agreed. "From my homeland. I scraped it off the boots of every trader just arrived. A symbol of how far you've come —and how far you have yet to go."

Cassia chuckled, torn between amusement and emotion. He played the fool so often, she sometimes forgot the depths of her debtor's intelligence. She set the box of dirt aside and reached for her own gift to him. A delighted smirk flickered across his face as he recognised the upturned triangle that was the icon of Erwyn.

"You seek to serve her yet you encourage me to mock her?" he asked. Cassia shrugged.

"The gods bestow favour on those with the stones to tempt their ire," she replied. Aldert grinned broadly and stretched the leather string around his neck. The icon rested against his collarbone.

"You're learning."

The pair were still exchanging mischievous grins when a hubbub rose from the street below. Cassia frowned and went to the window, ignoring Aldert's sudden tension.

"What on earth—"

"Ah, yes, I forgot to mention... Saffron said she needed to be with her family on the Hunter's Moon. So I, er, invited them all."

Cassia was about to scowl at him when she caught sight of the litter. All her neighbours and, it seemed, all of their neighbours had gathered around the noble conveyance. Excitement rose off the crowd in waves that felt almost tangible. For a second, Cassia was transported back to a time before she'd developed such antagonism towards the holy feast days. Her heart swelled at the gleeful cries as Saffron stepped down from the litter and passed out fruit and coins from her baskets. Aldert joined her by the window.

"Family..."

Cassia jumped and glanced around. Though soft as a breeze, she was sure she had heard Sofien's voice whisper to her. A cold, disembodied finger ran down her spine.

"Concentrate..."

Breath catching in her throat, Cassia tried to reach out with her mind into the realm of the dead. For a moment she faltered, and then her hours of practice and study paid off. She felt the dam break with a lurching rush.

"There she is. My Cassia..."

"Sofien." Tears slid down Cassia's cheeks, her heart aching. She could almost feel her mentor's effort to make the connection, her urgency to convey the message. For a moment Cassia was at a loss for what to say. After months of effort, now that she had achieved a death whisper, she realised she had not thought beyond mastering it for the sake of mastering it. But Sofien knew what she wanted without asking.

"Your brother is not here..." The words began to fade as the clamouring in the street below forced its way back into Cassia's mind, but she still caught her mentor's words. "Cuinn is still among the living..."

It was as though her blood froze in her veins as Sofien's words disintegrated in her mind. Cuinn was not dead. Her brother was out there, somewhere, alive and hopefully well. But then why had he not returned to the fortress? Where was he? Had he forgotten her? A thousand thoughts jostled for attention all at once.

"Are you angry, mistress?"

Cassia jumped at Aldert's voice. Even after such a brief connection, the receding voices of the dead left her hazy and rattled.

Then a sharp rap at their door chased the last of her first death whisper from her. She slid her usual mask of cold indifference back into place before she sighed and turned to her debtor. He was not Cuinn, nor would he ever be. But she could scarcely remember a time before he'd been at her side. She'd known Saffron even longer. She took his giant hands in her small ones and gave them a squeeze.

"No, Aldert. I am not angry."

His broad face cracked into a relieved grin, and he returned the gentle pressure on her fingers. "Happy Hunter's Moon, mistress," he said.

ABOUT THE AUTHOR

E. S. FURLÁN

Knowing she wanted to be a writer and artist a young age,
E. S. Furlán took the scenic route in life, travelling and
delving into every facet of society she could.
Her work often reflects this and doesn't shy away from the
more unpleasant aspects of existence. Faith, witchcraft,
ostracisation, and life paths deviating from the norm are
common themes. E. S. Furlán strives to include a wide and
diverse range of characters in her novels.
She now lives in Denmark with her wild-child, bog-creature
daughter and a surprisingly normal housemate.
www.esfurlan.com

 facebook.com/e.s.furlan

 twitter.com/Nefeliba_art

 instagram.com/neffiart

ACKNOWLEDGMENTS

Thank you to all those who worked tirelessly to create this book.

Thank you to our amazing editor, Adryanna Monteiro for never dismissing an email no matter how many times we flooded your inbox.

Thank you to Pam Hage for your beautiful cover.

And thank you to all the beta readers:
A. A. Warne, R. A. Darlinge, Michelle Crow,
Serena Dawson, Deanna Young, Tonja K. Johnson,
Ezra Raikes, L. R. Huseboe, Pam Hage.

Made in the USA
Middletown, DE
23 December 2019